Meritocrats

Stuart Evans

VP Festschrift Series:

Volume 1: Christine Brooke-Rose
Volume 2: Gilbert Adair
Volume 3: The Syllabus
Volume 4: Rikki Ducornet
(Edited by G.N. Forester and M.J. Nicholls)

Reprint Titles:

The Languages of Love
The Sycamore Tree
The Dear Deceit
The Middlemen
Go When You See the Green Man Walking
Next
Xorandor/Verbivore
by Christine Brooke-Rose

Three Novels — Rosalyn Drexler
Knut — Tom Mallin
Erowina — Tom Mallin
The Greater Infortune/The Connecting Door — Rayner Heppenstall
The Penelope Shuttle Omnibus — Penelope Shuttle
Conversations with Critics — Nicolas Tredell
The Utopian — Michael Westlake
Image for Investigation: About my Father — Christoph Meckel

New fiction:

Mirrors on which dust has fallen — Jeff Bursey

other Verbivoracious titles @

www.verbivoraciouspress.org

Meritocrats

Stuart Evans

Verbivoracious Press

Glentrees, 13 Mt Sinai Lane, Singapore

This edition published in Great Britain & Singapore

by Verbivoracious Press

www.verbivoraciouspress.org

ISBN: 978-981-09-9344-3

Printed and bound in Great Britain & Singapore

First published in Great Britain by Hutchinson (1974).

Introduction

M.J. NICHOLLS

By 1974, the year *Meritocrats* appeared, the experimental novel in Britain was slowly passing into obsolescence. The loss of B.S. Johnson and Ann Quin the previous year was a significant blow to a scene that briefly thrived in the 1960s, and faded in the subsequent decade: unsympathetic critics, hostile novelists still annotating *Lucky Jim*, and an apathetic reading public on a comedown from the free-love dream performed the *coup de grâce*. Giles Gordon's *Beyond the Words* anthology, featuring Quin, Johnson, Eva Figes, and Gabriel Josipovici, attempted a hearty resuscitation, but Britain had never really embraced the "scene" in the first place: publishers like Hutchinson, Allison & Busby, and John Calder would eventually narrow their output of innovative fiction, or stop publishing risky works at all, and many leading figures of the "scene" moved into writing more commercial novels, such as Anthony Burgess and Robert Nye.

Stuart Evans is not ordinarily associated with the post-1960s British avant-garde, however, his works are sprawling, ambitious, and unique, and while a project as monumental as his five-tome Windmill Hill sequence seems to have failed to attract a scrap of readerly or critical attention, his other novels (*Meritocrats*, *The Garden at the Casino*, *The Caves of Alienation*), are original, playful, and amusing. Critic Francis Booth likens his works to Nicholas Mosley "in both experimental form and intellectual seriousness."

Evans was born in Swansea in 1934, and raised in Ystalyfea in Glamorgan. He studied English at Jesus College, Oxford, and in 1955 won the Newdigate Prize for his poem 'Elegy for a Dead Clown', afterwards attempting to "make a fortune writing musicals" before serving in the Royal Navy in the Inspector Branch. Later he taught at Brunel College of Advanced Technology, and in the 1960s worked at BBC Radio in London as a producer in the Schools Broadcasting Department, where he met his wife, the journalist Kay Evans. His background tallies entirely with the scene lampooned in *Meritocrats*, his debut novel.

Meritocrats is a waspish comedy-of-ill-manners set in a nouveau riche milieu, and is a fantastic satirical performance and hyper-referential homage to masters past and present. Split into five sections, voiced by five members of the milieu, Evans spins various narrative styles and modes to brilliant effect. Paul Keller is the Stephen Dedalus of the piece, the son of Robert and Sylvie, whose internal monologue is spliced into the action, and whose incestuous feelings for his sister lead to an increase in tormented and histrionic imagery. Sylvie Keller's sections comprise of pastiches, some of which are of Victorian authors (Austen or Trollope?), and later more recognisable takes on the Penelope chapter of *Ulysses*, and an amusing riff on Alain Robbe-Grillet (who appears twice at one of the parties). Robert Keller, the paterfamilias, has more conventional narration sprinkled with the sexist opinions of the none-too-subtle Australian character—a coarse millionaire in the Rupert Murdoch mould. Eric Foster, "vernissage of the independent cinema", is the most intriguing experiment: a cinematographic narration, blending snippets from his screenplays, pieces of real-time dialogue, and more theoretical musings, mirroring the approach of his movies: New Wave French *à la* Bresson or Godard. Gavin McNamara is the final voice: a caustic internal monologue from an parodic Irish character, sprinkled with amusing portmanteau words such as 'marshgassers', 'simperjunket', and 'gabledecock', included self-consciously, more entertaining than embarrassing.

These narrations are sequenced in different orders over eight parts, mimicking the drunken headiness of the endless parties taking place. The end product is a fantastic intellectual romp that transcends its swinging '60/'70s setting and succeeds in impressing with each stylish sentence.

Evans's next work, *The Gardens of the Casino* (1976) is not as successful, with the repartee more stilted, the tone less humorous and more ponderous, and a less controlled approach to narrative position. A year later, his most well-known work appeared, *The Caves of Alienation* (leading to the suspicion Evans had been sitting on these manuscripts for a while), a "document" novel that expanded upon the philosophical musings in this work, veering into similar fictional territory as Nicholas Mosley, and into the more dated form of often pseudo-philosophical lyricism that blighted many writers of the period. Evans also wrote three thrillers with his wife Kay (work that Robert Keller himself might have produced), published as Hugh Tracy, all out of print. Evans is a fairly unusual, inconsistent talent, however this debut novel showcases the swaggering bravado and well-crafted wit of a stylish and playful writer well worth rediscovering.

MERITOCRATS

PART ONE

Paul Keller

Enemy Coast Ahead. There through a peep in the cloud, see the southern coast of the Dorset desert washed patiently by the cloacal sea. Clouds get dirty too. B for Bandit bumps and judders in the unwelcoming air, banking round to approach target.

Wartime wizard of a depot pay-office listens, hears the tell-tale whine in the second port engine and puts two grey-green old ladies in the horror picture. Objective achieved, wartime wizard settles in his seat-belt with the comfortable smile of one wearing bicycle clips on his balls. The old women struggle with their panic.

Rain on the green and pleasant workshop of the world, paradise of individuality. Reconstituted tyres on clearways from suburb to suburb hissing. The serious problem of central drift. Long-range forecast: a warm complacent drizzle. Paul Keller returns from Paris. I should never have left.

Late Summer. Morning. Nightmare. The technopolitan sprawl starts somewhere in North-East Hampshire as B for Bandit homes in. Unsuspecting, the elegant Athenians of this latter day go about their important work. Robert Keller, Duke of Athens, sits at his desk in a tower by a river over the city pro bono publico. (Ah, but let midnight strike and he is Faery King, with radioactive fingertips, defoliating earth-girdler, sucking up from the sea contagious fogs.) The fastest prick, to boot, in the Scientific Civil Service.

And in her pine room, some miles to the West, spinning her gossamer marvels, his rash wanton Titania smiles over her newest book review or modest appraisal. (Alias, a bouncing Amazon, buskin'd mistress and warrior love in Hitler's War during the great days of broadcasting.) Who is Sylvie Keller?

And turning and turning somewhere in the wilds of Boreham Wood (near Athens) master of the revels, the painful self-despising revels, Eric Foster labours at his next film, seeing only through the viewfinder . . . . What? A night when he will be Lysander and in the high lyric of his imagination, she will turn to him and stroke the monstrous donkey head.

Meanwhile Barbara listens to the complaints of those made mad with love, or imagination, or poetry. Hermia in a white overall, enduring the livery of a nun, cool and untouchable. While Jacqueline who sat in childhood innocence at the same sampler, worries over a possible authentic Caravaggio in a vestal vault of the national temple of art.

And elsewhere the mortal-immortal-mechanicals are spread over the city confidently, speaking in monstrous or little voices, proper men and women, earning the gratitude of an indifferent public. There doesn't seem to be a part for me in the play. Enough.

The ground rushes up. The old ladies sigh and regain their parlour. Everyone leaves at once. I think of them busy around me: Andrew Stone, gnawing at his pencil over a novel; Jack Rathbone, grimly ruling the waves of Whitehall; Laurence Bisset, narrow-eyed over defence estimates; Roger Lomax cursing his bloody hands that perhaps this time were not deft enough. And their tidy wives in their neat houses. Oh it is a long way from the soft-haired girl in the Café L'Atrium in St Germain whom I rescued from the waiter who was making her blush and who did not take me back to a 1950 idyll in Montparnasse with frank close-ups of naked faces in ecstatic proximity. A long way from Frankie, the whore who liked me. A long way from limbo . . .

It is good for the old ladies, after the wartime wizard has capered with a camera in the thin Hounslow rain (agile in spite of the bicycle clips), to see the clean, white collars of British Customs Officers, standing with the nonchalance of Bismark sinkers after passing through the emphatically un-alien gate.

Anything to declare, Paul Keller? Only guilt. A rather nasty mind. An emotional problem . . . Welcome home, old boy.

Look now, upon *this* picture! Not in his tower at all, but in the blood and sand of the arrivals lounge, steel-blue, lightweight, seven-and-a-half-feet of white-fanged, sanguine (though balding) kingdom of twilight's Margrave. Daddy. Robert Keller, C.B.E., massive assurance incarnate, inc.

Those sculptured teeth, the work of Brisbane Praxiteles, are precisely deployed in the greeting ritual. 'Good trip, Paul?' 'A bit bumpy. Good of you to meet me.' The consubstantial edge-hate sheathed.

Through the airport anxieties and doubts, he strides, allowing expressions of benign calm to chase one another across his ruddy features, untangling nervous old men, sinew by sinew, tenderly, from escalators; flicking infants from the skidding wheels of runaway buses. Calling to him the pregnant, the poor and the heavy-laden as well as those who are sure they are about to crash. Reassuring. Dispensing charisma from the government hip-flask. And yet not one of them knows his greyly eminent name.

As Keller the father steps through the doors, a pale but reviving sun makes the rain on his Rolls glisten. Of course, he drives himself. What chauffeur could match his serpentine guile, his aquiline alertness, his leonine resolution? What chauffeur with first class honours in Moral Science, Physics, Law and Management? Cultured with it, he writes light fiction. Now skimming the M4, offering laconic hints about the state of the Nation ('Harold will stick it out') and the well-being of his household ('Mummy's away at Edinburgh for the festival').

And Barbara? My sister, I will be pleased to hear, is doing unusually well: a senior registrar with every prospect of a consultancy in a year or so at only thirty. Dedicated. All psychiatrists, says Daddy, are a bit odd. The sun gathers confidence. The yellowed brilliance of summer days. Dark questions, whispered answers.

No, the riots in May were not comfortable, but I stayed on the Right Bank, like a sensible Keller. But then the majority said *oui* to the General, whom Daddy admires, and things are quiet again with grievances dormant and prices and standards rising. Rue de Bac is still where it used to be when young Colonel R. Keller (Military Intelligence) took his pretty wife there just after the war for a month or so. It doesn't miss them.

So to brass-tacks. Why did I secure myself a grass-green job at the Cricklewood College of Technology and never even visit them. (Mummy was hurt.) Well, he would know but let us not for the moment ponder on the sins of the father . . . . He must at sixteen stone be an awful weight to bear, the fastest and most discreet prick in the Scientific Civil Service. But let's keep to the point: I thought, Daddy, it was time I worked. I was not writing. Paris was at her worst in May. So I offered my buttercup-yellow first class degree, my three fluent languages, my handful of published poems to their Liberal Studies Dept. And was gratefully accepted. I did not want advice. Did Barbara . . . ? No, of course, Barbara has a flat of her own.

Have I asked about her? Yes, of course . . . '. . . rather amusing chap, called Fingal Grey . . .' (Fingal!) '. . . hard-hitting television interviewer. But it's not very serious. You know what Barbara is like.' Oh yes. Is she to live a barren sister all her life, chanting faint hymns to the cold, fruitless moon. The panic returns. Wild lament from a torn mouth. 'Mummy's pleased about it.' We will die with our kinky boots on swearing that Mummy and Barbara really like each other.

And so we approach the new house with rose-garden and pool in Barnes, which Daddy's fine brain and Mummy's sharp nib have acquired. He out of the lower home-counties middle-class, administrator for administration's sake, top-adviser to Roy and Tony, Dick and Barbara and Harold now as he once was to Reggie and Iain, Ted and Ernie and the Prime Minister. Daddy may not have lain the lino in the corridors of power: but he polishes it. (And to make up has lain a fine aggregate of secretaries, lady civil-servants and private citizens.) While Mummy . . . ? Mummy was a girl called Sylvia in Merthyr Tydfil. Now she smokes Gitanes and sips martinis among serious artists at festivals, charming all with her silky wit, her kind eyes, her gentle socialism. Seeing all life from the point of view of a heroine in somebody else's novel.

Why do I hate them so much? That isn't even true. So this is home in its own grounds. Lawn. Swimming Pool. Rose Garden. Sun lounge, din., 3 recep., kitch. well appt., W.C.; 5 beds., 3 baths., sep. W.C.; Woodsheds.

A lot of roses. 'Yes, Mummy has always adored them.' 'Who's that?' 'George, the gardener. He looks after them.'

This is the true beginning of our end. Very tragical mirth.

Sylvie Keller

'THE CONSCIENCE OF THE FAIRLY WELL-HEELED'

"I went immediately from the office to a dinner party at the Keller's. Their son had recently returned from Paris and Sylvie Keller, who had always been rather proud of him, wanted to celebrate the fact.

It was a pleasant rather smoky evening with the first hint of Autumn in the air and I looked forward to a relaxed civilised evening. Keller was usually seen to his best advantage with the other members of his family who were all exceedingly personable and who, he was perfectly confident, were unlikely ever to let him down. Sylvie Keller was an excellent cook among her many accomplishments and their circle of friends was varied and interesting, although chosen almost exclusively from people, like Keller and myself, who had acquired professional and, with it, social status from provincial lower-middle-class beginnings.

I had known Keller for some years when we had both been principals, although in different departments. In spite of the fact that he found me to be over-cautious, and, I suspect, a little formal and I thought him to be self-confident to the point of arrogance, we got on well enough. We shared an interest in music and architecture along with our enthusiasm for the work we did, and our politics were similar.

Sylvie Keller was always delightful and I suppose that a more positive friendship existed between us than between her husband and myself. She was extremely pretty still and looked much younger than her years. She had, for me, considerable physical charm. Over the years I had become her adviser as well as her friend, experiencing some difficulty in keeping our relationship on this footing. Not that Sylvie Keller, herself, showed the slightest sexual interest in me or in any other man that I had noticed.

On this particular evening, apart from the Kellers and myself, there were five others at dinner. Paul, their son, had always struck me as a supercilious young man who barely remembered to make a show of interest in most conversations. Keller, like a number of others of relatively humble origins, had compromised his liberal views on education sufficiently to send his own children to well-established London day schools. Both had inherited all the intellectual brilliance of their parents and did well at University. The boy had taken a first in English at Oxford, but had made no use of it and had gone off to France in order to write. Keller seemed to want to indulge him and the boy was able to live in comparative comfort while abroad. It was my own private opinion that Keller had no great opinion of his son's talent, but cherished a faint hope that he might be wrong and would one day be able to boast a writer in his family. The other four present were Laurence and Andrea Bisset, old friends, Jacqueline Benbow and a pretty girl called Jane West.

'David,' Sylvie said. 'It's been much too long. You remember Jane, don't you?'

'We haven't seen you for ages, David,' Andrea Bisset said.

Keller handed me sherry.

'The Board of Trade keep him far too busy,' he said. 'It's all this talk of productivity.'

We settled immediately into the sort of desultory chatter that precedes dinner and the relaxation of a good wine. I allowed myself to be cornered by Andrea Bisset who was a compulsive talker and this enabled me to watch the others in the room with more or less undivided attention. This helped me temporarily to put the disturbing news the Minister had brought back from Cambridge out of my mind.

We were in three groups: Keller was talking to the two younger women and his wife to her son and Laurence Bisset, who stood remarkably still watching with dark wary eyes. Of all the people I met fairly regularly, I found him the most enigmatic. He was a back-bench Labour M.P. of certain ambition though it was unlikely to be fulfilled since his majority was precarious in one of the Greater London constituencies which changed its representative every ten years or so. Before his election in 1964, he had worked in a business organisation, making steady but not outstanding progress.

Now I became aware of the attention he was paying to Sylvie Keller. She looked particularly charming in a plain blue dress and knew quite well that she was in no way overshadowed by the fashionably elegant Jacqueline or the unusually pretty child, Jane. She talked fluently and wittily always, but perhaps Bisset's dedicated attention was unduly emphasised by the indifference of Paul, who kept glancing towards his father.

I wondered how much the children would know about Keller's philandering. I supposed, in fact, that both Paul and his sister had grown into the cold, unsympathetic young people they were after enduring for many years the frivolity of their father and Sylvie's icy tolerance of it. Not many of their friends would have noticed as much as I had, and certainly few of Keller's professional colleagues knew anything of his amorous proclivities, for his appetites were unfailingly tempered by his ambition.

The Kellers always ate at a large round table which meant that there was seldom any embarrassed juggling of the sexes to upset the digestion. I sat between Sylvie and Jacqueline, with Bisset on Sylvie's other side and Paul next to Jacqueline.

'And how is the National Gallery?' I asked. 'Thriving, I hope.'

'We don't have enough money, David, as you know perfectly well. I wish that you and Robert worked in some useful department of the Civil Service . . .'

'I should lobby Laurence,' Keller said, with unassuming charm. 'He's much more likely to be useful than David or I.'

Everyone around the table noticed the hidden barb, except perhaps for Jane West, but made no sign. Bisset was able to laugh lightly and say something deprecating about his unreliable taste in art.

'Don't we all know it, darling,' said Andrea Bisset. 'Laurence has cloth eyes.'

She turned a somewhat knowing face to Jacqueline.

'Thinking of buying something interesting?' she asked.

'This and that. Bits and pieces,' Jacqueline answered.

I saw the minute tensions as Jacqueline straightened in her chair while making the rebuff almost at the same moment as I became aware of the sympathetic and silent exchange that was taking place between Sylvie and Laurence. Jacqueline Benbow had all the unconcealable dislike of the professional for a not very gifted and pretentious amateur in her dealings with Andrea, who had been left an antique shop unexpectedly by an uncle and had since assumed that her informed interest in art had become expertise.

The dinner was excellent and Keller served us with a decent Moselle and a decidedly good claret, which produced a comfortable glow rather at odds with the sombreness of our conversation. It had been a violent and depressing month with extreme violence at the Democratic convention in Chicago and the brutally swift subjugation of Prague by Soviet Forces, as well as the stock tensions, all giving cause for concern.

Bisset was something of an authority on the United States and travelled there frequently. He spoke confidently, prompted expertly by Sylvie, who refused to be distracted by Andrea's tangential forays into the environmental mores of different places. Keller, himself, of course, was well able to keep up and I had picked up odd scraps of interesting information in the course of work.

'Tell us about somewhere interesting,' Andrea Bisset said to Paul, at last. 'What's going to happen in France?'

'I really haven't much idea . . .'

'I thought all you young people were frightfully committed,' Andrea said.

'Paul is committed to a policy of total apathy,' said Keller. 'He spends his time contemplating some ideal object in a thoroughly retrograde way. He reads the most extraordinary people.'

I thought that the girl, Jane West, had been left out of the conversation too long and sought to bring her in.

'What about you, my dear,' I said. 'What particular barricades would you defend?'

'My God!' Keller said, buffoonishly, 'I do believe that David's making a pass.'

Keller's vulgarity was infrequent and since he often managed to invest it with an almost epigrammatic distinction seldom offended. Andrea Bisset and the child both laughed and I smiled politely along with Jacqueline, but a look of boredom passed between Laurence Bisset and Sylvie that was not far away from scorn.

Jane was a little shy of revelation but took her cue from Paul Keller whose family traditions of uninhibited discussion had banished any frets of embarrassment in infancy.

The French windows were open and the evening was mild and fragrant enough for us to stroll in the garden. There were flecks of pinkish cloud above the rustling trees. Keller was anxious to show off his swimming pool to Jane West who had not seen it, so led a group beyond the shadows of the trees to inspect it.

I sat with Sylvie Keller on a wrought iron bench, drawing contentedly on my pipe. After briefly complimenting her on the dinner, we fell naturally enough into talk about books. I had seldom read a quarter of the stuff that she got through as a matter of course in her reviewing, but she enjoyed discussing things she had recommended. On this particular occasion, however, I was able to be of some use to her as she was drafting a piece on novelists who wrote about the Civil Service.

'I must pick your brains, David,' she said. 'Robert is remarkably uncommunicative about whatever happens at Millbank.'

'No doubt the consequences of security,' I said rather dryly.

Keller's reticence was legendary and in my opinion exaggerated in matters of his work. We talked for a while and I found myself confiding in her about the brewing scandal over the textile contracts and the Minister's gloomy predictions that afternoon. She was, as usual, detached but understanding and though unable to offer any constructive advice she listened sympathetically, asking one or two questions that helped me clear my own thoughts.

I felt considerably more at ease after my conversation with her and when Sylvie departed to make coffee, I idled across the lawn in the direction of the rose garden, as suitably relaxed as I had expected to feel after an evening with the Kellers, even though the guests had not been as stimulating as I might have hoped this time. An owl swooped between two fine chestnuts and the grass was silvery in the moonlight.

Then I experienced a shock which was not so much unpleasant as unexpected, for I almost stumbled upon Keller and Andrea Bisset knotted in a furiously passionate embrace. Even then I was conscious that they made an incongruous pair, since she was short, even squat, in stature and he was abnormally tall. I withdrew in haste, perhaps inadvertently making some noise. A moment later I heard both their voices raised in laughter.

I stepped onto the verandah and tried to look as though I had been there for some time, but, in so doing, caught sight of Sylvie at another window. I had seen a number of people suffering emotional pain in my life, and it was not difficult for me to recognise that this woman was fighting to retain some composure for a while longer, as she watched her husband returning to the house with the person who, however unlikely it might have been, was undoubtedly his latest mistress."

Robert Keller

There was a red and white striped hammock slung between two young beech trees in the rose garden. It had been there throughout the summer and Sylvie sometimes lay in it to relax, but not often. Now there was an old man peacefully asleep in it. His face was red and wrinkled, not flushed but deeply red after many years in strong sunlight while most of the wrinkles were around his eyes. He was bald with a white fuzz of hair above his ears. On the grass under the hammock lay an empty bottle of whisky.

Paul grinned and shook the hammock, looking across at Robert Keller. The old man did not wake, so Paul pushed the hammock harder until it swung. Almost in rhythm to the momentum of the hammock, the old man opened first one eye and then the other. He wore a good but rumpled sports jacket, expensive twill trousers that looked as though he had slept in them many times before and an open-necked dirty white shirt.

'Very comfortable hammick,' he said.

He spoke with some sort of accent. Robert Keller said nothing, nor did Paul. They stood in affable silence watching the old man, perhaps expecting him to be a bit frightened. He was not. He farted lengthily.

'Better,' he said. 'I'm looking for a young bloke called Robert Keller.'

Then he swung himself out of the hammock with unusual agility and stood stuffing his shirt into his unbuttoned trousers, beaming. He was about five feet five, had a considerable paunch and short stubby limbs. Robert Keller identified himself and introduced Paul. The old man was delighted and shambled forward, pushing out a surprisingly lean, tough hand.

'Sebastian Jones,' said the old man. 'Does an old geezer's heart good to see that his niece had the sense to marry a man who looks after her in the style she was never accustomed to as a girlie.'

His accent seemed to be Australian. Robert Keller was about to explain to Paul that this was his great-uncle, when Paul, untypically, spoke in a friendly way.

'We used to send you Christmas Cards,' he said.

'And you'll never know what they meant to an old grey kangaroo stuck out in the blazing Yuletide of the Great Victoria Desert, son. Which brings to mind the fact that I'm just about parched,' said Sebastian Jones.

They paused, however, on the way back across the lawn to admire the roses. Robert Keller quite liked flowers but knew nothing about them, nor did Paul. But Sebastian Jones was able to christen them all with fantastic names. They were all in very good humour by the time they reached the French windows.

'Jesus, mate,' said Sebastian Jones, 'you don't have to be the philosopher Plato to work out that you're doing pretty nicely, Rob.'

Robert Keller explained that his wife was at a preview of an art exhibition with a family friend. The old man was interested. He described his niece's remarkable skill at drawing from a very early age and went into detail about an illustrated letter she had once sent to him in Australia. Robert Keller described Sylvie's successful career at Broadcasting House and in the great days of radio and her subsequent work as a freelance journalist, reviewer and pundit. Sebastian Jones slapped his fat thighs in rhythmic delight, pausing only to refill his glass.

'And what the hell d'you do yourself, Rob, to bring in all this?' asked Sebastian Jones, waving his free arm about.

'My father keeps the country safe and smooth-running in spite of politicians and democracy,' said Paul. 'He is a very senior civil servant.'

Sebastian Jones pursued his enquiries into the careers of Paul and Barbara. He was amazed at the passing of time on hearing that Barbara was thirty and Paul twenty six.

'Well is that true?' said Sebastian Jones. 'Then Sylvia must be pushing fifty.'

With a charged glass, he asked to be shown the entire house. His enthusiasm was copious extending to copper pans in the kitchen, prints in the hall, the deep freeze in the larder, the dining-room table, curtains and carpets, pictures and light-fittings. In all of these Sebastian Jones found evidence of the status and prudence and intelligence of Robert Keller, not to mention the infallible taste of his own niece. Robert Keller pushed open the door of his study. There were about five thousand books around the walls, all in hard-covers except for foreign editions, on physics, philosophy, politics, communication, law, management, mathematics, together with standard works of reference, some favourite classics and a shelf of Robert Keller's own thrillers and light works of fiction.

They moved into the second sitting room, which Sylvie called the 'pine' room and which Robert Keller wished she would find some other name for. Its walls were panelled and Sylvie had furnished it with light unaffected pieces. She worked there at an ordinary table (very unlike Robert Keller's own highly expensive desk) and the room was full of her books, all concerned with literature and the arts including a comprehensive range of contemporary books, plays and poems, and of her ornaments. These ranged from a Japanese sword to the carapace of a sea-urchin found on the beach at Le Touquet. All had some sentimental value or association for her. Sebastian Jones read in the room the wonderful character of his niece.

The tour was protracted and comprehensive. Sebastian Jones stepped into the room where Robert and Sylvie Keller still, however passively, slept together. There was a small dressing-room adjoining it where Robert moved when Sylvie was suffering an attack of mild insomnia. He was an easy and a heavy sleeper with an unfortunate tendency to snore.

Robert Keller noticed for the first time in manyyears that the room smelt of Sylvie and that, apart from the few bits and pieces that belonged to him, it was very much a woman's room.

They moved to Paul's room, where there were more books. Robert Keller noticed that Paul had done away with all the junk that had meant so much to him as a kid: soldiers from Hummel, games, maps and so on. He wondered what had become of them. He recalled with a surprisingly tender amusement the occasion when Paul had saved up to buy his mother an Arab dagger as a birthday gift. It had been the most beautiful thing the boy had, up to that time, seen. He saw too that Paul kept a photograph of his sister on his writing-table. Robert Keller supposed he was quite a nice young chap, though not positively likeable. Sebastian Jones was moving in the direction of the photograph when Paul bustled over to the table and began tidying it rapidly.

Barbara's room, seldom used, was very different. Of course most of her stuff was in her own place, near the hospital, but the room was remarkably bare. Robert Keller was fond of Barbara and respected her complete contempt for possessions, without really admitting that he did. Robert Keller reflected with some pleasure on his daughter, imagining her inevitable and fastidious distaste for Sebastian Jones, who was invoking the historian Gibbon to observe that his great-niece kept her room pretty bloody tidy.

They moved on to the other unoccupied rooms in each of which Sebastian Jones found something to admire and spent some considerable time in the bathroom and lavatory which the old man thought fit for the Royal family to entertain in. When the progress was over they went back to the sitting room and all took some whisky.

'Where are you staying while you're in London?' Robert Keller asked.

'Hotel called the Hilton, me old mate,' said Sebastian Jones. 'So I ain't doing so badly. But it's short of what you might call home comforts. And an old frill-tailed lizard like me sets great store you might say by such things as them.'

'I'm sure,' Paul said, 'that you would be most welcome here. There's lots of room.'

Robert Keller considered his son's pleasant, smiling face and listened to the even voice. In all decency he could do nothing but agree warmly to the suggestion, while realising that Paul was simply up to mischief. There would be hardly any doubt that Sebastian Jones would turn into a thorough nuisance.

'Well, that's really bloody good of you, Rob,' said Sebastian Jones. 'I'll shift my gear here today.'

'I'll drive you up and we can collect it,' said Robert Keller.

'I hold my hand out to you, Rob,' said Sebastian Jones, 'noticing, by Christ, that it's got an empty glass in it. That's generous of you, boy. I only ever say no to the elixir of Scotland when Good Friday falls on Trinity Sunday, and you don't need to be the poet Burns to see that I enjoy it. I'll drink to being in the bosom of a real family for once in a stone-arsed existence.'

'You never married, Great-Uncle?' said Paul.

'Spent me life grubbing in the dust of the G.V.D., son. Not that I'm complaining but the sheilas don't take to the rasp of sand in the sheets. I made the odd trip back east and drank the bars arid and shagged everything in sight. But that was when the blood was higher and I'm an old man now and the things I set a bit of store on are a home, a family, a few fucking flowers about.'

While aware that the sentiment was being laid on a little too thickly, Robert Keller found himself warming to the idea of the old man's staying with them. He was not sure how long he would find the visitor refreshing, but for the moment he did. He said that the Kellers must soon have a few people around to welcome Sebastian Jones, who thought it an excellent notion.

'Dinkum,' said Sebastian Jones.

Eric Foster

Absurd . . .

In the top left-hand corner, naked and impossible configurations of innocence, facing the praying figure.

Spoils the picture.

Her face is always calm.

Beside her I look ridiculous. Bald. Limping. Trying not to look tenderly towards her, ever. *O che sciagura d'essere senza . . .*

Absurd.

In the top left-hand corner, naked and impossible angels. Christ in an attitude of prayer. To his left eroded rock with hewn steps. To his right a beautiful city under two extinct peaks of rock, with pinnacles and spires.

I do not wish to make any more of my chaos. I wish I did not love her. I wish I was not now with her.

Her face is always calm. Today, she wears a black suit.

She stands away from the picture and my eyes close against her naked body. In an attitude of subservience. While she is completely still . . .

(This is Barbara, my daughter.

She can't be. You're much too young to have such a …)

Laughter and confusion. Twelve years away.

'…a job. Not particularly interesting.'
'Surely.'
'For most of us, there is only …'
'…fascination …'
'…squeak like dolls.'
'Tell me.'
'But you are …'
'About the films you make.'

Her face is always calm. Today, she wears a black suit. The skirt is not outrageously short.

Absurd.

Lame, ageing man. Not doubting reason. Though there is little else left to doubt and no hymns to sing for any reason. Looking at her. Robert Keller watching me, amused …

Spoils the picture.

'I don't understand.'
'…unconscionable …'
'Treachery?'
'…life.'
'Why not "yes" …?'
'…slowly opening …'
'No?'

In the top left hand corner the impossible angels. Christ in an attitude of prayer. Wrought and barren rocks. The beautiful city with its towers. Under the cowdung hill the sleeping friends. Some way off a crowd, one man pointing. A dying tree, foreground: cruciform. Perched on it a bird of prey.

Eric, you are always asleep.

A mute, nearly beautiful thing Is your face, that fills me with shame As I see it hardening.

Her face is calm always. Today, she wears a black suit. The skirt is not outrageously short. But every time she has to stretch her body, it rides higher and the tops of her tights show.

> 'It's true?'
> 'Yes.'
> 'But when? How long . . . ?'
> 'There is no when in chaos . . .'

It's been my experience, too, that the common occurrences of daily life are vain and futile and friends become quickly exhausted. Objects of desire and fear are only good or bad if they affect my mind . . .

Oh fuck off, Eric. You and bloody Spinoza.
Sorry, Ginny.

Absurd.

> 'Spinoza?'
> 'Yes . . .'
> 'No. I haven't. Tell . . .'
> 'The ordinary man who . . .'
> 'When, Eric?'
> 'I can't remember "when".'

Shake the superflux. Categorise. Rocks. Tell us in plain words.

> 'I'm afraid it's true. I love you.'
> 'But when . . . ?'

In the top left-hand corner the impossible . . .

Dancing to a cracked record somewhere. Always I am in this posture of supplication. You control the figures of the dance.

Your problem, Eric, is self pity. You're a weak person, Eric. I have never known anyone who is as weak as you are.

In the top left hand corner the picture *Agony in the Garden* by Mantegna. The praying man alone, kneeling on the coagulated cowshit hill of the ages. Sleeping friends. A group of people. The beautiful city. Under its walls, more distant, other people carrying on their affairs . . .

My friend, cut your own throat. Cut your own throat.

'This is absurd.'
'Yes.'
'. . . twelve years . . .'
'Not that long. No.'
' . . . when?'

The world's great men have seldom been great scholars. Cut your own throat.

'. . . your divorce.'
' . . . rituals of . . .'
'Wasn't there . . . ?'
'Of course. Hours. Years.'
'And then.'
'Then . . .'

In the top left hand corner we had a Dufy print.

Ginny liked Dufy. Prokofiev. Thomas Mann. Eisenstein. Understood none of them. Why don't you make films that people can understand, Eric.

'My problem has always been self pity.'
'. . . yes . . .'

Her face is calm always. Today, she wears a black suit. The skirt is not outrageously short. But every time she has to stretch her body, it rides higher and the tops of her tights show. Now, she crosses her legs, high up. Her even, blue eyes stare at me, interested.

Falling in love at fifty. Having bluffed my way from Plato to Proust. Erstwhile emotional sneak-thief. A hustler in the best intellectual pool-rooms.

Why confess, Eric? Why must you confess things that aren't worth confessing.
I don't know, Ginny. But listen, please . . .

'Sounds a bitch.'
'No.'
'Well . . .'
'. . . twelve years ago, I . . .'
'You. And my mother.'
'Oh no. Barbara, no . . .'
'Not funny . . .'
'. . . funny? . . .'
. . . used to drink together.'
'Yes . . .'
'And that was . . .'
'. . . all.'

In the top left hand corner there is always a picture. This one is by Mantegna, but it might have been Dufy or Soutine or Jackson Pollock. The man looking at the picture is standing still, but we know that he limps. He is bald. There is nothing supplicatory about the way he is standing, but there is something defeated about the sag of the shoulders. The calm, beautiful girl on the sofa lies there carelessly, her legs indifferently open. The man has his back to the girl and her face is blank. They stand to the left of a labyrinth, through which a number of people are moving. These all have names, but they do not matter. Sometimes they band together, but they lose each other quickly in the maze. When they meet at intersections, they show surprise, relief, pleasure and exasperation. Nothing happens. There is no way out of the picture.

> 'How?'
> ' . . . explosion . . .'
> ' . . . painful.'
> 'The attack upon Caen in 1944.'
>
> It was a question of saving my skin or damning my conscience. I was her brother's age then—twenty-six. At that hour of the day it was no good saying: 'Take away this cup' . . .

Her face is always calm. Today, she wears a black suit. The skirt is not outrageously short. But every time she has to stretch her body, it rides higher and the tops of her tights show. Now she crosses her legs, high up. Her even, blue eyes stare at me, interested. She moves one thigh along the other. Twice. Three times. Indifferent. Unaware.

(You never wanted to make love to me, Eric.
I've never wanted to risk anything, Sylvie.)

> So, now, God help me I have become crazed by your daughter. At my age. Laughter. Robert Keller watching me, amused.

> 'So? When?'
> ' . . . if there has to be a moment . . .'
> 'A party. Andrea's, I think.'
> 'Yes.'
> 'What . . .'
> 'It was very full and quite accidentally someone bumped you against me. My hand brushed against your breast. You looked at me and smiled . . .'
> 'Did they know her?'
> ' . . . six months after it was absolute.'

'I was eighteen then . . .'
'. . . twelve years . . .'
'Adultery?'
'. . . hers. My cruelty.'
'. . . not you.'
'Oh yes.'
'Then?'
' . . . emptiness. Cold rooms, dark . . .'
'Me?'
'Not immediately. No.'
'I'm glad about that.'
'Some years after. So . . .'
'Don't ask.'
'. . . slowly opening . . .'
'No!'

You can't Eric. You haven't a logical mind. Stick to the things you're good at. Don't think.

In the top left hand corner is a picture. It is out of focus. A man is looking at the picture, with his back to a girl. She is with a young man whose face is averted, but whose back is powerful, young, muscular. This young man and the beautiful girl may have been making love or fucking. We do not know. They are in a gallery built like a labyrinth. A lost group of people wander through its passages with names like Robert, Sylvie, Andrea, David, Paul, Jack, Jacqueline, Roger, Jasmine. When they meet they discuss the pictures. The man looking at the picture in the top left hand corner turns holding a long-bladed knife . . .

Her face is always calm. Today, she wears a black suit. The skirt is not outrageously short. But every time she has to stretch her body, it rides higher and the tops of her tights show. Now she crosses her legs, high up. Her even, blue eyes stare at me, interested. She moves one thigh along the other. Twice. Three times. Indifferent. Unaware. Then, unexpectedly, she blushes. And then she smiles.

A long-bladed knife . . .

Absurd.

Gavin McNamara

Well, a right bunch of thoolermerauns we have here. The women are biologically serviceable enough, and some of them a lot more than that, to be fair and upright. A scholar would describe them properly, but I'm just a dilettante, so let's be content with their softness, the silk sheen of them, their scents and earthy confidence commingling. Enough to intoxicate a man.

The mother. Sylvie by name. Looks thirty-nine and it's ten years since she was wished many happy neveragains of that. Short, dark hair. Pale face that never did have a lot of colour. Nice eyes, brown, if it wasn't for that gleam of intelligence. Neat round tits for the right sensitive hand. A grand eye for a flattering brassiere the girl has. Neat round bum and flat belly with a seductive roundness hinted at. Slender pretty legs so that a short skirt doesn't look like some shepherdess from old oak common tarted up for the trianon. A very high class of person. Sure, it's a long way to Merthyr Tydfil.

That Andrea is an ineluctable example of fruits de mer, and no mistake. Voice like a rasp. She's six years younger than Sylvie, but running over the rim a bit. Friendly enough bust and broad shapely arse. Short, overstuffed body and short legs which they say is a sign of passion. Fair fading hair; faded blue eyes. Very generous with the views, but I can never make my mind up whether they want you to look or not.

Jacqueline is younger. A quiet one. Thirty odd. I shouldn't be a bit surprised she goes in for golf or swimming or some other deviation, for she has the wide shoulders and strong hips. Average about the bosom and the legs are what you'd call elegant if it wasn't for a sharpness at the knees. Terrible sweet voice. High flowered dress of the oriental type and the quiet manners of a dormant volcano.

Ah, now. Elaine. A real open sandwich of Pallas Athene at the age of twenty-nine. Five children, begob, so her waist isn't exactly girlish, but the rest of her explains the five children: big wide breasts, hips that could swing a bloody election, blue eyes, dark, long hair falling to her shoulders and legs you want to worship. Eldobloodyrado. And I'm not settling for the Crystal Palace.

They tell me his sister's quite something, but she's not here.

And the menfolk ! There's the Da, himself. Six foot four and a half of patiently acquired privilege with more letters behind his name than I get through the postal services in a month. And when he has a bit of time spare from working out ways of bringing destruction to others and technological progress to his own, he writes thrillers under one name and humorous novels under another. Grey-eyed and ruddy triton. Cuchulain of the Thames Embankment. But with an eye for the ladies, and no mistake. Not that he makes it obvious at all, like some. He hasn't cast a single glance at that enticing triangle of white peeping between the fine thighs of Elaine, but the way he hands her a glass of wine sets up vibrations. Now you'd think his son would admire such a handsome, successful, sympathetic, virile da as Robert Keller is: but the poor bloody gawp resents him and his mother too for being bourgeois hypocrites. It's all come too easy.

Then there's the M.P. As saturnine an arse as ever polished a back-bench. Laurence Bisset, friend of comprehensive education, the United States, consenting adults and the Campaign for Better Broadcasting. As fair-minded a mixture of political paradox as mild and bitter and at least as honest as the shortest day of the year. Well-dressed and with a quiet eye on the hostess.

The naval sea-faring captain now. There's a fine example of belligerent intelligence. Behind that granite brow whirs a turbine of a brain. As silent as a close-shave with a cutthroat and straight as a good briar. Cool and clear of eye, grim visaged until the face creases slowly into one of the ugliest smiles since Nelson got his column. Ah, but he's handsome in repose and he's performing the fine service of drawing off the old scalybreeches, on his second bottle, whose had his hand on three thighs and one buttock to date.

The other one worries me. Eric Foster. Bald, limping, uneven teeth. Of course, we've all heard of him, making fine intellectual cinematographic poems which make Robbe-Grillet's look like the tale of Pigling Bland. Watchful eyes, this one has. He doesn't miss much and there's the mark of pain on his face. He worries me.

And here they all are. There are two centres of interest. One is, naturally enough, myself. I'm a witty profound devil at times, I must admit. The other is that old blubberguts from Australia. Oh Jaysus, it's a real bloody banquet of talk for some poor mendicant like myself to gorge on.

And the hints, the veiled suggestions, the innuendos, the witty jibes! It takes a connoisseur to figure all the pussyinthecorner out. And me thinking only to discuss an exhibition of art at the Cricklewood College of Technology where I do a bit on the side in the way of liberal studies and where the bloody mooncalf, Paul, tries to prove there's poetry in thermodynamics as well as poetry. I can't tell you what the society of the deserving cultured does for a chap like me. And they're not a bit mean with the whisky. I'm sure I'll find their company very educational.

PART TWO

Robert Keller

The inner office was a large comfortable room with a vast desk and a tall black-leather swivelling chair. The desk was set at an angle so that, while seated at it, Robert Keller could make use of the extensive console of knobs and switches to his left and right. There were three deep easy chairs in the office, all of black leather and about half-a-dozen straight-backed chairs with black leather seats. Seven in fact. On the wall opposite the desk were two television sets, one closed-circuit, flanking a small screen. The projector was concealed in a cupboard above Robert Keller's head and to the right. Along another wall was a massive cocktail cabinet, of teak, matching the desk.

Everything on the desk was squared-off meticulously. There were two trays made of a refined black wood, a black rack for pens and pencils, a small but clear calendar, a leather-bound diary (black), two Sèvres paper-weights, and a small glass egg-timer containing pink grit which took two minutes forty-three seconds in which to empty the substance from one compartment into the other. In one of the black trays were three files. In the other tray, to the right of Robert Keller, was another file. Two of the files in the first tray had buff folders and one a red folder. The one in the other tray had a yellow folder.

The door opened. A tall young man with straw-coloured hair grown rather long, and a humorously mobile face which he had carefully rehearsed came in, his face humorously mobile. Robert Keller lay down the yellow file he was reading from and greeted the young man pleasantly. The young man's name was Christopher Jarvis. He had a promising career ahead of him.

'Do you know an old man called Sebastian Jones?' asked Christopher Jarvis.

Robert Keller asked pleasantly if the old man had stolen the statue of Boadicea near Westminster Bridge or had attempted to rape it.

'At least you've heard of him. We were afraid that he'd heard of you and was some sort of crank. He's down below, raising the most frightful rumpus and calling the sergeants puffed-up pommie tits who couldn't have fought their way through toffee bags.'

Robert Keller asked his secretary to go down and sort the matter out by giving Sebastian Jones a temporary pass. He then proceeded to discuss with Jarvis an imminent visit to the Porton research establishment, touching rapidly but clearly upon matters of policy, politics and executive detail. Jarvis's mobile face was still and composed as he listened intently. Loud noises penetrated the room from the outer office.

The door opened abruptly. Iris, one of Robert Keller's junior secretaries, stood near it, scarlet in a miniskirt. Beyond Iris, Sebastian Jones was to be seen kissing Hilda, the most senior person in the office, forty-three but comely, and a third girl whose name Robert Keller, for the moment, could not remember stood further off, grinning.

'Mr Jones is here,' said Iris.

Robert Keller asked Sebastian Jones to put down Mrs Marsden and come inside. The response was ebullient. Sebastian Jones, whose easy agile movement in spite of his bulk and habits again impressed Robert Keller, capered towards the door, waving a battered hat. He offered the hat to Iris, but, as she reached for it, held it high away from her. The unwary girl stretched, causing her skirt to rise. Sebastian Jones slapped her buttocks heartily with his left hand. The poor girl empurpled. Christopher Jarvis mobilised his humorous features unreservedly.

'Bob, me old mate,' cried Sebastian Jones. 'It's a bloody nice set-up you have here, nephew, and no mistake. Except for the plummy poofs dressed up as soldiers in the bastard lobby. Jesus love us all, mate, you don't need the memoirs of last year's harlot to cotton on to the fact that you're the guardian of state secrets, sport. And no mistake. Strewth, what have I married into, I ask meself. Hullo, sweetheart. Who are you?'

Robert Keller introduced Christopher Jarvis to Sebastian Jones. Jarvis excused himself almost immediately.

With a reasonably composed, tolerably amused air, Robert Keller explained the status and function of his female office staff; and asked what Sebastian Jones wanted.

'Very kind of you, Bob,' said Sebastian Jones. 'Whisky's me usual tipple, as you know. After years of shortage in the Great Victoria Desert.'

There was no alternative left to Robert Keller, who accordingly served his wife's uncle with a large glass of whisky and took one himself. Sebastian Jones took a cordial gulp.

'Hope you didn't mind my giving that little sheila a good slap on the arse, Robbie. Like it, you know. Little things mean a lot. Shows them they're appreciated. How about a spot of lunch. The Ritz, the Savoy, the Hilton. You name it, mate. The tucker's on me.'

Sometimes Robert Keller found it difficult to believe in Sebastian Jones. He declined the offer politely, explaining that he was eating with an M.P.

'Is that straight?' said Sebastian Jones. The old man grinned.

'Course, you're a bit of a pink-arse yourself. Seriously, though, Bob, the reason I've come around here, disturbing you in the office like this, is that I want a tot of advice. Man to man over the roast and veg. An old feller like me gets a bit low sometimes.'

This confession seemed implausible. Robert Keller politely doubted that Sebastian Jones was often depressed.

'No, mate, I'm not. I made it a rule early in life not to be depressed. But I'm not above a word of advice. And another snort of the wild west wind would go down a treat as well.'

While Robert Keller poured Sebastian Jones a further generous measure of whisky, they digressed a little into the nature of Robert Keller's work as a very senior scientific civil servant. Sebastian Jones was satisfied by vague references to general co-ordination of the nation's efforts and resources and stated that you did not have to be the historian Livy to see that Robert Keller held a bloody responsible job. He expatiated on Robert Keller's fine brain and attractive family, becoming adiposely sentimental about the welcome afforded to him. He then, shrewdly, asked permission to put to Robert Keller a personal question.

'It's meant kindly,' Sebastian Jones explained. 'And no mistake. Things are O.K. between you and Sylvie, are they?'

The question was something of a surprise, but Robert Keller found it highly improbable that Sebastian Jones would acquire any evidence to the contrary and said that his relations with his wife were excellent. Indeed, in their way, so they were. They were highly civilised people with an unaffected understanding of each other's problems. As far as the rest of the world was concerned, there was no necessity at all of delving into the intimacies of psychological, physical and emotional adjustment. Sebastian Jones, with admirable avuncular concern, expressed relief and pleasure, but, he went on to say that the Kellers moved in, for an old wallaroo such as himself, sophisticated circles inside an infinitely permissive society. Some of the women, he continued, whom he had met were powerfully attractive.

'That Elaine, f'r instance, mate. She'd give a eunuch wet-dreams,' he said thoughtfully.

Smoothly and with a great display of amusement, Robert Keller, filling the old man's glass, asked him why he thought that he (Robert Keller) might be having a liaison with Elaine Rathbone.

'Strewth!' said Sebastian Jones. 'Is that what you call a fuck around here. I can see why you need all this co-ordination, son. No, seriously, Robbie, and it's nice of you to take it the way you are. A lot of blokes would start chucking the furniture about. It's some great furniture you've got here, by the way, and no mistake.'

Further assurance was offered but when Sebastian Jones inquired about the morals of his niece, Robert Keller sheltered behind the umbrella of Anglo-Saxon gentle-manliness.

The reason for Sebastian Jones's highly personal questions eventually became apparent.

'I ain't just an old kangaroo rat who don't know any better, Rob. I landed with both feet in the loot out there in Australia, I don't mind telling you and I'm not getting a day younger and that's for sure. You don't need to be the prophet Isaiah to tell you that. Well, I don't want the lot to go to the bloody bolshies in death taxes or whatever the bare-arsed robbery's called. I found the goddam stuff they wanted and that's enough . . .'

Robert Keller was interested but, true to his brief, Christopher Jarvis appeared and announced it time for their departure. Before Jarvis could be appropriately dismissed, Sebastian Jones had surged to his feet and stumped towards the languid young man wagging a bottle of whisky.

'Have a snort, young Chris,' he said.

The order of mobility of Jarvis's face was impeccable. He glanced ironically in the direction of Robert Keller, contriving to lace his aroused sense of irony with familiar deference. Robert Keller remained pleasantly impassive. Jarvis then called into action half the languid humour at his disposal, sensibly keeping a manoeuvrable mass in reserve. His pale blue eyes became friendly.

'I didn't mean to burst in,' said Jarvis.

'Think nothing of it, me beauty,' said Sebastian Jones. 'Just talking man to man with your gaffer. Telling him how to run the place.'

'I'm sure he's grateful,' said Jarvis, taking a glass.

'You don't have to tell me, mate,' said Sebastian Jones. 'I bet you had a fine education, son?'

'The very best,' said Robert Keller.

It gave him pleasure always to talk about, even merely to contemplate, the education and advantages of his subordinates. He was perfectly aware of it and thought it a harmless indulgence.

'As a matter of fact, I did,' said Christopher Jarvis, whose mouth slackened into a self-mocking smile that knows it is right. 'I went to Eton.'

'It's right there in your bearing, mate,' said Sebastian Jones. 'You've got the Etonian stance and no mistake. A great place. I hope you're doing something to stop the blasted bolshies buggering it. Still that ain't my affair, as you've every right to tell me. Go on, son. I suppose you went to college in Oxford or Cambridge, like your guvnor here.'

Sebastian Jones listened with frequent interpolations of admiration and enthusiasm to a brief account of Jarvis's academic and military (National Service) career, his attainments and his current position. Robert Keller, himself, contributed benignly, relying on Christopher Jarvis to read the situation accurately and go away. It was not that Robert Keller was avaricious or even acquisitive, but he was interested in the old man's story of having struck it rich, partly for its own sake and partly because Sebastian had hinted at finding minerals useful to governments. It was Robert Keller's job, at least a part of Robert Keller's job, to know about such things. He was being asked advice from a man who, in spite of the variety of a richly coloured life, would be unsophisticated in financial matters and he was prepared to offer it. If some of the money came Sylvie's way, or the children's, or even his own, Robert Keller would welcome it. Between them they earned a great deal but they also spent freely. Sebastian Jones refilled their glasses, Robert Keller caught Jarvis's eye. Jarvis immediately rang up an expression of forgetful alarm and bustled in some remark about discussing strategy for the impending meeting with the M.P. When Robert Keller replied that it could wait, Christopher Jarvis misconstrued the answer and turned a sceptical but amused smile back on to Sebastian Jones. Robert Keller said that he did not want to keep Jarvis from any pressing business. Sebastian Jones, however, was eager to keep the young man. On learning his age, thirty-six, he pronounced Jarvis an excellent match for Robert Keller's daughter.

'Not that I've set eyes on the girl yet,' said Sebastian Jones 'but she's a real little boomer from her picture.'

Christopher Jarvis said that he had met Barbara and that she was attractive and intelligent.

After a short, lachrymose spell in which he talked of lost love, Sebastian Jones began again to recall the good times. He then told them a series of scandalous stories. Robert Keller glanced at his watch. Unfortunately he really did have an appointment with an M.P., a P.P.S. who could be useful to Robert Keller and who, in turn, desired a discreet favour.

'I'm afraid I have to go soon,' said Robert Keller.

Sebastian Jones seemed inclined to broach a second bottle but Robert Keller was able to mobilise Christopher Jarvis into seeing the old fellow out.

When they had gone, Robert Keller reflected philosophically that he would have many opportunities of reopening the subject of Sebastian's financial problems. He glanced round the large spacious office, taking stock of its few but exemplary fittings with customary appreciation. He had never wished to be a millionaire and found those who vowed to be vulgar and, on the whole, stupid. Robert Keller was a different kind of self-made man. Nevertheless he enjoyed being moderately rich and owed it to his family to see that opportunities were not missed.

He finished reacting the yellow file, wrote a few notes with a throwaway felt pen in green on a sheet of clean white cream-wove paper, enjoying the texture and sensation. Then he took a paperclip out of a box in the top right hand drawer and clipped the notes to the first sheet of the report. He transferred the file to the right hand tray.

Eric Foster

There can be little doubt that he will find a place on the last plane out of the disaster area. Slightly amused, perhaps. An invisible public man whose public duty it is to save his skin. The conscientious coward.

— We're ready to shoot now, Eric.

> The Managers. Shot seventeen. Take eight. Waterloo Bridge. Pan from right (St Pauls) around in slow arc to Westminster Palace. The streets are empty. Autumn flowers. Trees shedding leaves. Sunlit. Begin panning back in slow arc from left, jarring to stop when at Lancaster Place. Cut.

> Many of us may die. Remember, statistically, It is unlikely to be you. . . . Unlikely to be my friend, Robert Keller. England confides this day that every manager will do his public duty. . .

> Now an aeroplane passes overhead.

> > 'My father knows a lot about death . . .'
> > ' . . . sentimental . . .'
> > 'Truth . . .'
> > ' . . . not exist. Rationally . . .'
> > 'You Eric, do not . . .'
> > 'I will not judge anyone.'

The Managers. Shot eighteen. First take. 'Q' appears round corner, from the Strand, running. He slows to a walk. He walks towards camera along the middle of the road, shoulders heaving, exhausted, gazing around in a concussed way. Cut.

Cold breeze. Five fifteen on an autumn morning. Aeroplane overhead. Long take of the Temple gardens.
Temple lawns. 'Q' alone. Gina alone. 'Q' and Gina. King William Street and St Mary Woolnoth. Lombard Street. I am never delighted by the triviality of my own mind and constantly amazed. But the work goes well. *Cela est biers dit . . . mais . . .*

'A job. Not particularly interesting.'
'Surely.'
'. . . squeak like dolls.'

London Wall. The Managers. Shots twenty-three, twenty-seven, twenty-eight, thirty-three, fifty-one, fifty-six, fifty-seven, eighty, one hundred and three, one hundred and thirteen, two hundred and twenty-one.

Think well, deeply, generously. An old nonsense. Twitched into every moral posture by the invisible strings of desire. Jointed ethically to respond to tugs of guilt. The intellectual dummy's dance working to the frenzied flicker of ambition.

«Of course, you're in a position to do so much, unlike the rest of us.
I suspect you of disingenuousness, Robert,
No, I'm being perfectly serious.»

You're not meant to be the leader of the pack, Eric.
Why aren't you satisfied? Why are you never satisfied?
I don't want to lead the pack, Ginny.
You're the sort of person, Eric, who uses reason like the electric light. You turn on a switch, but you haven't a clue what happens to make the light come on.

That sounds remarkably clever.

Reason can be a labour-saving device. When it goes wrong, you can telephone a logician to fix it. Laziness rather than good sense is, of all things among men, most equally distributed. The logician, even, will ask for overtime pay.

Aldgate, Minories, Tower. That'll take us the rest of the morning.

—We'd better break now for an hour, Tim.
—Right, Eric. Break for an hour. There's a coffee shop just around the corner, Eric, if you . . .
—No thanks, Tim. I'll just walk around for a bit.

Poor 'Q'. One moment in front of his shaving mirror and then waking up, running, in a holocaust. Where have all the bodies gone? Forked animal, poor 'Q', whose nerve-ends wince in anticipation. In empty London, out of which the managers have flown, he thinks of Gina waking, getting up, dressing. And someone else, someone else still alive, watching her.

'How long, for Christ's sake?'
'. . . no when in chaos . . .'

Barbara Keller is a decent girl, a controlled woman, an honest person.

For 'Q', whose nerve ends wince, Gina's absence means that she has flung out her thighs to the first passing berserk. Seven five. The Spitalfields sequence.

I have no claim on her loyalty, affection, love. And she is not Gina. Poor 'Q'. Crassly promiscuous imagination.

'But why?'
'Madness.'
'I didn't do anything . . .'

Good shepherd, tell this child what 'tis to love.

'Q' rubs his chin with his thumb. Having always enjoyed shaving. In the shaving-glass: shot seventeen. 'Q' is twenty-six. I am forty-nine. An aeroplane passes . . .

When we heard about the Hiroshima bomb, in hospital, a man whose name was Batchelor told us 'I'd have gone home to fuck my wife.' Given warning. The bald head nods wisely in the shaving-glass.

Barbara Keller is a decent girl, a controlled woman, an honest person.

It was a successful evening. We walked up the Charing Cross Road until we found a taxi . . .

'I don't know why, but you enchant me . . .'

She kissed me. (Gina kissed 'Q' as she left him on the evening before, in the taxi. 'Q' got out, holding her hand. She did not ask him up for a drink.) Then immediately. Absurd. The idea suddenly struck him that Odette was expecting someone else. Poor Swann tapping at the wrong window. The wretched Marcel waiting for inevitably miserable moments with Gilberte. (When he woke up, 'Q' had become mad. Or London had become empty.) Tolerantly Robert Keller smiled in the VIP lounge . . .

«It's been a good autumn.
Good light.
Been getting a lot done?
Yes. Film about you.
I'm not flattered. I don't suppose I'm the hero.
No.
The humanitarian conscience and the work of national importance, I imagine?
The conflict.
What's it called?

The Managers.

You forget, Eric, that I claim Hegel as a formative influence. I have this talent for dialectic.

I cannot in any degree approve of those restless and busy meddlers who, called neither by birth nor fortune to take part in the management of public affairs, are yet always projecting reforms . . .

I suppose you have never contemplated anything better than the reformation of your own opinions?

That's about it.

Interesting. Talented chap, Descartes . . .

Too lazy to catch the last plane out, Robert.

Sorry? What was that? Have some more wine . . .»

> 'Q'. In his laboratory studying slides under a microscope. In his shaving mirror. The image of Gina. Smoothness of a hand. Rustle of clothing. The ultimate value is reality.

Absurd.

> 'What's it about?'
> 'You and me and the rest of us.
> Your father . . .'
> 'I thought you made no judgements.'
> 'I don't . . .'
> '. . . merely observe?'
> 'Merely record.'
> '. . . time I went . . . busy . . .'

> Leaving the pub, we walked over Waterloo Bridge towards the Strand. She held my hand and, for her, became suddenly lyrical about London. And I fell most foolishly in love.

> 'Q' screaming towards up appeared. In the sky overhead the navigation lights of an aeroplane twinkled in sequence.

What are you going to do? Eric, I said: what are you going to
do?
I don't know, Ginny. Work . . .
Do you think you'll marry again, Eric?
I doubt that I am ever likely to fall in love again.
Perhaps you won't. You've done a very good job,
Eric. It's what you're good at.
What's that?
Isolation . . .

> 'You know, my dear, for an intellectual you're not
> desperately intelligent.'
> 'You are enchanting . . .'

"The places that we have known belong now only to the little
world of space on which we map them for our own convenience. None of
them was ever more than a thin slice, held between the contiguous
impressions that composed our life at that time; remembrance of a
particular form is but regret for a particular moment; and houses, roads,
avenues are as fugitive, alas, as the years."

'Q' is a man of twenty-six, a qualified physician who works at
a research hospital. Gina is twenty-two, a secretary. The ultimate value
is absurdity.

Gavin McNamara

If ever there was an enterprise that, like the ass of a hoss with the bobo flies, attracted to it every throb-throated papblather for miles around, it's bloody Television. And when you hear what a nice class of gentlemanly person there used to bein Radio, with a pork pie and a glass of Macon at any time of the day or night and no ugly talk about money, it's a great pity that times have to change the way they do. But I must say from Forty Winks to Cockles Alive, there isn't one of them I wouldn't give the red rosette for Bastard of the Year against the clock and in the puissance event too.

The fact of the matter is, though, that the young dew-piddle, Paul, is powerfully well connected through his da and his daarlin' mother. So that when we put on this exhibition at the Cricklewood College of Technology, that Louvre of NW2, damn me if all and sundry don't turn up to say that it's rather good and before I know which way the homely mule of Munster is facing here I am at the Television Centre aself with a glass in my hand and a merry quip, casting an eye around for an outlet for my raging Celtic talent.

Well, Jaysus, it's difficult to see how they can have herded together so many marshgassers all at once. And out there the great English audience, every head rustling with crisps, is drinking innocently in every methylated drop, going mad and blind and helpless. Though I daresay it sounds ungrateful to be going on about it all, especially when there is a fine selection of macarons croquants, swinging daintily amongst the equipment, and I'm the guest of Fingal Grey, no less.

Now you'd think a boyo with a name like that would be handsome and aggressive to all comers, working on a hard-hitting programme; with the blue eyes, steel-blue, the straight nose, the firm jaw, clean brow, ears that know their place, thick hair and thin smile; a soupçon of the twilit accent to taste. Not a bloody blind bit of it. A short, round wee fellow with a smile on him like the man in the moon and a face just as scarred by time and experience. He has his hair mowed regularly to disguise its creeping absence and plastic teeth that would turn the Transylvanian undead an even greener shade with envy. And he has other remarkable gifts like eyes that can change gear—from sincere to sexy to shifty in three slick movements, not to mention great powers of laughter.

But when it's a question of some enquiry of the hard-hitting class, there is no one at all to beat your man here. On account no doubt of his relatively humble start in life forty-two years ago in Ipswich as the son of a family grocer.

Take tonight, now. There's a commotion lined up for the coming Sunday where several thousand people are expected to march round the arse end of Kenneth Tynan to Trafalgar Square and back again by way of Hyde Park in order to put pressure on the government and the Americans in the matter of Vietnam. Well, I've got opinions myself of course, being after all a compatriot of Conor Cruise O'Brien, no less, but these sensations are too strong for me. So I daresay I won't be doing the actual marching. Anyway, we have a confrontation of about half a dozen of these proud walkers and the British police, represented by a senior spokesman a bit grey in the face, and Fingal in the middle smiling incisively all round. And then to complicate matters, there's a clerical eminence without his puttees, a metrical high tory who was in the International Brigade and two cordial politicos with grenadine voices and cyanide eyes.

Now while Fingal, himself, is asking how peace is served by kicking in the balls of a British bobby and how law is served by the introduction of tear-gas and machine-guns, deferring now and again to the panel of pundits, up in the gallery, where Paul and myself are, in the flickering dark, there are mysteries going on that wouldn't have disgraced Eleusis, except that these are all in aid of the goddess of sterility. It's a fine technological sight and no mistake with Gabriel Da Costa in charge of the whole wondrous electronic miracle at the age of twenty-four and a half; as junior a patriarch with the charming boyish gaucheness of that strange article in Kubla-Khan-by-Shelley as ever left Golders Green for Putney. There are also two delicate morceaux of charlotte russe shouting out things such as numbers and jargon.

Towards the end, with everyone yelling bloody murder and old Fingal shining on like the harvest moon, in comes a snakehipped whizzkid in polaroid goggles and Roman hair, who stands obtrusively in the background. This turns out to be Emery Herrick, who runs the whole weekly space-probe. And when it's all over in a blaze of incoherence and a few of us go down to the lavish bar, this thirteenth muse himself graces us with his company and opinions. You name it—the tragedy of *Othello*, wine gums, the educational system, Her Majesty the Queen of England, the standard manhole cover, fishnet stockings, *Finnegans Wake*, the Church of Rome, insecticide, the dairies of Katmandu, bar-billiards, deodorants for men, the Democratic Party and *As You Like It* on ice—your man has an instant opinion, delivered with the compassion of Bugs Moran. I must say these brave classless pixies in their sunglasses act on me like itching balls in a garden-party.

So there we were among a host of dangerously personable personalities of television, who all regularly receive packets of crisps through the post from the great British nation, out there, watching and chomping as steady as you like; personalities ranging from the lowest kitchen farce to the higher theocratic realities. And in walked a real, seven-star, high-fidelity, by-appointment miracle. She was called Barbara Keller.

She walked across the room with the rhythm and class of the Modern Jazz Quartet and I can't say fairer than that. But slow and unexaggerated, not an undulation out of place, the supple-stiff walk of a goddess with perfect hips.

Soft, fairish hair; cool, steady eyes; not quite perfect features by any means—her nose turns up too far and her mouth is small, but the rest of her—from the retroussé tits to the delicate ankles—would have any decent heterosexual rushing to the bar for bromide on the rocks. She gives a cool, indifferent smile to all assembled, very unlike the flashing benevolent sunrise of her da or the vin mousseux of her mother.

Then Fingal Grey kissed her, uninvited, and I thought the young droop, Paul, her brother, who had sponged up a quantity of the hard stuff, had a bad twinge of catalectic arsis in the octave. Sensitive plants these poets. But his confusion was adequately covered by the bolting thunder-burps all round.

The reason for her appearance was that Fingal Grey was taking her, later that same momentous evening, to a film première, but they didn't have to depart for the moment and Fingal Grey was unwinding after the catch-as-catch-can with copious guffaws and slapping the backs of all concerned and laying a friendly hand on whichever parts of Barbara Keller were compatible with such decent surroundings as the lavish bar of Television Centre and the company of M.P.s and clergymen.

Then, to the general surprise, bang in the middle of an epigram from the gums of Emery Herrick in person, who should enter but the wary-eyed scop of the modern cinema, Eric Foster, in company of a nervous velvet waistcoat recognisable to the cultured as Andrew Stone.

Sure, this elfin fellow was to the novel what the tall, bald limp of a stuffed ollave was to the film, but strange to say, in spite of his drastic nerves, he had made a great success with the television as link-man for a programme about the arts, and had received his share of crisps in the weekly mail, which proves the British public isn't as thick as you find yourself believing. But more important, he turned out to be another of the ring of the Kellerungs. And he did a wee skip over to us and kissed Barbara in a civil way without the slightest offence.

Well, now, a master of nuance and atmosphere would be able to describe the subtle tensions that ensued in grand style, affecting almost everyone present except Emery Herrick and Gabriel da Costa. You'd think that Herrick would know his place in the presence of two genuine creative zombies like these, but not a bit of it. Herrick babbled away and bickered on down the bloody valley regardless and da Costa looked his unusual bewildered self. Meanwhile you have Eric Foster looking at the beautiful lady like some good and faithful hound of the buskervilles which leads Fingal Grey, who is a great lad for contact at all times, to lay a proprietorial hand upon the upper reaches of the glorious hip furthest away from him which causes the gloomgulp, Paul, to twitch so that he doesn't listen to the wee Stone gnome and that upsets him seeing that he has a sensitive nature and likes to be listened to. Jaysus! It would need Henry James, himself, to do them all justice in one of them long, wise, refined books where there's more going on between the lines than the sheets. I'm too coarse a hand for it.

She, of course, as befits a real ambrosial presence is quite calm and cool about it all. A couple of times I notice her eye playing over me own not unhandsome but rugged enough features like a gentle flurry of summer rain. Fingal Grey is on the defensive because he is giggling at the slightest remark especially from Eric Foster; the wetlegs is pissed; little Stone is rolling perturbably on about Alain Robbe-Grillet, who sounds a complicated class of chap to me; Emery Herrick, da Costa and the other winds and dragons are not listening to anyone at all. To the casual observer without much sophistication in these matters, it looks a tolerably jolly gathering. But from where I am there's more high tension than you'd find on the national grid.

But I fell into pleasant chat with a couple of boyos and the wee author, Stone, and got a couple of commissions for designs for some bloody brouhaha or other, so it wasn't entirely an unimproving evening.

Sylvie Keller

'THE HEART OF THE BATTLEFIELD'

"When young, one never knows where a love-affair will begin or end. There is an arbitrary moment at which one decides to start seeing someone clandestinely or to stop seeing her at all: but the attraction happened long before any word was spoken and the decision to bring the affair to an end was taken before the final meeting, in which some of the pain is real but as much of it is sheer pretence.

When I first saw Sylvie Keller, I wrote in the journal I used to keep in those days: 'In ordinary circumstances a rather unpleasant woman. Lyrical but intelligent with restless eyes and a waspish tongue that she controls with difficulty. She tries to give the impression of world-weariness, but I suspect has remained coldly faithful throughout her marriage. Emotionally she is probably a little frigid and, while needing the fillip of flirtations, has no real enthusiasm for sex.'

I used the phrase 'in ordinary circumstances' because I was taken to the Kellers' house by Eric Foster, who had known them for some time and whose work Sylvie admired.

What happened later would have been less of a surprise to me had I recognised both Kellers immediately as collectors. If only I had, it would have perhaps saved a lot of trouble.

If you are to understand this commonplace, rather pathetic story, you must have an impression of the background. The self-conscious and certainly self-satisfied sub-bohemia of Hampstead in the mid-fifties throve on the up-and-coming heterogeneous hopefuls who had already moved quite a long way beyond the gentility principle. At that time, property was acquired by politicians, advertisers, broadcasters and what have you, who were determined to be two things—promising and civilised. Consequently they welcomed all those of us who were struggling with novels or plays or pictures, whether or not we had talent. And they were unfailingly patronisingly generous. Now that I live there myself, some thirteen years later, it seems a much more bourgeois, sedate place. The Kellers, of course, have moved on.

In all these years, Sylvie Keller showed no more than the most casual interest in me and I don't remember giving her more than the odd thought when I was to go to their house for dinner. I'd try to call to mind what I'd read of hers in recent weeks, in much the same way as I imagine she tried to remember what I liked eating and drinking. She was always a perfect, immaculate hostess. As soon as I became successful professionally as a writer, I stopped keeping my journal—for one thing, I had less time and for another less reason to write for the sake of writing—so the relationship that developed between us is obscure in my mind and I have no recollection of actually starting to like her.

It was a surprise that particular morning, however, in late November to hear Sylvie's voice on the telephone. This was partly because I knew she hated telephoning—any arrangements were always made by Robert or, in latter years, Robert's secretary; and partly because I had been thinking about the Kellers earlier that same morning after a chance meeting with both their children a few evenings before.

'Andrew,' she said, 'I want to pick your brains. Will you let me buy you lunch?'

When I arrived, she was already waiting, although I was if anything a little early. She smiled at me and I remember thinking for the first time that there was as much allure as there was poise in her manner.

'I'm so glad you were able to come,' she said. 'I've got to do a piece on writers under twenty-five and to my horror I don't know any. So I want you to suggest a few for me to read.'

We talked about new authors for a while, but I soon discovered her real purpose was to interrogate me about Catholic writers. She was doing one of her long, perceptive bits for an upper middle-brow magazine and she knew that I had been a Catholic and that I wrote. It was a rather typical deception of the kind that Sylvie practised almost automatically and quite unnecessarily and I felt unexpectedly affectionate towards her because of it. I think I laughed at her at this point and when she asked why, I told her.

By the time they had fetched our *quennelles de homard* and brought the Montrachet, we had left Catholic writers and novelists under the age of twenty-five a long way behind. I told her about Leningrad and began to talk quite animatedly about the Nevsky Prospect, when I met her eyes smiling in a quietly tender way. I reached forward on the table for something and she took my hand gently in hers and kept it there for a moment as though we were very young lovers.

If I wanted to describe a moment of abruptly felt unhappiness I could probably do so more minutely and perhaps to greater effect than I can that moment of unexpected happiness. But pain seems to give things sharper outlines and although I remember what we were eating, what the room looked like, even what we said almost to the last word I still cannot put down what I felt at that moment.

We talked and made a lot of jokes and we ate and drank a great deal. She described her Australian uncle who had suddenly appeared from nowhere amusingly: he seemed to have infected the rest of the family with his irresponsible high spirits.

'Always excepting Barbara, of course,' she said. 'Who is untouchable.'

'I met her the other evening, at Television Centre,' I said. 'She was with Paul and a rather farouche sort of Irishman.'

'I'm sure she wasn't,' Sylvie said. 'She's far too intelligent to mix with interesting people.'

Then we were both silent. Jane West, a very pretty girl, whose mother, Sally, had once been Robert Keller's dentist and mistress came into the restaurant. She waved to us and joined two young men at another table. I don't suppose that an eighteen-year-old girl today would find it at all remarkable that two middle-aged people were falling in love over *profiteroles.*

'She's a pretty girl,' Sylvie said.

'Not very intelligent.'

'No. But, at that age, she doesn't have to be.'

'The young surprise me, Andrew. I had her round when Paul got back from France. They might both have been carved out of plastic.'

'Paul's twenty-six and decidedly intelligent.'

'I expect he'll have another chance at Andrea's party.'

'Are you going to that?'

'Of course.'

'Then it's something to look forward to.'

'Don't you feel like a party?'

'I'd rather talk about books.'

We both laughed at this feeble joke and I had a sudden sense again that I was seeing a woman I had not ever met before. I don't know what she saw in my face but when I put my hand on her thigh under the table, she held it there tightly.

After that there was no kind of tactical game. We found a taxi and I told it to go to Hampstead. We sat apart from one another in the cab and I don't think we exchanged more than a dozen words. I almost laughed aloud when I thought of the times in the past when this might have happened and how my conscience would have troubled me for days and nights.

Once in my flat there was no question that we both wanted each other very badly. I made love to her on the studio divan without unusual success, but that did not matter. I think we were both very happy in the sort of mood when people do inconsequential, perfectly commonplace things and find them marvellously charged with humour and excitement. We went out onto the Heath, beautiful and brilliant in the autumn, and walked across it very close to each other until we reached the Highgate side. She looked up at me, smiling. I had seen her smiling in the same way a thousand times, exchanging polite conversation.

'There are quite a lot of people who might be hurt,' I said.

She looked out over the City, stretching below us in the Hazy sunshine.

'A lot of people are hurt,' she said. 'We can't afford to waste our lives because of the risk of hurting and being hurt.'

'It's a question of conscience,' I said, smiling.

'I was forgetting,' she said. 'You're a Catholic writer.'

'I was.'

'Perhaps it's just as well,' she said.

We turned back the way we had come. At that moment when we might have hesitated neither of us had any doubts. That afternoon mattered, not next year or last weekend. When we had whispered to each other about love in those breathless, clumsy moments of desire, I think we had both meant them. I wondered when their memory would return with anger and bitterness."

Paul Keller

O ps. Room, Cricklewood College of Technology. Seventeen forty-eight hours. Visibility zero; cloud-cover dense. Bandits at three o'clock. The Head of Biology in southern English brogues that squeaked along corridor parquet as though it were cloister stone turns his tight little eyes upon us and quotes R. L. Stevenson as evidence of his culture. He shares an American moment with us and an African peril, in all modesty, and suggests (someone has whispered the magic name of Daddy in his crucibles) that our young colleague, Keller, might have something to say from his first-hand experience of riots.

Meanwhile Les Cohn of Parsons Green and Stan Bendit of Goldhawk Road whip up a sizzling revolution in the main canteen that gurgles past in the pipework along with toxic fluids and corrosive effluent. Poor Les and Stan beating their pointed Maoist heads against the plastic-pudding wall of our educational system: a four-square obliteration wish: three bedrooms, car with garage and the uniform gadgets of a street in Cookham, an avenue in Hillingdon, a crescent in West Ruislip. Decent lads, nice girls, waiting to come into their birth-right.

Silence for Groupie. The Principal. Thomas Hoopoe, Ph.D., Erasmic of Rotherham, not too little, not too much . . . in fact a leavening of bread, circuses, stones and serpents in streams not unreasonable. We must not, he tells us, expect young people today to be as acquiescent as we were; of course, our young colleague, Keller, co-opted onto the strategic air command, doesn't need telling. All because Les and Stan want beer in the canteen and the right to grant themselves and their best mates automatic first class diplomas. He foresees, he tells us, serious trouble at the London School of Economics and it might spread like wildfire.

The Head of Liberal Studies, Pontius Probert B.Litt., puts us in the action politics picture as published by Pelican and heads wag sadly but wisely agreeing that the time will come when students must have a large say in their own government. Our young colleague, Keller . . .

At the age of twenty-six has no ideals and no illusions. He does not give a damn about equality of opportunity, appetite, envy, lust or gratification of same. Ethically kitted out for a career in commerce, he suffers from undropped ambitions and so is unable to adopt the necessary stand. Lubriciously pissed with a grubby old Australian most evenings, he aspires to lechery and fastidious poems but.

Odd to see her suddenly in that way. Perhaps she arranged it.

And Fingal Grey! A cathode beam in each eye, sabre toothed tiger burning brightly into the immortal subtopian symmetry and laughing and pawing her and laughing. Slack skin under the jaw. Eric Foster shuddered. I like him. But has he . . . ? And poor little Andrew Stone, sensitive and gentle as some perpetually worried animal, whiskers twitching this way and that wanting only to talk about meaning and essence, leaving the grunting and sweating to others. Friend of less bitchy Mummy. But not I think of the protector of his people, shadow-walking, joyful in heart, terrible visitant, nobly adorned with gold and terrifying in his variegated colouring. Who would seize the cowering novelist by the scruff out of the filthy heap of bones and have him expose his neuroses. *She* is less bitchy. Easier with Barbara out of the house. The spirit of competition is diluted. Even mother and daughter. You would not catch steel-blue Dad circling the sacred Whitehall groves with drawn sword and furtive expression, waiting for the tanist, Paul. Women tear at each other like hot peasant girls in dirty books.

I haven't heard a word of this. Keller? No comment, Principal. (We're just good friends.)

The Barbaric Queen. The May Queen. It is only the innocent who are fooled. Gavin says, 'You have a very beautiful girl for a sister, Paul.' Eyes I saw in nightmares take us in coolly, temperate, sure. Take in too Fingal, Foster, who else . . . ? Unter goldnem Gezweig . . . die blutenden Häupter.

A committee. The Head of Biology, scourge of microbes, one-eyed gazer into truth magnified to two thousand to one; Jem Crusoe, the plebiean student's friend, the dipole Ariel who wouldn't die; Pontius Probert and his B. Litt. (a committee all on their own); Les; Stan; a faceless student who owns several shirts and is president of the Union; our young colleague, Keller . . . 'who will no doubt have inherited a talent for committees.' Laughter. The backslap of jesting Probert. Already it is seven thirty. Burnt-out end.

And I have faked it all. Faked everything. My reputation among friends, an image, a job, an intellect. Emotions, exultations, agonies. A master's degree in extemporal self-pity. The diagnosis for my kind. Better the self-deception of Les and Stan because they'll grow out of it. At twenty-six one should have found something to believe in other than lechery and writing poems. But.

Sebastian may be coarse and loud and pissed—but at least he's honest and coarse and loud and pissed. Now how do I get from Cricklewood to Hampstead. Sir, it is not possible to get from Cricklewood to Hampstead. Through the light rain muffled in the dark, the killer a youngish man of medium height wearing a short white mack, probably foreign, no visible scars was last seen dangerously at shouting distance moving through Kilburn. Trying desperately hard to look like someone turning to nod goodbye to Rochefoucauld he mounts the steps and rings the bell of a house in Southill Park Gardens and Hullo! It is darling Paul! Our young colleague, Keller! Son of Da-Bog, degraded in some places to the status of a demon. Who'll be there? The usual smug crowd. Why can't I be *nice*? The trouble with a memory like mine is that it files away every imagined insult, every real blow, catalogues enemies. Blandford, Aylmer, sneering. The shock on their faces as the knife went in. And dirty secondary moderns on the way home. Keller ran away. All burned when the school caught fire. I shall discipline my mind and not hate for the rest of this filthy, wet walk. I shall magine undressing Jane West. No, her mother.

Damn, Daddy got there first. I suppose I had better donate my mind to *Hamlet*.

Bisset greets his guests like attractive business propositions. He studies their faces with narrowed eyes looking for the small print. Five backbenchers, a junior minister, three critics, eleven journalists, two nice young men in the same line of business as Andrea and the sexiest dentist of the English speaking world, Sally West. I wonder why Da-Bog changed to Brisbane Praxiteles. I've had some lovely fantasies in that chair with the spit-sucking gurgler hissing away and a mouthful of felt plugs and those tits hovering above my frozen jaws. Stands there: body slightly turned, one hip jutting, one leg slightly bend, sardonic. The wickedest trouble shooter in Wimpole Street, exciting David Lawson so much that he has almost wet his moustache.

Jane waves from the long yellow yonder, surrounded by the junior El Vino's—big brown eyes, very white slightly projecting teeth and small lines about her young eyes that eighteen-year-old girls did not have when I was eighteen.

'Now, you young jumbuck. Stop exercising your eyes on that beautiful version of the female form that you don't have to be the poet Ovid to leap to attention for and come and have a drink.' The latest curiosity, perched on his own pedestal of homely aphorisms, obscenity and outrage, has arrived ahead of the family into whose cleavage he has crept.

The door opens. Here! Now! The valiant one advances, matt-finished in his corselet of charcoal grey, cunningly woven by the cloth-smith. Three junior ministers stop looking bored. For it is Eleutharian Dad and with him (Good God!) Jacqueline of the welded knickers. They must have met accidently. (Surely!)

Imperceptible amusement crosses the grant-maker's face as he takes administrative steps into the mead-lounge. But the entrance is spoiled by Fingal Grey to whom flock tomorrow's guests like the beasts of the jungle to an ululation of Tarzan. Every party should have its Television personality. Fingal amiables around, immaculate creases of good humour ...

And then Barbara.

O Christ. She is superb.

A distant smile. Then Fingal has her elbow and Eric Foster stoops into the frame. The charcoal chieftain smiles over Andrea's faded hair. Now at the young lord's side, the functional-finical-pathetical David Lawson extending downward his upper lip over huge hippic teeth. 'I always enjoy Andrea's parties,' he says. 'One meets such an unlikely cross-section of people.' And tells me about airline complexities that are bothering his department, a protozoic eye fixed upon smiling Dad and Andrea.

Now Mummy. A discreet entrance, but an entrance. Eclipsing the slightly agitated Andrew Stone who happens to be in her progress. Mummy is warm, for the Welsh lilt creeps into her voice and eyes, and patronising. Eric Foster, at a conversation tasting, deep eyes smiling, sips, considers, rejects, chooses . . . Obviously Barbara.

Roger Lomax, saturnine socialist consultant, and his pastel shaded cologne scented wife, Jasmine. 'Hullo, Paul. How's technology?' Flatter, dimmer, rougher cut that most of them, trying to make the Welfare State work. And Jasmine always smells fresh and dew-washed. I could get quite pastoral about Jasmine if it were not for her three children and their little ways.

Andrea enlists me. Small sausages on sticks, canapes, croques and croutes, bouches and tartes and galettes. A Welsh dresser and an oak table. Wedged between them against her big soft titties, she giggles and rubs against me. 'You had no idea helping could be such fun, had you?'

Last one up the north face of the Eiger's a rice pudding. It is the warlike-tusked night-stepper, charcoally creeping up. The monster—Nigel Elliot Carew Sinclair. (Nigel Elliot is the pseudonym of a higher civil servant who brings a delicious authenticity to his ghoulish stories of murder and malice.) (Carew—it rhymes with 'hairy'—Sinclair is the pen-name of Robert Keller, whose sophisticated comedies have long charmed the white knickers off Western Civilisation.) And poor Andrew Stone, who wants only to talk of purpose and meaning and theory, finds himself at grips with the moor of Little Venice, dripping battle-icicles. Daddy has a

Nietzschean loathing of the timid, the gentle, the sensitive. But Mummy will caress them in sibilant Welsh. Mothering.

I know as Barbara approaches again the bite of that full mouth curved in anger and contempt. Now smiling, now. The steady eyes. Like them she has the instinct for the top, the inborn sense of status. Perhaps, I am a foundling. Then she would not be my sister . . .

'How are you? Settling down?' She explains why we have seen so little of each other—she has been busy on research. And I have to explain why the Cricklewood College of Technology and that it's not a curious job for someone who wants to be a writer because of the free time and unexacting standards. 'I should have thought,' she says, 'that you could have got something at a University.'

The instinct for the top. Her work, I know, fascinates her. There is no point talking about that. In a moment of silence she scans the room with the impersonality of radar. Eric Foster sidespying her from a neo-stoical rock. Fingal Grey chatting up Sally West, one watching the other with eyes of a gourmet cannibal. She does not flicker, except passing over Sebastian, then the slightest, merest spasm of distaste. That slight curl of the mouth. The sweet, sick feeling seeps back. Hysterical, exhausting, destroying. Passion is to love, my dear pupils, what heroin is to Haut-Brion.

I wonder if I still sicken her. 'What are you writing?' 'Not much. The odd poem.' Holiday chalet. No. Talk about Paris. It's a wonderful place, I tell her, for wandering around having profound ideas that never work on the page. Holiday chalet. The yellowed brilliance of fine summer days. I don't know whether she notices the panic. Talking feverishly. 'I've always thought your great problem is boredom, Paul. Let's go to the theatre or have dinner one evening.' Oh, goddess, yes! Smiling, now. Yellowed sunlight. She was nineteen, standing there only . . . 'I understand from Daddy that you were kept fully occupied by that mythical giant.'

'Fingal?' She laughs a lot. It makes her breasts move.

Holiday yellow, nineteen, standing there in thin white pants, bare breasts, stretching up to turn on the shower. Turning, tearing back the curtain, looking down where it was red and swollen in my hand . . .

The cold curl of her mouth and silence. Vomiting and waking up (even now) sweating with cold shame. Oh, my goddess, yes. After eleven years the wine is pressed.

Smiling now we look at each other. Our eyes meet and it is an effort but neither looks away. The wine is pressed, the mild stillness resolves dark questions with whispered answers. 'I go out with him sometimes, but it's not important.' When?' Some rosy, ribald shout from Sebastian interrupts and she sweeps her eyes icily towards him. 'How long is that idiot staying?' I think it is indefinitely and he is not so bad, darling, let's not worry about him. Eric Foster can keep away no longer, chasing the pain into the back of his eyes. She is kind to him. He wants to know about a type of madness.

She answers and he stores her frame by frame to gloat over the rushes and lovingly edit her into his private masterpiece. But Mummy comes and darlings us into docile emptiness.

Eric watches Barbara. 'I've got to go, Mummy. Fingal wants me to meet someone or other he has to interview.' Foster does not wince. She touches his arm briefly, kindly. 'I'll fix something for Wednesday, Paul.'

Sebastian cuts her off and slurps his hand onto her side one thumb trickily massaging upwards to her breast. She removes him as she would a spider.

Now the sly Rhiamon, wife of Pwyll (see also Nimue enchantress of Merlin), turns laughing eyes on the son who learned the myths at her smooth Welsh knee. 'What on earth are you two up to on Wednesday?' 'We haven't decided.' It'll be a change whatever it is. You know, Eric, I've always rather suspected that my children don't like each other. Still, I won't bore you with that. You can both help me. What d'you think of Iris Murdoch's novels . . .' Andrea shrills 'For Christ's sake, Sylvie, why are you so bloody intellectual all the time. I want to borrow your son.'

In the kitchen, heaving more plates. Again the manoeuvre of bodies in confined spaces and a husky giggle. My trouble is I'm bloody bored.

PART THREE

Sylvie Keller

'AN UNOFFICIAL SANDCASTLE'

"I was lying on the black leather sofa in my room in the house at Barnes reading Ayer's *The Concept of a Person* and wondering why it was that Sally West's cooking did not give me indigestion. The trouble was that I always returned, even now, from an afternoon with Sally in a mood of restless elation and I could not concentrate properly.

I drifted into the sitting room and switched the lights on, taking pleasure in the soft yellow glow on the dove-grey walls and noticed as always the faint smell of lilac which Sylvie contrived to hint at in every room she herself used. I dare say I felt absurdly complacent at that moment as I moved towards the drinks table to mix a martini for Sylvie and myself. The irony of that moment of unregenerate self-satisfaction was not something that I was ever to forget.

I delighted in the rare moments I spent alone with Sylvie. Sometimes when I was weary of the intricacies of my adventures into love with other women, I thought the anxiety of intrigue hardly worthwhile. At these moments, however, I knew that it was. I imagined, as I prepared the cocktail, and carried it through to the refrigerator, the calm, relaxed, witty conversation we should have when she came back from *The Sunday Times* and congratulated myself for realising how much she still meant to me. I was living in another age.

Sally had been silent driving me to the station, probably wondering whether I had chosen to lunch in a restaurant which she (and therefore I) knew that Jacqueline went to. Of course, the idea had been ridiculous but her feigned attack of nausea had been convincing enough for me to think that she was sincerely upset. It had also meant that I had been forced to endure her frightful cuisine.

As a younger man, I should have found no difficulty at all in forgetting my problems by reading something intellectually exciting, but on this particular evening I could only prowl restlessly around and wait for Sylvie to return and make me calm again.

I was glancing impatiently at my watch, when I became aware of her at the doorway. She moved everywhere very quietly, with a graceful lilt which even people whom she knew very well could never quite take for granted, but she usually entered a room with natural assurance. I could not remember her hesitating in movement in all the years we had been together. Now she stood at the doorway, staring at me, her eyes tense and strained.

'Hello, darling,' I said, smiling at her, 'I've just made some drinks. Sit down and I'll bring you one.'

I went out of the room for a moment and returned to find her sitting on the edge of an armchair in a compact, cramped position. When I offered her a cold, inviting glass, she made no move to take it. At first I was not alarmed. I knew quite well that she might have read of some disaster in an evening paper and that this would have been quite enough to upset her, but to merit this display of numb despair it must have been of immense seriousness.

'There's something you want to tell me,' I said.

'Perhaps,' said Sylvie. 'Have you any idea what it might be?'

'For God's sake, Sylvie,' I said, 'no. You've such a subtle mind, I have always found it hard to know what might be troubling you. Is it something I've done?'

She shook her head and turned to look directly at me. She went over to a bowl of roses. Taking one of these, she began to twirl it between her fingers.

'There's no way I know of breaking it gently,' she said. 'It's Andrew and me. I think we're in love. I don't think we ever intended to be and I don't think we either of us wanted to be. It was just something trivial that became important. I'm sorry.'

I watched the rose between her fingers as though mesmerically fascinated, gradually becoming aware of an ache of relief creeping through my limbs.

'Aren't you a bit old for desperate passions?' I said.

She darted her head at me and for a moment there was a flash in her eyes, but then they saddened again. She put the rose down.

'Anyway,' I said, 'we surely don't need to be too dramatic about it.'

'Robert,' she said, 'please understand. It will save us both a lot of weariness.'

I swallowed my drink and moved towards the table, driven for some reason to pick up the flower that she had put down. But as I approached she picked it up with a fearful, childishly possessive gesture almost crushing the petals between her fingers. Some deep-running feeling which I did not remotely understand made me say:

'I suppose I've always disappointed you, Sylvie. But, darling, this is absurd. You can't mean you want a divorce.'

She twirled the rose again. It was becoming intolerable and I wanted to forcibly snatch the flower away from her and shred it. Then she shook her head.

'What would be the point?' she said. 'I don't want to hurt you, Robert. That's not why I have spoken about it. It's just that I want it to be clean and honest.'

I looked at her. She looked like someone painted by Matisse. I knew that in this mood she was not likely to burst into tears so I allowed myself to laugh bitterly.

'Of course, you've already been to bed with him,' I said.

'Several times,' she said.

We stared at each other in silence for some time. Her finely chiselled face was calm again, but there was unmistakable grief in the eyes. I realised that it was probably the first time she had been unfaithful to me. She threw the crumpled rose down onto the highly-polished table, but I no longer wanted to pick it up. Quite suddenly, I stopped feeling rational and mildly amused about it all. It did not matter how many times I had deceived her. I had paid in pain and remorse for all of them. I could only think of that delicate, shy little man in her arms and a feeling of bitterness and anger invaded me and seemed to freeze my heart.

In this mood of torment, I rushed out of the room and out of the house, not quite sure what I intended to do. I suppose that there was some improbable notion at the back of my mind that I should go around to Andrew and knock his teeth out. But as I was making for the blue Rolls, someone called my name.

It was Jacqueline Benbow. As I saw her I pulled myself together and assumed some semblance of rationality. She was with another woman, whom I had met briefly some time before, Annabelle Finch, a tall, dark-skinned, striking woman who was a lecturer at L.S.E.

However distraught I might have looked, I apprehended at once that neither of them seemed to have noticed and Jacqueline explained that they were collecting Sylvie to go to an exhibition at Richmond of paintings by a young man she wanted to encourage.

'Sylvie very kindly asked us to have a drink,' said Jacqueline.

I took them into the house, making as much noise as possible. In the pain and excitement of the moment, Sylvie must have completely forgotten her invitation and the private view. I took them into Sylvie's own sitting room, with its inevitable faint perfume of lilacs and the light pine panelling. Here I found a bottle of excellent brandy and insisted, somewhat to their surprise, that they have some. A moment or so later, Sylvie came in with that radiant confidence that I knew so well and could have hated so readily.

Still in a state of some confusion, I allowed Sylvie to take charge of the conversation. Annabelle said little but in spite of the shock of what Sylvie had just told me, or perhaps because of it, I found myself fascinated by her. She appeared to be paying very little attention to what the other two were saying and sat still in a straight-backed chair, watching them with quick movements of her dark eyes. She was quite relaxed, her strong thighs crossed, her dark face in repose. I found her strangely challenging and exciting, so I waited until Sylvie and Jacqueline were talking animatedly about a painting and drew my chair closer to hers.

'You're obviously very interested in art, Miss Finch,' I said.

She kept her eyes on the other two women, deliberately indifferent.

'No,' she said. 'Not particularly.'

Sylvie glanced towards us and smiled at Annabelle with great charm and brilliance. The smile was not returned. Annabelle Finch looked across the room with the impervious arrogance of Corot's Roman Odalisque.

'I want Jacqueline's advice about those drawings I bought,' Sylvie said. 'I don't think they can be Ben Marshalls.'

I saw immediately that she was for some reason playing up to me, contriving to leave me alone with Annabelle. I resented furiously her indifference and her attempt to control the rhythms of my own plans. As she went out, she turned:

'Give Mrs Finch another drink, Robert.'

I went over to the drinks on the plain table and filled both glasses. When I turned round, Annabelle was smiling. Her lips were drawn back tightly and very white teeth showed in the thin space between them.

'*Mrs* Finch?' I said.

'Divorced, of course,' she said. 'My husband was a psychoanalyst. I wasn't good for him.'

We sat in silence for some minutes. In such a brooding presence, the whole room seemed to be unbearably trivial. Annabelle leaned forward from the waist and picked up the Arab dagger that Sylvie used as a paper-knife. She laid it on her thigh and stroked the curved blade with one finger. The weapon gleamed silver against the dark blue stocking and I found myself leaning forward.

'I think I can believe that,' I said.

She kept her eyes on the point of the knife, stroking it, smiling slightly.

'It was not pleasant,' she said.

I was by this time in a state of high sexual excitement and improbable though it may seem I wondered seriously about attacking her. She would undoubtedly fight me off and I should be able to hurt her. I wanted that.

'You are a remarkably civilised man, Mr Keller,' said Annabelle. 'This is very tasteful.'

She made a circular movement of her head, her dark eyes mocking me, then uncrossed her legs and sat with her knees pressed tightly together, the left foot slightly forward, the right poised on the toe with the bright-bladed dagger along the line where her thighs met. I got up and walked around behind her chair. I stood there, trying to control my breathing, not moving.

Annabelle Finch sat perfectly still, then she gestured with the dagger towards a bowl of flowers, white roses.

'In mediaeval literature the rose was a symbol of earthly love,' she said. 'But Dante made it a white rose and the symbol of divine love.'

Her voice was cool and factual. She sat, with her back to me, looking towards the flowers, holding the dagger by the hilt so that the curved blade pointed upwards.

'I'm not desperately concerned with symbols,' I said.

Suddenly she laughed and the sound maddened me. I stepped up to the back of her chair and gripped her shoulders. She became charged with stillness but did not even turn her head. I moved my hands roughly over her breasts. She made one slow writhing ripple from the shoulders and with terrifying violence flung the blade of the dagger into the plain wooden table. I was unable to control an involuntary movement away from her. The bright blade quivered. She said nothing but got up and faced me with dark, savage eyes.

A moment later Sylvie and Jacqueline came back into the room. I don't know what they thought seeing us standing there, glaring at each other, like two gladiators about to tear at each other.

'Have you finished your drink, Mrs Finch?' Sylvie asked. asked. 'I think it's time we were moving.'

She turned her dark face towards them. I looked at the three women. Next to Annabelle, the other two were like Dresden figures alongside an erotic Hindu idol."

Robert Keller

The December afternoon was pleasantly sunlit. From the window of Robert Keller's study, the prospect of light falling through the bare branches of chestnut trees onto the winter-coloured grass was relaxing and irrationally delightful.

Robert Keller turned from the window and contemplated with regrettable self-satisfaction his book-lined walls, the magnificent and tidy desk to his left in the centre of which was a page of good plain paper half-filled with Robert Keller's unaffectedly neat handwriting, the black leather sofa and the chairs and the good oak occasional table on which his mistress, Sally West, sat.

Sally West looked opulently attractive as usual in a black two-piece suit and light-blue roll-necked sweater which was probably a size too small. She was smoking a long cigarette.

'You never know,' said Sally, 'perhaps she's discovered she's a lesbian.'

Robert Keller laughed but purely to please Sally. He did not regard her as intelligent and he found her sense of humour, as well as her sensibility, crude most of the time, but occasionally it jarred especially. To keep in check his spasm of irritation, Robert Keller focused his attention on his mistress's long powerful thighs. He asked her whether it was certain that Annabelle Finch was lesbian.

'I'd have said she was as queer as a rubber cucumber, darling. Not that she's ever approached me. Her sort and mine keep out of spitting range.'

Robert Keller assured Sally that his wife was not likely to have developed Sapphic propensities, whereupon Sally West mocked at him for being pompous and in a knowing, worldly-wise way said that stranger things had been heard of. There were times when Robert Keller found her very banal.

'I've always thought,' she said, 'that there's something odd about Jacqueline.'

While she talked inconsequentially about Sylvie and the fantastic relationship she had dreamed up as soon as he had told her of the visit by Annabelle Finch, Robert Keller studied her, pretending to listen. There was no question about her being the coarsest, most earthy woman of his acquaintance—and this had always struck him as odd since she was the daughter of a country doctor and came from the middle-to-upper-middle-class, unlike Sylvie (daughter of a miner), Andrea (daughter of a blacksmith), Jasmine (daughter of a plumber), Elaine (daughter of a post-office official). Even Jacqueline's father was a poor parson. Robert Keller was placidly exploring once again his interest in social origins, continuing to look directly at Sally, when he realised that she had misinterpreted the look and was playing up to him. She had placed her hands on her hips and was thrusting her breasts, already struggling against the light-blue woollen sweater, forward. At the same time she uncrossed her legs and sat with them slightly apart, inclining to the left with one knee a little lower than the other.

Robert Keller, uncertain of the movements of his family on that particular Saturday and feeling no particular urgency, affected not to notice and made some unspecific noise in his throat to suggest that he had been evaluating semi-seriously Sally's theories. He knew perfectly well that she would cover up the provocative drill and that neither of them need be embarrassed.

He got up and walked over to one of the book shelves, reading the titles: Sikes *Peter Abailard*; Aquinas *Philosophical Texts*; Gilson *The Christian Philosophy of St Thomas Aquinas*; Coplestone *Aquinas*; The Works of Aristotle; Ross *Aristotle*; Jaeger *Aristotle*; Augustine *Confessions*; Augustine *The City of God*; Augustine . . .

He enjoyed enormously reading the titles of his books and reminding himself that he had read them all. As he let his eye move over Averroes, Avicenna, A. J. Ayer, onward, he made some expertly non-committal comment on what Sally had been saying. When he turned round again, she was standing at the window, looking out into the garden, her arms placidly folded. The moment of challenge had been postponed.

'What did *you* make of her, Robert?' she said.

Robert Keller joined his mistress at the window and they both looked out in an abstracted way at a few dead leaves which had escaped the gardener scuttling about on the pale grass. He said that he had found Annabelle Finch fairly unremarkable, commenting that she was undoubtedly good-looking. Sally West interrupted to say that she was not surprised that Robert Keller had noticed that. Ignoring her, he explained that in the time he had spent alone with Annabelle Finch, while his wife and Jacqueline had been out of the room looking at prints in order to establish their authenticity, they had talked about economic affairs. She was an able, if academic, woman—academic in the sense that she tended to place enormous weight on theoretical solutions —and he had found her forecast of economic recovery in late 1969 optimistic but encouraging. His own grasp on these things was a little rusty. As he had guessed, Sally West was soon bored by the account of this conversation. Robert Keller did not tell her that, while it had been taking place, he had found himself powerfully attracted by Mrs Finch. He would have been wary of admitting as much to another man and was certainly much too wise to say anything of the sort to Sally. He described Annabelle Finch's manner as distant but polite.

Sally looked up and sideways at him, no doubt with the well-worn irony that she commanded so accurately. Robert Keller continued to look at the winter sunlight scene with intact unruffled pleasure, half-smiling contentedly.

'He's made a bloody good job of your teeth,' Sally West said. 'Is it all over now?'

He was amused and put his arm around her shoulders squeezing her affectionately, murmuring something about professional jealousy. Sally laughed.

'He may be a better dentist,' she said, 'but I bet you don't put your hand up *his* skirt when you're in the chair.'

She seemed determined to tune onto a sexual frequency. Robert Keller was reminded of Sylvie and the appalling little man, Andrew Stone. With effortless insouciance he walked over to one of the armchairs and sat down. Then he mentioned it casually to Sally West.

She turned quickly to face him, grinning.

'You don't mean it! Little Stone . . .'

Robert Keller told her of his wife's confession and how she had enjoyed making it.

'Well, good for him!' said Sally.

'Oh, Robert, love! You can't pretend that you care. I mean, you've been fucking about like an old goat for years. It's all right, darling. I know there must have been a few dozen others besides me. Why should you care if Sylvie has it off once in a while? Though I must say I wouldn't have chosen Andrew myself . . .'

Somewhat guardedly, Robert Keller intimated that he agreed generally with what his mistress was saying about his wife and his wife's choice of lover. Andrew Stone had always seemed to him to be a moderately talented but absurdly pretentious aesthete. Disliking theories of art, obscurantist fashions, elitist presumptions from his earliest years at Cambridge, Robert Keller had always taken pleasure in his own crisp prose which set out in thrillers to entertain by means of well-etched characters in exciting situations; and in light fiction to amuse by means of interesting characters in precisely observed environments. He spoke a little of this to Sally West, noticing her unashamedly happy grin.

'I confess it's a real turn up for the book,' Sally said. 'Fancy, Sylvie! God, can you imagine them . . .'

Since the picture caused Sally West such amusement, Robert Keller was determined not to show her that in his own imagination it roused him to something approaching fury. He was not in the habit of losing his temper, but he was anxious to forestall Sally's inevitable description of a love scene between Sylvie and the ridiculous Stone.

'Come here,' said Robert Keller.

As he had guessed, she responded readily and walked slowly towards his arm chair, dawdling at the hips and smiling like a she-wolf. She hitched her skirt up and sat across his legs in such a way as to enable him to easily slip his hand between her thighs. Knowing his preference for stockings she always wore them rather than tights on these occasions. Robert Keller was therefore in the act of feeling the sheer, plump, firm, warm texture give way to the momentary coarser softer instant of the stocking top before reaching the cool, pliant, bare flesh, when the door was flung open.

'Say, Robbie, me old son, there ain't a drop of bloody whisky in the entire estate, mate,' said Sebastian Jones.

It was not possible to tell for certain what Sebastian Jones had noticed upon his sudden entry. Robert Keller, a little flummoxed by his sudden appearance, was nevertheless able to remain calmly seated. For the brief instant possible, he wondered, clinically rather than anxiously, how Sally would react. She behaved well. At the moment of Robert Keller's withdrawing his trembling hand from her crutch, coincidental with the first hint of the door opening, she swung her knees together and levering with both arms against the sides of the black leather armchair raised herself to a position where she was kissing Robert Keller's forehead lightly and in the process of pushing herself away.

'Strewth,' said Sebastian Jones, 'you must have had a winner come up, girlie. I'd drink to that and no mistake if I could find a single drop of the Northern rainbow.'

Robert Keller, remaining seated with a clear sense of physiological diplomacy, offered the old man the facilities of his study where he kept a few bottles. Sally West said that she would be delighted to help and cleverly asked where the drink was to be found.

'Showing off your etchings, eh, Rob, mate,' asked Sebastian Jones. 'Can't say that I blame you. Thank you, sweetheart. This'll get the pipes working again.'

The uncle of Robert Keller's wife plunked himself down in the other armchair, looking red, benign, hot and unperturbed. Robert Keller's most permanent mistress poured drinks for all three of them in the most feminine way imaginable. Robert Keller, gradually losing tension, sat back in his armchair comfortably.

'There's no ice,' said Sally West. 'And I want some if you don't.'

She went out.

'That's only my joke, you understand, Rob,' said Sebastian Jones. 'I know you're straight where little Sylvie's concerned. But you don't take no notice of an old kookaburra screeching away, anyway, do you, mate?'

They both laughed and took a sip of whisky.

'That's the taste of civilisation, sport,' said Sebastian Jones.

As the old man was listening to Robert Keller's explanation: that Sally was worried about her daughter's university prospects and had come to him for advice, Sally returned. They both declined ice, but Sebastian Jones took advantage of Sally's proximity by patting her bottom appreciatively. After discreetly allowing him to do so, she moved over to the sofa and sat down.

'Fine looking girl you've got there and no mistake,' said Sebastian Jones to Sally. 'And if you take my advice the best university she can go to has four posts and springy mattress.'

Interpreting Sally West's baffled look in good time, Robert Keller explained. Then while Sally exchanged something like conversation with his wife's relative, he sipped his whisky, a good single malt, and wondered why he was going to such trouble to allay the suspicions of Sebastian Jones. Robert Keller had not become the very senior figure he was in the Civil Service by fooling himself either about other people or about himself: He was consequently able to see that he was cultivating the old man's good will, in spite of the fact that Sebastian Jones was absurdly coarse, excruciatingly boring and a distinct nuisance, because he hoped that some of the Australian's wealth would come to Sylvie.

On the pretext of drawing the curtains, he got up from his chair and wandered over to the window, aware of both pairs of eyes following him. Sebastian Jones was liberally counselling Sally invoking at various intervals various sages, philosophers, poets and divines. Robert Keller looked out into the evening and saw his daughter standing alone in the garden. She was wearing a black and white coat and her fairish hair was disarranged. She had her hands in the coat pockets and looked, as usual, self-contained, unmoved and untouchable. He thought that he respected his daughter. He arranged the curtains and stepped over to the desk.

'It's a great thing to be young at heart, sweetheart,' said Sebastian Jones. 'It keeps the spirits up which puts me in mind of another small snort of the elixir. Shall I tell you something, Sally girl? When I sit here surrounded by all these damned books, an old burrowing wombat like me, I feel overbloodyawed. And do you know, when this boy, Bobby, ain't reading, he's writing the damn things? Now that's quite something and no mistake.'

Smiling her sexy smile, Sally West refilled the old fellow's glass.

'I don't suppose even your travels have taken you to the GVD, eh, Robbie?'

Robert Keller said that although there had been some talk of his going to Woomera many years before, the trip had been postponed and ultimately the work had fallen to a subordinate.

'Woomera,' said Sebastian Jones, reflectively emptying half his glass. 'There's a place. Desolate, mate, It's all below sea level around Lake Eyre. Pretty fair hell that can be. Like the Quattara Depression.'

He then fell into a condition of medial alcoholic lyricism, describing the fine, fresh and clean cities of Australia, and the fine, tall and healthy men and women who lived in them. He digressed on the subject of cricket which happened to be a passion of Sally West's. Robert Keller was able to defocus his attention.

Games bored Robert Keller, so he gave his mind to the forthcoming evidence he was to give to the latest committee, looking into the Civil Service. Robert Keller was aware that his voice was a significant one. He was a natural administrator able to exercise charm, power, persuasion, force and he believed firmly in the permanent, problem-solving core of the first-rate men who made government work, but his grasp of technical detail was slack. He reflected that he was a strategist in terms of policy: he saw things with a broad, imaginative sweep. In this way he would be able to put certain proposals to the committee, which he was in little doubt would impress them: but it would not be a bad idea to have dinner at his club with David Lawson. David Lawson was stuffy but he had a good mind. He was an excellent administrative mechanic. A REME major. Or in Naval terms, the electrical commander to Robert Keller's officer. The conversation would prove useful. Robert Keller smiled at the thought of David Lawson's ancient and meticulously undeclared longing for Sylvie. It reminded him of Stone. He had not realised how much he detested Stone until recently. Such emotional concerns, however, were unprofitable. He shifted his eyes from the books on the shelves opposite to his mistress and picked up the conversation.

Under the influence of a new drink, Sebastian Jones became sonorously dithyrambic about the natural marvels of Australia.

'I'll never forget the time,' he said, 'I went into a cave, poking about generally. Couldn't see a bloody thing but me ears was hurting me. Then I saw thousands and thousands of tiny red spots in the blackness.'

'Bats with baby faces whistling and beating their wings,' murmured Robert Keller to himself.

'Sharp as an echidna's elbow!' said Sebastian Jones. 'That's what you are, Bobby, sport. You got it in one. Millions of bats. Bloody vampires. Well, I don't mind admitting it gave me the creeps and I pissed off out of there at a hell of a spurt. Fell over. Caught meself a crack on the conk that was a bonzer k.o.'

The interminable tales, amusing enough in certain circumstances, continued. Robert Keller was now in a mood to make love to his mistress, to read peacefully alongside a glass of cool beer, to get on with his thriller, best of all to make a few brief notes about what he would say to the committee. He became aware of what Sebastian Jones was saying again.

' . . . Ethel Creek, Horseshoe, Mount Vernon, Wittenoom Gorge. You name the spot . . .'

'I take it,' said Robert Keller, 'the government were grateful.'

'He's a sly bastard, this one, Sally girl,' said Sebastian Jones delightedly. 'I'd watch him in the dark on a spiral staircase, sweetheart, if I were you. Of course, that's a joke, Rob, lad, and you know it. You enjoy one better than most of us. Well, we won't go into State secrets, Robbie. Not for the moment at least. And I dare say you youngsters have had enough of listening to an old brush-tongued parakeet like me by now. Anyway it's opening time and that fine boy of yours is taking me around the East End with an Irish mate of his.'

Predicting that Sebastian Jones would make his son, Paul, a drunkard, Robert Keller encouraged him to be on his way. The old man insisted on kissing Sally, lasciviously rubbing her thighs as he bent over and planted his wet, red lips on her forehead. Then he went out.

'Is he as rich as he pretends Sally West said. Or is he every bit the shocking old fake I think he is.'

Robert Keller cautiously and prudently told his mistress that there had been some interesting discoveries in the regions mentioned by Sebastian Jones in the way of strategic metals. If Sebastian Jones had had a hand in the initial strike, he might have found ways of making a handsome profit.

'You don't fool me, Keller,' Sally said. 'You're using him for one of your books like you use everyone. You don't need the money, if it's even there.'

Laughing indulgently and aware that he was very tall, Robert Keller arose and consciously towered over Sally West, round and compact and plump, looking up at him with clear blue eyes and eyeballs shot with fine irregular red lines.

'You,' said Sally West, 'are a conniving shit.'

Her tone was matter-of-fact and without acrimony. Robert Keller knew exactly why she was spiteful—his earlier indifference to a direct sexual gambit had annoyed her—but he was nevertheless affected by the unnecessary violence of the words, combined as it was with a stillness and dispassion in delivery. He turned away and moved towards a bookshelf, where he read: Kant *Critique of Pure Reason*; Kant *Critique of Practical Reason*; Kant *Critique of Judgement*; Kant *Prolegomena to any Future Metaphysics*; Kant *The Moral Law*; Paton *Kant's Metaphysic of Experience*; Paton *The Critical Imperative* . . .

'That's ugly, Sally,' said Robert Keller. 'It doesn't become you.'

She laughed and he knew that she was laughing at him for pomposity.

'The only thing that you think becomes me, lovie,' she said, 'is frilly pants.'

Robert Keller, in spite of himself, moved towards her, but she was quickly and neatly on her feet.

'Good heavens,' Sally West said, 'look at the time. I am going out to dinner. Hullo Barbara.'

When Robert Keller turned round, he saw his beautiful daughter standing coolly at the door.

'Hullo, Sally,' said Barbara. 'Have you seen Paul, Daddy?'

'I understand,' said Sally West, 'that he's going on a pub crawl with your uncle. How are all the nutters?'

Robert Keller's daughter ignored the remark and addressed her father. She was wearing a fawn dress of some coarse woollen fibre with a belt of the same material. She wore light stockings and fawn shoes with higher heels than were currently fashionable. Small garnet stud ear-rings. To her father she looked remarkably impressive.

'Mummy's out, I suppose?' she said.

'I think she was going somewhere with Eric,' said Robert Keller.

His daughter looked very briefly surprised.

'Barbara, love,' said Sally West, 'I know it's bloody boring, but can I ask you a professional question. Christ, I don't know what I'd do without Kellers. I've been asking your father about Jane's education and now I want to ask you about one of her friends that she's worried about. See you, Robert. Thanks for the advice. I'll ring Sylvie about the theatre.'

Watching the smaller, softer woman guide away the younger and more perfect girl with the snub nose, Robert Keller experienced briefly anger which very quickly became laughter, long unobtrusive laughter. He told himself, aloud, that it was all a farce. There were more important things to consider.

He sat at his superb desk and opened his brief-case, ignoring the litter of used glasses, cigar stubbs and cigarette ends behind him. He took out feasibility reports from three of his most immediately trusted subordinates and set them neatly and squarely down on the desk.

On the black surface were three red pens, one black pen, two blue pens, all felt disposables, two red ball-points, one green ball-point, four HB pencils; the uncompleted page of manuscript for the thriller he was writing; small card-index drawers; a large shell from some Mediterranean beach; the feasibility studies; a ruler.

Robert Keller put the unfinished page of the thriller in a buff folder with the rest of the book, so far completed. He sat down and picked up the first report. Then he got up and began to collect glasses and ashtrays, methodically tidying the room as he moved about it. He thought of ways in which he might humiliate Andrew Stone.

Paul Keller

Flowering Carpet.

In the bleak midwinter, artificial roses round the door. London rooks alight on the slender, yawning arms of heath and common. Young lovers arrange timetables. In the frost of fourteen fifteen, to the minute, a colder afternoon than average for the time of year, Hampstead lies cosy in a thousand infidelities. Small-toothed animals venture into deciduous coverts, fallen leaves crisp underfoot.

The arrangement is good. Thursday. Early closing. What does she want to hear? Certainly not an essay in shame. Such laboured nothings, in so strange a style. It has been this way since antiquity. Your breasts are as suet dumplings, your belly is an apfelstrudel. 'What do you do on Thursdays, Paul?' Come, Andrea, you would be bored by stories of my electrical engineers and their amusing sayings but the afternoons are free and lunch might be a good early closing idea.

'You must be very lonely, Andrea.' Wise child. Frankie never wanted me to speak, but she was a professional and *I* was early closing day. Frankie hated talk and it was the only amateur thing about her. Now, this! Wise child! Sexy brat. Kiss and the grand canyon yawns open. On early closing day.

The questions cooroo. Ten Gallon Dad rode here. Well, howdy ma'am. Mind if I kinda water my Rolls. Coyotes slink along the gaunt ridges of Highgate and buzzards circle over Archway. How did she get so desperate, on the flowering carpet legs flung out and writing, still fully dressed. Cooroooroo. I am thinking really nothing. 'Yes, lonely.'

The Vale of Enna was in Gloucestershire. 'Be a darling and fetch us both a gin.' But picture that innocent girl, not twenty, yearning for beautiful things. Smooth textures in roughened hands and London at war. Crumph. The wail of sirens. Suddenly from the underground. Up periscope, I say! Lieutenant Laurence Bisset, submariner, sweeps her off from Hippodrome Corner in a taxi to the Stage Door Canteen. A lone a tlast a long at the digs in Notting Hell Gate, Mrs Haggerty the landlady thought she heard a cry. (Rape!) Not loud, but piercing. Then he crashdived, surfacing again months later, full of new torpedoes.

(Christ, though, she has a son about eighteen or nineteen, drifting somewhere.)

Married in Caxton Hall, June, 1945. Lt. L. F. Bisset, R.N.V.R. and Miss A. Cory. Square shouldered together, a bunch of flowers and lonely together celebration with rationed cheer and utility hope. And, then, a lot of love. Now good bare-breasted below me. And tears. 'Go and get the gin, wise child.'

I suppose they were all the same. War-waging and intelligent Dad, sam-browned and brassoed, calling at sandbagged Broadcasting House for warworking, slender Mummy coming to him from the heart of London. Miss A. Cory wondering if the V2's would get her before Lieut. Bisset, going without knickers in his memory, at sea somewhere. Keeping a lone at last a long vigil. Rathbone winning his DSC in the icy straits of Denmark, when Elaine was pigtailed still. Captain David Lawson, Royal Army Educational Corps, teaching desert rats to vote Labour. Eric Foster lying wounded in a hedgerow storing up a nightmare vision. Grey city taken quite for granted, crumph. Crash. Gin and tonic. Leading Seaman Lomax hating his officers. Sally West happily landing the Fleet Air Arm in Earl's Court. Carry on, Third Officer.

It's enough to make you weep. Now she is as faded as Parliament Hill Fields in the white afternoon. 'Now,' she said, 'I'm going to shower. Cheers, darling.' Oh God, this was a mistake. Had me unzipped in the front hall. Rough stroking hand. Kissing my hairless chest. I certainly do not have the right to smile. Running to fat, she still used her hips and thighs like a belly dancer . . .

Uncle was right. 'Paul, me young sport, if you're looking for a bit of plump experience on the side, I don't think you need look further than that Andrea. If she doesn't drop 'em, I'm a Colonel in the Jehovah's Witnesses.' Her idea. Spiting Daddy, perhaps. My God, I bet imperial crown prince of icecream doesn't compare with hell-bonded hearth companion, brave in fight and hostile in mind, whose deeds are sung in the penthouses of influence. Oh, for God's sake, why don't I read a good book? I have a feeling that I'm not going to get out of this gracefully.

Now I ask myself: do I want to know about the private life of the *capo di tutti capi*? No it's sick. It has been that way from antiquity . . .

She re-enters in a dark green dress, looking pale but pleased. 'Pour me another gin, darling.' She sits down and draws in her belly and looks imperious. 'You make love beautifully,' she says. Go on: I bet you say that to all the boys. This is that good Pelican that to feed her people spareth not to rend her own person. So, let's have enormous gins.

Paul Keller is a bloody fool. One thousand times. She sits with her legs all over the place. What happened to the endearing elegance of female friendship for Christ's sake. Cheers!

'It really was rather embarrassing. But your father can be bloody annoying when he is really making an effort.' Yes. I can see him. Lord of the microbes. Gamma-ray Gandalf. The nerve-gasser with the de-luxe radioactive smile. 'So they made this absurd bet. Which was *my* idea. Well, darling, I really did think that Andrew Stone was going to chuck his lager at your father.'

'Do you mean that Andrew is going to write a thriller?'

'*That* was the challenge. Well, it was better than a scene, if you know what I mean.' Although she likes Andrew Stone, there is no love for Eric Foster, thin-fingered she calls him and puritan and crazy about my sister but who can blame any man for that. 'What's it like, having a ravishingly beautiful sister?' she asks, but I cannot see her eyes behind the gleam of her spectacles.

Let's talk instead of the charming Irishman . . . named Gavin. Then Suddenly it's Bisset. Narrow and dark eyed. Unexpected. Wise. Weary. Bored. Covertly fierce, maybe jealous of his rights, Bisset only visits the upper air on business or overcome by lust. He considers his pulled-together wife, demurely cross-kneed, with a sardonic grin as she explains the nature of my visit. 'It's good to see you, Paul,' he says. 'How are you settling down at Cricklewood?'

'The point is,' says his wife, 'are you going to agree to give one of his lunchtime lectures?' Tailor-made Bisset considers me with his shrewd dark eyes, fingers the little greying wings of hair above his ears. He says why not. So I suppose our young colleague Keller will have to run a series of bloody lunchtime lectures. We talk of Daddy's thrillers—jolly clever chap Daddy—until it is time for me to go.

She sees me out with a quick, sentimental kiss and invites me back, soon, to the drawing board; but I think she's glad it's over too and it is only vanity and compassion, because she has some compassion. Except for him. She detests him. Why?

'Darling, Paul. You make love very wonderfully.'

A needless Alexandrine ends the song.

Gavin McNamara

Some people have no idea at all of the Christmas spirit. Take the auld bitch of a landlady I had, for example. Built like a Slav javelin-thrower, with a bold and lonely look about her, I didn't think that after a while there would be any animosity about things like the rent. Then she took up with a little ferret of an income-tax officer by the name of Mr Elwyn Lamprey who was a canting preaching Welshman who I got a surfeit of long before the first scene change. I accordingly got smoothly into arrears and a few days before the feast of the nativity of our Lord she gave me the bullet and showed herself in her true colours which were lavatory pink.

Everything was going nicely according to plan, so I rang up the young campwallower, Paul, and suggested a pint of double x, adjusting my features into long furrows of Celtic gloom. The point is, of course, that I was angling unashamedly for the goose-dripping and Gevrey-Chambertin. And whatever their faults, I could see that the Keller family were great ones for handing round caviare to the general with or without chips and since that old Australian frothfirkin was putting down gallons of the stuff, I thought I'd get in on the act.

True enough the invite forthcame. I waited until Mr Elwyn Lamprey was getting out his sand-wedge for the final approach to the green, then I was in and out with my humble personal effects like a radiophonic engineer in a science-fiction serial. That same evening I was in the elegant surroundings of Barnes, sipping the paterfamilial liquor and giving me views on op, pop and wilfred. The ancient blusterguts was giving me the odd ragged-arsed look, but as soon as he saw I was a mate of the goody gumdrop, Paul, he was suitably diplomatic.

I suppose it's only fair, seeing that I've been fairly free with descriptions of the all and sundry so far, to say a few words about my own nature and deeds. I'll be objective but the fact of the matter is I'm a fine looking fellow, six foot tall and lithe with it, fair wavy hair and bright blue eyes, supple muscles, lean long face that takes the sun without having to be battered, twelve stone two pounds.

I don't look a bit Irish, but I was born in a Western thunderstorm of great ferocity in 1937. I feel pretty ageless and the way I look at it I'm reborn every new place I go to.

The point is I've never had anything so dignified as a career. There's a natural asceticism in me that's always prevented it: every man should deprive himself of something or other—and I decided on a foreseeable future. As a consequence of this courageous course of action, I've been in any number of interesting situations and jobs—washing dishes in Detroit, selling candyfloss in Calcutta (which as a business enterprise left something to be desired), hawking horoscopes in Hamburg, driving long-distance lorries along the Limpopo. And there haven't been many heathen rumpuses where I haven't been the only representative of the English speaking union with full syndication rights tapping out the lurid details on an antique typewriter. I admit I'm fond of a glass, I smoke French fags and I am an active member of the heterosexual class.

Leaving Ireland at an early age I went to France. I had been put into the horny hands of the Christian Brothers for education who are great battlers against the sins of nature and innocence; but I was fortunate enough to meet several of the benign old soaks who can still satirise a man to death in ancient and modern tongues, with a warehouse of learned lumber in them and they advised me to travel.

I spent a great summer one year on the Côte d'Azur where the climate is very suitable for anyone of a naturally sybaritic metabolism recovering from the spiritual sauna baths of the Christian Brothers. Sure, it was a great sight to see me lepping about the *plages* of Cannes in front of them grand hotels after the bronze goddesses with yellow swimsuits and flying hair, skimming the glitter of the waves with pearly-toothed aplomb on a single ski, rising to the occasional jeu de ballon, the life and soul of fragrant nights in the country of tamarisks and acacias with lights twinkling around the bay and glitter on La Croisette and boats bobbing on the midnight blue of the harbour. Although I say it myself, I seem to encourage the party atmosphere wherever I am, even in North Wales. Anyway I had the good fortune here to meet a film-star who was rich, bored, beautiful and deserted by some Brazilian playboy or other, so I was able to console her and she turned out suitably grateful.

But on a visit to Marseilles, I'd left her for a moment in a delightful cafe in the Rue des Trois Mages, when I heard a voice say: *Le voilà, le petit bizet.* Whereupon a filthy old sack is flung over me and I'm chucked roughly into a car and handled with the same consideration I thought was over with my education. The next thing I know I'm aboard a ship and we're slipping away from the opulence of thought word and deed that was Francesca. After a while I hear these rough voices again, talking some lingo that I don't know, which turns out to be modern Greek.

It was clearly the moment of unveiling and when they did and I had a look at them for the first time, I almost withered out of fright. Enormous, swart bastards every one of them, and brutal with it. And I thought they were going to tear me limb from limb. But if I was destroyed with fear they must have had the shock of their lives, because I turned out to be the wrong article.

I pieced it together as best I could over a few games of pontoon and poker. They were drug-smugglers, a class of person I had not met up with before and very low I'd put them on my list of new year's honours I can promise you, with television entertainment and building societies. It appeared that a certain JoJo had performed some paganini type fiddle on them, involving substantial dividends and that this merchant of scorpions bore a striking resemblance to myself when young. The upshot was that they'd made a mistake and the best thing they could think of to do with me was to dump me in the Mediterranean sea. But by this time, I'd won a good few hands of poker and a nice wee fellow by the name of Mikos pointed out that they ought to win it back before tipping me into the wine-dark dregs. I was grateful to Mikos, because he knew as well as I did that it was theirs for the asking once I was the plat du jour for the langoustes, service et boisson non compris.

Anyway we kept on course for Greece and by the time we were turning left at Milos, they were satisfied I was innocuous but lucky at cards and just as decided about burying me at sea. Now your men were great ones for the life of leisure and had very poor manners, so I was expected to serve them with their potations of a night. I didn't discourage their expectations, having had a visit to the medicine chest for stomach powders and found a quantity of tranquillising pills that are very effective against sea-sickness and also against consciousness, so I tipped the lot into the drinks, sharing them out fair and square. It was one of those Aegean nights that might convince you there's laughter in heaven, so the boys had taken the game topsides and was lounging about like pigmen on a bank holiday. I gave them their share and took some up to the driver. They nodded off in no time and I slipped over the side of my own free will and swam to an island we happened to be passing, where I was lying exhausted on the beach until a slim girl with some goats came up. She and I got on fine for a while, and she took me home to her da.

I stayed with them for a bit, during which time there was this language problem, until I learned that there had been a medium-sized boat run aground further up the Cyclades and I got the old man to run me over to Athens.

Well, I hardly knew it at the time of course, but me travels was only beginning. I didn't have a penny so I was obliged to accept what work was going. You might say I drifted eastwards. I had the good fortune in Smyrna to meet a travel-writer, feline in thought and movement, purring and spitting by turns, an olive-skinned panther of a woman who taught me a lot and disappeared one morning without so much as a line of regret. Francesca married a king of some class in due course, but I never heard a word from the other one.

Moving in to Istanbul, I got into fearful trouble by picking up a little blonde schoolteacher from St Paul, Minnesota, but she was travelling with a sorority of bloody schoolteachers and after I'd secured a slight loan from the little blonde one, damn me if the rest of them, seven in number don't come riding round like the James gang in nylon girdles to reclaim it. One by one I daresay I'd have managed to make a fair barbecued kebab of them, but as it was I slipped out of the back landing and dropped into the street below and took a taxi to the Bosphorus where I got a job as wine-steward on a ship for Beirut. I wasn't a bit sorry to leave my digs on account of the walls being prolific with bugs.

The Lebanon is a very aromatic little country. And it was there that I actually took up with painting, finding also a moment or two for a spot of genteel journalism. It was surely a great blessing to be an Irishman in the Arab World round about 1957, since the name of the English was in pitiable esteem and I had a fine time there before moving on via Iraq to Pakistan and India. Well now. Both these places are a gift to your man who has just taken up painting. All you need is the eye for it and a touch of manual facility plus a bored widow to ship your canvases back for you to London in return for a few hours of civilised discourse.

It strikes me I've already indicated that I am accident prone, good company and never wanting, so far, a touch of velvet comfort from a responsible female source. So that's briefly how I got to London and extramural duties at the academy of Cricklewood and a very comfortable room in the house of the moonmilking Paul and his successful ambiance. Where we take up the yarn with me on one side of the argument, the Australian gasgasket on the other, young Paul pissed out of his skull, and the paterfamilias himself limp and in neutral.

We sat there for quite some time the four of us, sipping delicately and exchanging ideas about the state of the nation, before the first hint of uncivilising femaleness was upon us. But then it was suddenly as overpowering as a prime lion's home thoughts from abroad, what with the trim Sylvie, arriving in the company of a dark fury with full, contemptuous lips, who turns out to be a financial witch of some class and they are going to the theatre together. Then the beautiful sister herself who gets a dark-eyed going-over from the economic piece that should have left her bruised in several soft areas, not that I claim to know anything about it. And finally a sexy dentist with violet eyes who, for all the hell sense I can make of it, has come to check everyone's teeth.

Sylvie is delighted that I'm staying but the beautiful sister gives me a decidedly psychological look and unless I can show her a bit of haute cuisine I think there'll be trouble there.

It's the work of a moment with me to slip in a short lyric about inconvenience, the difficulty of it all, exile and gratitude, which touches the heart of all concerned except the fiscal sorceress, but even then I had to beat out the rhythms for the other two. Sylvie seems to be a pushover, but I never saw in my life a harder faced triad than these otherwise magnificently fitted out escalopes de foie gras a la ravignan in front of me. By the time I'd finished the dentist was laughing and even the beautiful Barbara was in a state of smiles, but the money-bunny didn't flicker. No, not a bloody bit of it. She swung one towering leg over the other in a flash of black and white and, before I could help myself, my eyes were ferreting into her like Mr Elwyn Lamprey tweaking the secrets of a tax-dodger. I think I recovered my composure eloquently, but she wasn't fooled herself. I can feel the sneer now right under the wallet. Still I managed to hold my own charmingly and amusingly in conversation.

The young wanhope, Paul, is telling them what a fine gift I have for the piano-playing and so nothing will do but we have to troop off to the next room where there is a beautifully finished bit of mahogany. Taking a quick look around I thought the paterfamilias would be a Django Reinhardt man because he remembered the name, the old rotjawer probably couldn't tell the Matthew Passion from Waltzing Matilda, Paul liked anything when he was pissed: so I need only consider the ladies. The lesbian was probably all for Schoenberg in jackboots and the sexy dentist's tastes would either be vulgar or traditional, or perhaps traditionally vulgar—there's always hope; Sylvie might be a shade too refined for anything louder than early English lute music; so what about Barbara . . . ? I played them some Modern Jazz Quartet originals.

When I looked up, Barbara had drawn up a chair and was watching the keyboard. And when the pretty grey eyes turned onto me, she'd melted. We smiled at each other. Then I turned my attention to the piano again, controlling the arabesques I was tempted to. Somewhere off I could hear general murmurs of approval and the old crapjabber telling some tedious yarn how he'd lost his false teeth in a piano in the pestilent bloody outback to which no one was listening, but as I took that in, I noticed the flushed scowl on the face of Paul, the young jackadreams, who was after all my host. So I thought, taking good care not to look at his holy sister again, I'd finish off the tune and pack it up, but the mother of earth and plenty more where that came from, Sally West, spotted him too. It was poetic to watch. She got up, ran her hands tightly down her hips to her thighs as though smoothing her skirt down which takes a lot of nerve in a roomful of women, clapped her hands in front of Paul's glassy fuddle and swung her gorgeous hips into a dance. He didn't have much choice, poor young marsh-mellow. The paterfamilias thought it was a grand kick and rung up his number on Annabelle who was a bit awkward and the guffhawk gyrated and capered around his niece, Sylvie, in a manner that was grotesque.

That left Barbara listening as long as I was playing and I got dangerously inventive all of a sudden.

'You like this stuff?'

She nodded and smiled again. You understand there was nothing come hither in her manner, but there was bugger all go hence either. And all the lacing of frost had gone. She was smiling still. Not talking. I played, showing off a bit at the edges. She laughed.

'You're very good.'

'Not really. I play for pleasure most of the time. I worked with a band in Paris for a while. That's why I know all this stuff.'

'You've lived in Paris?'

'I still do. Up here.'

'I thought someone said you were a painter.'

'I'd call myself an art-teacher. It's not quite the same thing.'

'I don't believe you're modest at all. You know you're good.'

'Listen to the music.'

I hit a marvellous undulating vein of left-hand work, so that even the statuesque investors' playmate was looking graceful and young Paul was staring fascinated at the tremors of her tits, so the whole operation became decidedly therapeutic as long as his interest stayed academic. The paterfamilias was teamed up with Sally who used her hips like a terrace waitress on a busy evening: and they looked a handsome pair, right enough. The pisspother had blown himself out with his thoughtless shinanikins, so was lying back getting smithereened and the elegant Sylvie had come to lean on the piano. There was a ring at the door and Fingal Grey aself was there, bright-eyed, brush-topped, his face a jovial prune of energy. He'd come to take out the lovely Barbara, who it turned out was moving in also for Christmas. (So why should Christian men be so sad, I suppose.)

Because it was such a great hooley, they decided to stay and the party was made complete by the arrival of Sally West's daughter in a motor for to fetch her ma at about ten, having herself been out for the day. And young as she was, about eighteen, it had all arrived and arranged itself to advantage. Of course, she having youth on her side and her mammy's natural grace she danced great. In a slip of a skirt at that, that disappeared up above her flowery panties rhythmically and Fingal Grey had to sit down with his hands on his lap with the strain.

Then Sylvie decides that if there's anyone dipping out on the festivities, it's meself. And since she's kind enough to claim that any other piano-playing after mine will be a bloody anticlimax, she switches on the gramophone. And leads me onto the floor herself. Now, I'm not boasting but I can look after myself well enough in the average palais, discotheque or barn whether it's long distance gymnastics or the hand-to-hand stuff and Sylvie favoured the tender grip. The tune was *How long has this been going on* and we had a lovely synchro-meshing of the centres of both our worlds which made her look delighted about the whole thing.

But I was dead careful. Having spontaneously paid her the hidden compliment myself, and her fully aware of its sincerity, I left her to Fingal of the foxy eyes, murmuring in his best voice. It was a different faster tune by the time I got to Sally and we did some pretty sinuous work on it. For her daughter very fast: and I suppose I have to confess I did a spot of showing off since most of the other contenders sat it out to watch. The males were watching without a doubt the dainty swivelling arse of Jane and the flashing thighs of her. I daresay the womenfolk found something to interest them also. Young Paul tried to compete, with his sister, but his heart wasn't in the dancing and he got quite pale with effort. Then Annebelle. Looked me in the eye all the time on *Someone to watch over me* and got me in a hell of a state for Barbara and *They can't take that away.*

When the tune finished neither of us wanted to dance for a bit, so we went and sat on a sofa, some distance apart. We didn't talk but sat there peaceful-like, relaxed as though we'd just made love. Then I became aware of the rest of them still agitating furiously and realised I'd done it again. A fine emancipated family like this one, as nice an upper-income group as you could find in the British commonwealth, lepping and jigging like young goats. I just carry the party spirit round with me, it seems. She layed her head back against the sofa and turned it towards me: soft fairish hair, grey eyes.

'Why d'you just drift?'

'Why are you a psychiatrist, for God's sake?'

'It's interesting; worthwhile.'

'It's a waste of a lovely woman.'

'That's patronising. I can be a woman and a psychiatrist.'

'What's this tune called?'

'*You go to my head.*'

'I don't think you're a doctor, at all. I think you're a sleeping princess that needs awakening.'

'Who's going to. . . .'

'Hush. Listen to the music.'

She laughed but not at me, though she wasn't fooled. And turned her head to watch them dancing.

'Anyway, you're my host's daughter and an M.R.C.P., and that savage from television would come and flay me into a briefcase if I attempted to touch you.'

'Fingal?'

'Let me take you out one night.'

'Yes. Where shall we go?'

'Not to your theatres or your art movies or your expensive restaurants. The rest of them can take you there. I'll think of something.'

'I'll look forward to it.'

Then Paul, who had been dancing with his mother, came across and took her away at a lurch.

Well, I don't think much else happened except that everyone got pretty pissed and hot from the dancing. Sally West undid several buttons of her blouse but there was nothing wild or abandoned and about two o'clock, they drove off most of them into the dangerous breathalised night, or went to bed. I sat up another hour or so with my hostess talking quietly about Paul's prospects, what I thought of his poetry which thank God I'd never seen, what Sylvie thought of his poetry, Barbara's job, old Sebastian, Robert's importance, Sylvie's childhood in the mining valleys of east Wales, Sylvie's socialist principles, my rapidly-acquired socialist principles, Sylvie's work reviewing and gassing about books, more worthwhile work, the desperate state of the world, what Nixon would do now that he was elected, and a comprehensive tour of Biafra, South Africa, refugee Palestine, Kerala and so on, somehow leading back to Sylvie's family. She was very struck on the young water-lily, Paul, and had nothing but praise for her daughter—but to the shrewd observer like meself I thought there was no love wasted in that direction.

We turned in, chastely of course, at about quarter to four. And I was up again about eight and had a fine walk in the stale air of S.W.13. I have this great gift of never having hangovers so I was full of good news when the rest of them came down to the devilled kidneys and sherbet. Sylvie wasn't too bad and Barbara only looked a bit pale, which made her even more beautiful, clear skinned and without make-up. The paterfamilias, the daffydowndilly and the rumbleballocks was destroyed! I had a grand breakfast.

Eric Foster

A trite tune but it fixes the emotion neatly. As the needle sticks in a groove we have six different images. The sweep of conifers up a steep hillside brushed heavily with mist; a beautiful girl alone in rumpled lingerie; four people at a bistro in London smiling; close up of a face with heavy lines, bearded, a patch over one eye; turbulence of stormclouds; a khaki jacket with medal ribbons worn by someone whose face we do not see, holding a long-bladed knife. The tune is called *I'll be around.*

—The point I'm making, Eric, is that none of us bloody know. We're all comparatively privileged. Jacqueline with her pictures and Jasmine with Eng. Litt. And you're so far up an ivory tower you need a bloody fire-brigade to get you down.

> The intellectual dummy's dance. . . .

> You've no aptitude for reasoning, Eric, but my God! you've got a creative imagination that's worth all the reasoning ever . . .
> You're very sweet, Ginny.

—The point I'm making, Eric, is that it was difficult enough for us and it's a bloody sight more difficult now. Because half of these bloody kids don't *want* to be educated, which at least we did, and they're being pressured into it by bloody society.

> '. . . really some kind of hothouse plant. . . .'

'Surely they were very relaxed with you?'
'Outwardly. . . .'
'. . . not your mother. . . .'
'. . . there's never been a lot of love going spare.'
'. . . your brother. Does he . . . ?'
'. . . mixed up.'
'You're an unlikely family, I suppose.'

A trite tune played over and over again. The sweep of conifers and the lined, bearded wanderer. Out of the mist and dark trees came four hooded murderers. Close up of the mutilated face of the victim. Next time we meet him (on the Marseilles waterfront) he wears a patch over one eye and the scars show beneath it.

Absurd.

I'm not sure, Eric, that you're not too Romantic for comfort.
What the hell is that supposed to mean?

No, my darling, as you lie there on the stained sheets of my imagination in disarranged silk, it is I who am in the supplicatory posture. You, my darling, control the figures of the dance. Your confident fingers stroke the scars and lines scored by unshed tears.

—The point I'm making, Eric, is that we've got to get away from the whole idea of competition and privilege. I mean it was still bloody there in our day at Oxford. It didn't matter so much to you, but it did to me. Grammar schools are just forcing-houses for the lower classes, by which I mean the bourgeois as well as the working class. Let's get rid of the lot and have people educated together.
—I'm going to quote Russell at you, Roger. And he's your sage not mine. What's the thing about rubbing up against all and sundry in youth as a good preparation for life? He says it's rubbish. No one in later life associates with all and sundry.

—Russell said some bloody strange things in his time. He was never afraid to change his mind, though.

Jacqueline smiling. Gold-haired Jasmine anxiously smiling too, half-listening and always afraid Roger's anger is serious. Narrow plush and gilt; gleaming mirrors, highlit metals also brassily gleaming; dirty floors, scuffed wood. Actors in a corner walking through an evening at the pub. Two mild eyed bookmen from the review pages with two chiffoned young men.

> '. . . you and mummy . . .'
> 'Attracted, certainly . . .'
> '. . . and . . .'
> 'No.'

(Perhaps we should go to bed together, Eric.
Perhaps
It might cure us both of this . . .
What's *this*, Sylvie?
Well, it's something. A sort of adult infatuation.)

> And so, God help me, Sylvie, I became infatuated by your daughter. Laughter. The managers file out into the corridors for the last time. All flights are cancelled: the runways are clear for the last important departures. 'Q' searches a deserted building.

Jasmine's white mac has fallen open revealing a long thigh in black, snagged nylon. She has beautiful legs. And now blushes, pleased. I was staring. Lop-sided, happy grin from Roger. Jacqueline rustles unruffled, coolly attacking me for helping to botch a civilisation.

> The articulated and macabre dance of a nude dummy.

> Eric Foster's work has always seemed to me to lack intellectual coherence. So that while there is always something in his films to delight (indeed to ravish) the

> eye, one's experience is never complete, seldom satisfying. His eclecticism suffers from his habit of apparently stringing images together haphazardly, often arbitrarily. No doubt there is a pattern, but for the life of me, in *Wanderer* (Academy) I couldn't see it. . . .

You can't Eric, you haven't a logical mind.
For God's sake, shut up, Ginny, and listen!

A mute, nearly beautiful thing is . . .

Jasmine shyly smiles. White mac, fine gold hair soft about the pale rather trite face, clear blue eyes, black beret, black tights. Chaste mother of four. Roger the father, good father, will love his kids even if they grow up tories and catholics.

> No, *I* don't. But don't you, Eric?
> Certainly not.
> Are you sure? You'd make a terrific father.
> No, I'm sure, Ginny.

> It would have meant sharing her at a time when I could not bear to. And then sharing myself, sharing what was left over from Ginny.

> 'Neither of you wanted any?'
> '. . . shrug it away easily enough.'
> 'Later did you . . . ?'
> '. . . a kind of residual bitterness about having cheated her . . .'
> '. . . still a lot of pain. Isn't there?'

Jasmine nervously watches the argument between Jacqueline and Roger, conservation versus activism. Gold hair curling under the beret, looking younger than thirty eight. Roger pleased that she is pretty grants her his ten-years-senior smile in passing, she lights up, listening to the talk of tradition and change which she seldom joins, thinking no longer of Jane Austen, Fanny Burney, Thackeray, but of Christopher's shoes, Lucy's cough, Alan's heat-rash and Lorna starting school. Since after all we were born to marry strangers. . . .

—The point I'm making, Eric, is that unless bloody art means something to reasonably educated people, then you can forget it.
—Leaving us with bloody television, Roger. What time did you book for?
—Quarter to nine.
—Then we'd better be moving.

Dark cold night. Walking with Jasmine. *The Managers*, a film about Robert Keller. She laughs and asks about Barbara. What does she know: am I obvious or is she especially sensitive? The acts of kindness that destroy. Something the rough kindness of Roger has made of her: frightened of her own slightly better intelligence. The photograph of a child he has begotten. And forgotten? It is also, you, Ginny. It is what I did, destroying you.

> 'Q' approaches Gina, who is fantastically attired in a thin light blue slip, light blue knickers, long black stockings held up by light blue garters. He tears the slip down off her breasts and sinks along her body to his knees pushing his head between her thighs and gripping the thinly silken haunches. Gina puts her head back, lips parted, clutching her own breasts. Her eyes are open and the expression in them tells more of weariness than desire. Barbara Keller in a light summer frock caught in a shower so that it clung to her tight
> And a plushy black girl, that Roger Lomax said he could fancy, huge in a see-through white dress and pink underclothes

> . . . squeak like dolls . . .

Absurd.

My love, my love, thy hair is one kingdom, the king whereof is darkness thy forehead is a flight of flowers.

Absurd.

> 'I'd have gone home to fuck my wife,' Batchelor told us, grinning through bandages. 'Given warning.' 'It's your wife who'd need the bloody warning, Batch.' Laughter. In the VIP lounge Robert Keller, her father, checks the final arrangements of overkill with quick biological follow-up, as the last plane takes on fuel

Dark and cold gives place to blinking light. *Ca va? Oui, Ça va très bien. Et vous monsieur et madame?* Jacqueline's elegant French in a National Gallery accent.

—The point I was making, Eric, is this . . .
—Oh Roger, love, give your conscience a rest.
—That's the bloody woman I married. If I could, lass, I'd give your bloody conscience a course of isometric exercises to do, and even then they wouldn't give it much stamina.

Habitual humiliation by now she is used to. Mock on, mock on, tis all in vain: there's Christopher's shoes, Lucy's cough, Alan's heat-rash and Lorna starting school. Do you know a really good pre-school school? Poor, soft, gold-haired child. Smiles.

—What's this about Robert Keller challenging Andrew to write a thriller?
—*Beaujolais Villages.*
—I don't know, Jasmine. Do you Jacqueline?
—Yes, I heard they had something of a row. But it was Andrea who said so and I'm not sure how accurate it all is.
—What's on the bloody blackboard, Jacqui? Is that *blanchaille.*
—Yes, it is.

—And Andy's accepted?

—Has he Eric?

—He says he's going to write a thriller. I don't think it's very wise of him.

—Well, that's it then. I'm going to have *blanchaille*, *tornedos chasseur* and *tarte aux cérises*. What's this about Andy writing a bloody thriller?

—He never listens to anything, do you, darling.

—What's come over the bloody Kellers anyway. We went over the other night and it turned into a right orgy. They've got this old uncle staying with them and now some Irish chap who works with Paul at Cricklewood. You know how bloody sedate it all used to be going round there: well, mate, you should see David Lawson doing a knees up with Sylvie. And the old Australian pinched Jasmine's bottom, didn't he Jaz? Oh it was a laugh a line.

A trite tune. On the evening before 'Q' woke up and saw the future in his shaving-glass, Gina was at an orgy. The obscenities were skilful. 'Q' worked in his lab with coloured slides and cross-cut to the party. All the scenes are reflected in some kind of black, shiny surface. We move back and forward from party to lab until the last shot of Gina delightedly preparing herself for a figure wearing an animal mask.

> Eric Foster's handling of sex is made all the more sinister by its obliqueness. I cannot remember a single instance of orthodox revelation (Perhaps there is very little orthodox, chez Foster, to reveal!) But the use of distortion, cross-cutting, disarranged time-sequences and quite often facial expressions, usually reflected in a glass or a vase builds up a certain hysterical tension and often creates a powerfully erotic undercurrent. In *Scipio's Friend* we have just such a sequence when the latin teacher meets the whore (a negress) in a waiting room. Focussing on the prodigiously calypigous swing of the whore, we cut to the street in Pompeii where the teacher and his young group are standing, to a page of tabulated grammar torn out of the

book, back to the boys giggling pruriently, to the whore again but still at the same level now from the front, sitting carelessly and wearing patterned stockings; next to an Italian hillside and the prim, bespectacled woman whom the teacher helped with a suitcase, to Pompeii again; back to the whore at thigh level. The camera slowly travels up her body and very slowly back down to her ankles and back to her thighs. A single held shot of the face of the bespectacled girl follows. Then we have another back view of the tart's swinging hips, as she moves to the ladies' room. The giggling boys and the torn page again. When the tart returns she has removed her tights. The camera slides towards her pants: her hands move to her hips. . . . Then we realise that the body revealed is white not black. Foster allows the briefest glimpse of pubic hair before we see something of what is about to happen reflected in a pair of discarded spectacles, eventually blotted out by the glare of the sun. But sex plays an incidental indeed a minor part in Eric Foster's work . . .

Your trouble, Eric, is that you've got a dirty mind and you won't admit it.

Oh . . . Ginny . . . can't you understand . . .

—Bloody pseudo-intellectual rubbish, most of the time.

—I'm going to have the *entrecote Mon Plaisir*.

—Salad?

—Yes.

—I don't mean you, Eric. Or Andy. But to hear that Irish lad talk and everyone swallowing it, with bloody pickled cabbage. Sylvie, Robert himself, who you think would know better.

—*Salade pour tous, alors, s'il vous plaît. Avec de l'ail.*

—Mind I've always found Paul a bit bloody pretentious. The thing that really surprised me was Barbara getting taken in . . .

—Barbara . . .

—Eric, will you ask him for a fork.

—Sorry, Jasmine. *S'il vous plaît. Madame désire une* uh er fork.

—The word is *fourchette*, Eric.

—Thank you, Jacqui. What were you saying about Barbara, Roger?

—Bloody nice girl. That's why I was surprised she was so struck by this bloody Irish harpist . . .

—I thought he was an artist, darling . . .

—Oh for Jesus Christ's sake, Jaz. It was a bloody joke!

> You know what I like about you, Eric? You're funny. You make me laugh and I like laughing.
>
> Thank you, my love. Now listen. The film . . . *Song in Late November?*
>
> Yes. They're going to give me the money . . .
>
> Oh, Eric, love! Darling!
>
> Thank you, Ginny, Thanks for believing . . . I've not been able to keep still all day. I couldn't wait to tell you.

> A trite tune.

> Since we agreed to let the road between us fall into disuse, and bricked our gates up, planted trees to screen us, and turned all time's eroding agents loose . . .

—Now if the young were all people like that bloody charlatan, I'd see what you had against them.

—I've got nothing against them, Roger, they just frighten the hell out of me. They don't want to know. It's what I've heard called the witless arrogance of late adolescence. The only difference is they expect *us* to obey it.

—Oh, Foster! Bloody roll on. When d'you get your C.S. gas and riot helmet.

—Let's have some more wine.

—Adolescents are getting later every year.

—How's your steak?

'I suppose it's adolescent . . .'
'I don't understand why.'
'. . . twenty years . . .'
'. . . shouldn't matter. Look, there's no need to rush anything, is there? Can you wait? Be patient'?
'. . . what . . .'
'Me.'
'You mean you . . . '
'Yes. I will. When it's right. But not just casually. As though it meant nothing . . .'

I do not know if it affects others in the same way but I have noticed an unmistakable souring of talent in the films of Eric Foster. No one could ever claim that this director's vision was flippant or over-optimistic, but the skein of compassion that interwove itself around the rich imagery of his early pictures has distintegrated, leaving a fragmented tapestry of misanthropic attitudes, loosely associated. *Reciprocals*, his latest effort now showing at the Curzon, is deeply pessimistic. It is the merciless dissection of a marriage between a mild, serious intellectual and an intelligent but extrovert actress. Both become embittered: he by the cheapening of standards in our society; she by the more sordid chanciness of her chosen career. They take their disappointment out on one another until, by the end of the film, Foster leaves us wondering whether there is anything for us to look forward to but degradation. . . .

It's over then, Eric.
What else is there? I'm sorry I hit you . . .
If *that* was all . . . You're right. What else is there?

—All right. Then you tell us what you believe, Jacqueline.
—Certainly. I believe in moral struggle . . .
—Gawd elp us . . .

—Oh do shut up, darling, and let her finish. We've been listening to you all night.

—I believe in the necessity of overcoming desires. I think there are some naturally virtuous people who like being naturally virtuous and who aren't sanctimonious or wet.

—I wish I'd ever bloody met one . . . No. There's Eric here.

—Eric isn't. Eric is a Jansenist.

—Well, I never knew that. What have *you* to say to that, then?

—I think, Sir Henry, that this lady is worthy of our close attention. It's interesting though. Think about our friends, the people we know. We're all ripe for a spot of moral anarchy.

—Who? David bloody Lawson? Jack Rathbone? Us bloody lot around this table?

Laughter.

Absurd!

'No, Barbara, honestly. I don't have a point of view. I merely observe.'

'. . . believe?'

'In not hurting . . .'

'Some people don't mind . . .'

'. . . would . . .'

'. . . have to. Have to.'

I am even the natural fool of Fortune. Use me well. You shall have ransome. Let me have surgeon. I am cut to the brains.

The old khaki jacket with ribbons. A limp. The circumstantial knife. The scarred traveller.

—Well, I think Eric's right . . .

—Do you, Jaz. D'you hear that, Eric? Jaz is on for a touch of moral anarchy.

—Shut up, darling. I think nearly all the people we know are terrific at intellectual virtues; including you, Roger; and no good at moral virtues at

all. I'm sure we'd be at it like knives if we thought we'd get away with it.
—D'you hear that? 'At it like knives', she said. That's a very swinging saying, Jaz.
—Well, we would. You fancy Elaine, don't you? And Sally West? So what stops you? Not moral virtue, Roger. Just knowing the chaos that might come of it. Do you remember a film you made called *Reciprocals*, Eric?
—Yes, of course. I was thinking about it earlier.
—What was that about?
—I see what you mean, Jasmine.

Gold-haired, pale trite face a little flushed, determinedly ignoring the lop-sided smile of Roger . . .

> If we can conceive that any person takes delight in something, which only one person can possess, we shall try to see that the person in question shall not get possession of it.
> These passions distract us and obscure our intellectual vision.

By God! She's right. Clever, little pale girl.

> 'Q's business is disease. He works at his microscope and having some talent as a painter, he constructs huge glass facsimiles of great beauty, all of which represent death. 'Q' loves Gina.
> Before the day of the war (or the day of 'Q' 's madness), some time before, there was the Sunday in the country-house of one of the managers. After the storm, Gina was wet through. Her light dress clung to her. Searching for her, 'Q' found her behind a gazebo being roundly violated to her obvious and extreme pleasure. 'Q' worked her out of his system and then the war came.

> You're bored with everything, Eric. You can't stay awake.
> I'm tired, Ginny. I work hard.

It's true, though, isn't it? You don't care.

quel grand genie que ce Pococurante! rien ne peut lui plaice.

Oh you have a genius, all right, Eric. You have a bloody marvellous genius for isolation.

'My dear, I promise . . .'
'. . . I . . .'
'Say nothing. No one will be hurt.'

—I can't imagine Barbara Keller becoming a moral anarch. She's a bloody iceberg, that girl. Sorry, Jacqui. I know she's a friend of yours. But it's bloody true, isn't it?

Outside it has started to snow. The heavy fat flakes settle in Jasmine's fine gold hair. Perfunctory kisses. They hunch away to their car and Blackheath. We set off for a taxi. Not speaking. Not touching. Jacqueline looks up at the sky: clouds and desultory snowfall. The pink city glow illuminates briefly vast, infinite, eternal silences.

PART FOUR

Gavin McNamara

I had a grand time in the homely Kellerzeitgeist with poultry, game and bakemeats of a high order; wines, spirits and alka-selzer of impeccable nobility; and the highest class of guests ranging from the tooth-tickling hamadryad of Wimpole Street, Sally, to the cynirammer warlord, Foster, giving us his kind, jawbreaking smile with all those peripatetic teeth that could have used a bit of sculpture, with representatives of television, the novel, the Board of Trade, Her Majesty's armed forces, cardiac surgery, journalism, scholarship and the fine arts, government, education and psychiatric medicine all crowding around the cold buffet and hock at any given moment. Not to mention the ancient artefactory and his coarseness, nor the young puttylustre who spent most of the time, in the presence of his sister, scowling like Ghenghis the Hun.

Still it was a great pity that that vernisage of the independant cinema, Eric Foster, has to behave so badly on the one occasion with that television god of tumult and confusion, Fingal Grey, and no less a piece of pattisserie than Barbara Keller. Why it's necessary to trap people into the most humiliating conversational labyrinths and show them off is beyond me and I'm not going to dwell on it, except to say that Barbara was naturally very grateful to be rescued by me and my magic piano. A smile and a song at all times.

What with this kind of disreputable conduct and Paul going round looking as though he'd like to make canapes of everyone in sight, it wasn't a bit surprising that Sylvie was drawn to me for the more lyrical moments of an undoubtedly festive season. Many was the quiet moment we spent together in decent and civil conversation while everyone else was sleeping off some excess or other, or destroying themselves with the gratification of appetites.

Understandably Barbara herself was in great demand. Not only did Fingal Grey lay siege to her with the cunning of a carved Odysseus every other night, but there was the celluloid troubador, Foster, caterwauling under the bloody balcony and any number of married men whose thoughts should have been mortgaged twice over, looking hopeful about what they might manage to raise. Since she never mentioned our own projected evening out, I didn't push myself forward. The welcome was warm enough for the time being and if I felt a cold wind blowing across my instant porridge that would be time enough for decisive action of that sort. I played the piano, though, with the patient stamina of water wearing away a semi-precious stone, if you'll forgive a moment of anthropomorphic excess.

In the course of the merrymaking, I was the object of some delighted attention myself, though I don't wish to make a cantata of it. On one evening in particular the woman called Andrea, married to that digit of government Bisset, took a dangerous fancy to me and though I behaved with a kind of terpsichorean politesse that wouldn't have raised a black eyebrow among the Inquisition or twitched the red nose of a sadist Roundhead, everywhere I went she was haunting, startling and waylaying like the phantom of the Rue Morgue. I was glad enough for the cool, Welsh spring of Sylvie's discourse that night, myself, right enough.

The sequence of events ran something as follows: we got back from some celebration or other at which the aforementioned revelries had been taking place, the dramdrain and the twinkleprick were both in fragments, the paterfamilias was exhausted by something that must have taken place off stage and turned in. Barbara hadn't been with us, since she had been dining tête à téton with one of her many admirers. She, the immaculate wife of Casar's top scientific civil servant, told me to help myself to a nightcap.

Returning, herself had slopped into something loose, a kind of satin white robe with a matt finish, elegantly shaped to suit the preserved matron. A cigarette and a smile and we were off.

'Do you know . . . It's very funny. Do you know what Barbara calls you? A talented vagrant.'

'Well, there's something to be said for that as a point of view. I'm not one of the three magi. Following a star in a hopeful way.'

'How do you follow it?'

'I've never noticed any star at all, to speak of. Does she mean I have a talent for vagrancy or that I'm a tramp with talent.'

'She's not a romantic.'

'No. And I'm not the scholar gypsy.'

'You're a funny man. I don't mean peculiar. I mean funny.'

She put her cigarette out and crossed her legs so that the white garment fell open discreetly, revealing a tantalisingly full thigh and what looked excitingly like a stocking top. Thank all the powers of nature and normality, I'm old enough to have known such things in a blissful adolescence and I pity the young of today and the sweaty fleshiness that is the only alternative to frustration.

With the education that I've been through, it wasn't difficult at all to preserve a devastating calm and keep up a class of light banter that goes down well enough in female circles. She reached forward for another cigarette and when she leaned back again the gown fell open just a shade more and it *was* a stocking top. I got up to light the cigarette for her and we stood there, quite close, for a few seconds breathing at one another before I resumed my chair.

'We must strike you as a pretty odd family, Gavin.'

'You're a remarkably well-endowed family. Good-looking, clever, successful, reasonably well-off.'

'But not particularly affectionate or close?'

'I'm surely not in a position to say. I imagine you're united enough when it comes to the rest of the world.'

She laughed in a low lilting way favoured by all the best seductresses in Celtic folk-lore. The kind of laugh that has soft, Western, summer rain in it and the sound of leaves at twilight and the light of the sun catching a clear running brook. All about as sincere as a lay-preaching second-hand car dealer and signifying as much amusement.

'I suppose you're right. My daughter is certainly more than just good-looking . . . Don't you think?'

'I haven't thought much about your daughter at all.'

'I don't believe that.'

I smiled at her and shrugged in the most ambiguous way possible that was consistent with good relations and such was her effortless sophistication that she didn't give a damn. You need a steady hand for intricate crochet of that sort and no mistake.

'I understand there was some sort of fuss.'

'A fuss?'

'The other night. Between Eric and . . .'

'Oh that.'

It was the work of a moment with me to infuse into my carelessly articulate chuckle a wealth of meaning, all the while watching her with the concealed tension of a psychoanalyst at a golf-club. I was wondering if the Cecil B de sixteen Mille meant more to her than a stoop of pessimistic compassion at a cocktail party and I was looking for the vulnerable wince you sometimes get in sophisticated eyes when people expect to hear something that's going to contribute another couple of cuts in the Chinese torture of personal vanity that some philosophers are pleased to call existence. But her enquiry was clinical.

'You were talking to Barbara. . . .'

'It wasn't very important.'

'Wasn't it? I've never known Eric Foster shout ever before.'

'I don't remember at all well, now. There was quite a large group of us : your husband, Paul, Andrea and a few others. I can't make out Eric Foster, anyway. What sort of a man is he?'

'Gentle, slightly embittered. He had a marriage that ended unhappily. Susceptible.'

A certain class of Celtic contralto can make a word like 'susceptible' sound like an invitation to sensual nirvanahs in the most perfumed of gardens. But bearing in mind the fact that Sylvie could qualify for an Evening Standard drama award on her free Sunday mornings, I persevered with adamantine dispassion, believing that knowledge is a string of priceless pearls particularly where other people are concerned.

'He seems to have it in for Fingal Grey.'

'Really? It was Fingal . . . What did he say?'

'Well, I think it started with your husband making some remark about overt sexuality in the arts, which led to Foster agreeing with him about restraint and Fingal Grey making a warm-hearted and tolerant defence of liberal standards in society. So Foster started to attack him, though I don't think anyone realised what was happening until Grey found himself defending the position of a moral degenerate over-compensating for a deep phobic lack. Foster did it very skilfully and with a fair wit.'

'Was that all? It doesn't sound like anything that Fingal wouldn't laugh off.'

'Are you sure you want to know? It's not in the least important, Sylvie.'

'Oh, Gavin! Don't be funny! You can't tell me so much and then leave me up in the air.'

'All right. The deep, phobia-type, lack turned out to be impotence. There's a certain type that can't stand innuendos relating to that. Grey forgot himself and turned . . . I hope this won't distress you . . . to your daughter. . .'

'To bear witness. How ridiculous!'

It speaks marvels for the free and civilised nature of modern life in Britain that a mother can hear about her daughter's minor promiscuities and think it only another colourful component of life's vast comic jigsaw.

'That was the idea, I think.'

'Well, God knows, I didn't think they spent every evening playing ludo . . .'

'Fingal Grey is a great fan of war-games . . .'

'Yes, dear. I was being ironic. Of course they go to bed together. Is that what upset Eric?'

'It did. He shouted something. And your son wasn't too pleased either. But I managed to catch his arm. Sure, it wasn't a very gentlemanly approach on the part of Grey, now, was it?'

'Paul's that sort of boy. He's tremendously loyal.'

'Anyhow, your daughter preserved a marvellous calm and sorted out the whole situation, in spite of the fact that she was clearly deeply embarrassed.'

'Was she? It's perhaps an odd thing for a mother to say, Gavin, but I can't imagine anyone finding much . . .'

Perhaps I'd better not . . .

'She has perfect self-control.'

'Yes, let's leave it at that.'

'I don't suppose you're sorry you missed it, anyway, Sylvie. It'll sort itself out quickly enough.'

'I hope it will. These things can be very tiresome in the sort of social life we have.'

'I'm sure it will. How is Andrew Stone getting on with this challenge thing, by the way. I think it all happened while you were talking to him.'

'The whole thing's ridiculous. I don't understand why Andrew bothered to accept it . . . '

She got up. The brown eyes flashed for all the world like an ancient princess of the Merthyr Tydfil district, and there must have been some in a land so prolific with sadomasochistic feys after all, before the Industrial Revolution. Then she smiled. I stood up. There was, you might say, a moment of understanding between us as she laid a white hand upon my sleeve and gave a soft laugh.

'I shouldn't worry. Fingal Grey went off looking white to the lavatory. And I took your daughter to the nearest piano.'

'We must have a long talk some time, Gavin. Good night.'

It's a certain sign as soon as anyone says they want to have a long talk with yez, that they're either going to roll golden sexual apples all over the Olympic track, or else treat you like a confessor with a slow fuse. I watched the dainty swing of her away, poured myself a final glass, and lay back like a literary gentleman out of another age to blow cigar-smoke at the ceiling and contemplate the jest of it all. Not that it hadn't been a lavish, entertaining time, but tomorrow was New Year's Eve and I was in no doubt that something would turn up, of a suitably elevating nature.

The trouble is that I have this knack of picking up a crowd of people and since the old showerdrivel had a similar way of drawing attention to himself by telling raucous stories, it wasn't long before we had quite a circus rolling about the bars of Richmond, normally a genteel place. Mind, we made a joyful procession and brought a hint of jollity into people's lives on a night when they are traditionally hopeful that next year is not going to be the unholy banjax that this one is.

There was myself, the old gushbollox, the moondrunk, three of my own countrymen all called Kevin, Jane West in black tights, a coloured friend of hers by the name of Ziz in pink tights, a sad, blonde called Natasha, four girls who didn't seem to have names, only thirst, a Scottish road-maker, a Welshman with a guitar and a mouth organ, a drunken doctor who kept bees, two French bums and a randy old vicar who, having been unfrocked himself, was doing his best to pass on the favour to every reasonable dish of cavoli in agrodolci that came his way.

I didn't think it was a good idea to inflict such diverse company on my own generous hosts, but the old prattlekeg had a notion we should sing in the garden to the mouth organ. And of course when the paterfamilias heard the frightful bloody row, nothing would do for his nature as generous as the rainfall in Kerry but to invite us all in. Two Kevins, Ziz, Jane, Natasha, the Welsh chap and his mouth organ, the drunken physician, three nameless girls with unquenched thirst and the French bums.

Well, we go in and there are a sedate few friends in for a New Year drink like Rathbone, the fearless sea-rover, and his opulent Britannia having her usual trouble concealing her knickers; Sally, mother of Jane; David Lawson who was almost filled in in triplicate by the two remaining Kevins and one of the French bums; and Barbara. And there was yet another party by all that's wonderful on a May morning in Connemara.

As luck would have it my own poor musical gifts were not in demand on that particular evening and so I had the opportunity of a quiet chat with Barbara, herself, since, for once, Foster wasn't tracking in from long shot; Fingal Grey was giving Manhattan back to the Indians; and gossamer-balls was contemplating the ascent of the south face of Jan West. She was as cool as a well-played vibrophone. She smiled, I smiled back to the base-line.

'You seem to have a portable party at your disposal, Gavin. Where did you find all these people?'

'It's your uncle. He has a devastating gift for friendship.'

Coarse as an old sack, the artefactory was shouting things like 'fasten your chastity belts for the knees-up' and it wasn't at all appropriate.

'It's devastating. I'll go that far.'

'By the way, a happy new year.'

'Thank you. I'm sure that your new years are all inevitably blissful, but the same to you.'

'This is beginning rather better than most. We still have an unconsummated date.'

'Yes, you're going to take me somewhere interesting.'

'I didn't say that. I said somewhere of my own.'

'I'll go on looking forward to it.'

'Have you been busy?'

'Fairly. It's a bad time of year for depressives.'

'I hadn't seen you since that ridiculous evening ...'

The remark made her blush proving that the old touch was still as deft.

'Yes. I didn't thank you properly at the time. You saved rather a difficult situation. Perhaps I should say that it isn't quite as . . . complicated . . . as it sounds.'

'You don't have to explain yourself or anything about yourself to me. Let's forget it.'

There were sights and sounds of revelry all around by now with the paterfamilias on the horns, as you might well put it, of a terrible dilemma. Paul had his tiny frozen hand warming up nicely near the appropriate crux of Jane West. Frenchmen and Kevins were ubiquitous. The Welsh chap was playing the piano in a pleasantly amateur way and the bee-keeper healer was asleep under it.

'Does my brother often get as drunk as that?'

'She's a very pretty girl.'

'Oh, don't mistake me. I'm . . . I'm not sure that you're a very good influence.'

'No? Perhaps I'm not. I'm not a professional like yourself at sorting people out, but I help whenever I can. They're the right age for each other. It makes me feel almost sentimental.'

'I don't trust you.'

'Why not?'

'I don't know. It's to do with dispassion. Wherever you are there's a lot of noise and laughing, but you are never a part of it.'

'You think I lead people on.'

'Only where they want to be led. I'm talking nonsense. Sorry. I didn't mean to be rude.'

'Think nothing of it.'

'I've never seen you frown. Or scowl.'

'It's an easy going nature.'

'You have a sort of serenity. God, I must be drunk myself. I don't make a habit of saying that sort of thing.'

'Thank you.'

She lobbed the smile back. But had no chance with the cross-court volley of my return. Game and set, as far as I could tell in the general excitement, to me.

Paul Keller

There is no doubt about it: I have an unusually nasty mind. But, Officer Krupke, my parents was twentieth century enlightened eggheads. Drink, reform and more poems. The point is have I or have I not a conscience: to pang or not to pang, that is the question. Now Sebastian Jones, playboy, richman and uncle, has no conscience; and Gavin McNamara has no conscience with his fifteen-year-old, peat-tasting speech-potheen. Not only do they not give a damn for the world, they don't give a damn for themselves.

'Here, Paul, I want you to meet Suzy. She doesn't want to be bothered by an old black-faced kangaroo like me. She's a stripper.' Worthy pioneer, is it any wonder I am such a mixed-up little prince? Thank God, Christmas is over at least. Chestnuts roasting by a multitude of heavenly hosts saying have a spot of goodwill in your peace-on-earth and just a thimbleful of ethic realism while I covet your wife in the neighbour room. At least, Sebastian is not a fake in their way. Or even McNamara, though I don't believe I said anything to him about her. However pissed.

Suzy is talkative enough for two of us.

Anyway what right have I to sneer? The Cricklewood College of Technology tries to affect traditions that *they* have imposed by affecting and accepting. The Head of Biology: 'Ah, Keller, I must say that having a young chap like you on the committee improves staff-student relationships, no end. By the way, I keep missing your father on various committees where I act as adviser. Haha. No doubt I shall meet him one day.' What? The protector of warriors who bears himself honourably and never strikes down his boon companions at the drinking? Brave in battle, but guarded with the greatest human liberal gifts? You are joking. Head of Biology, you *earn* my father's society! By brilliant achievement or youth. The deserving meritocracy of England is as exclusive as only those who have struggled in a stratified monolith of privilege, to emerge volcanically at the bloody summit, can make it.

'Sorry, Suzy, I'm not very marvellous company.' 'Are you depressed, then, love?' 'Yes, a bit depressed.' Not that it will mean much to a healthily ebullient girl like Suzy, who has probably had to fight every inch of the way to any kind of survival. It is interesting, looking at her, to think that our measurable intelligence is so much in my favour and that I am, compared to her, such a total idiot. Strip away the books from the walls and you will see the leprous spots. Suzy laughs.

It's not as simple as inverted snobbery or romanticism. It is as though some poisoned hormone that makes me love Barbara makes me loathe all the others except Jane West and her mother. That at least is normal. To want them. 'I lived in Paris for a few years.'

Suzy would like to have lived in Paris. Once the promise of a job in a classy strip-show off the . . . Champs-Elysées? . . . that's right. Turned out to be a horrible dump in Montmartre. But Suzy liked Paris. Yes I liked it too. Frankie, quiet, soft, with sad eyes. Careful, young colleague. Always amazing, her pleasure. Poison in the blood that did not infect her, a whore. Afflicted with a neurotic spinal convulsion of guilt. Now, a smiling strip-tease girl in a pub. Sebastian is less cunningly outrageous in pubs, rubbing his thigh against a tight-skirted, round-bellied Amazon, shrieking with laughter. Reminds me of Mrs Annabelle Finch.

Curious friendship. The nightmare goddess, accused by her women of destroying her son, lilting affectedly somewhere with her. Blandford, Aylmer: Have you seen Keller's mother, Aylmer? Diddums, snookums, wantums mummy. I've seen Keller's sister, Blandford. Oooooofff! Ever had a peek, Keller? No one survived. I smashed each of them to pulp, exulted while they slowly burned. Your sister's got big ones, Keller. D'you ever have a feel? Hung on meathooks, starved. To this day, I would kill . . . . I say, Aylmer, Blandford's pissed in Keller's gumboots.

'No, Suzy, I don't think we'd better go. I have to look after my uncle.' 'It's just you looked very miserable, love.' 'Are you miserable, too.' 'I'm not happy.' The soft sell about drinking too much. Nice boy with brains, good job, writes poetry, being saved from alcoholic collapse by golden-hearted, sequin-nippled damsel from wrong side of bump-and-grind tracks. No one would believe the fiction, the supreme fiction, of it. I owe you something, Suzy, Tell me about merry hell. 'Hey, Paul, son, I've got us a lift. This is Tarzan Cohen, he's a bookie.'

Jaguar smooths its way to Roehampton where Tarzan swings to his treetop home. Real name Tarjan. Born Budapest. Got out 1938, presciently. Purrs sleekly along the Cromwell Road, cigared and generous, sharing his good fortune. No complaints. Nice house with small pool. Keeps tropical fish. Two kids at Grammar School. None of your public schools, no, but none of this comprehensive rubbish either, mate. Mr Chapman, schoolmaster, up the road, has told him the British Grammar School is the backbone of the nation. Famous products, Mr Cohen, as follows: R. Keller, Mrs R. Keller, Miss Barbara Keller, Captain J. Rathbone, Royal Navy, R. Lomax, Mrs R. Lomax, A. Stone, D. Lawson, L. Bisset, M.P., Miss Jacqueline Benbow, Mrs. Sally West, F. Grey, Mrs. L. Bisset and many others, in business, in the professions, in the communications racket, in publishing, in government and administration, in journalism, in science and technology, in medicine, in the armed forces, in education (Charity begins at home and is not puffed up) and in the arts. To what purpose, to underwrite the bourgeois philosophy of ownership with intellectual respectability. Not that I am a conscience-stricken revolutionary, sir. I am an elitist. Perhaps my only hope is that I am an elitist who does not care whether he is elite.

She is alone. Sitting alone, reading.

She has been waiting up for me. Daddy and McNamara playing chess with lidless eyes in the study. Mummy out. Sebastian sniffs the air. The whisky is not where my frost-kissed sister sits. He pads away, fat and friendly mastiff. Heart thump. 'Shut the door, Paul, and sit down.'

It bores you. Then, darling, it bores me. But it is harmless enough. Our respectable environment enjoying a seasonable knees-up, pretending it is part of the licensed society: what harm is there in a show of panties and a disgusting old man. 'He's all right, Barbara. A bit ribald, but he doesn't mean any harm. I'm less sure of Gavin.' Sharp look. Pain under the heart. The indecision in her eyes as she speaks his name: I watch. The naturally deceitful who are bad liars, can never control that split-second shiver of the eyes. Or perhaps it is fear and means nothing. Fear of misunderstanding or possibilities. This jealousy has never died.

'He's all right, I suppose.' But, surely, my dear sister, you find him attractive. Most women do. The spirit of the black bog, primordial thing from twenty thousand conquests. Heart thump. Blood pound behind the eyes. A rushing noise in my years of wanting, longing. She sits primly: knees pressed fast together, left foot a few inches in front of the right, hands loosely folded on her lap. 'Do you want a drink?' No. She does not. 'Nor, do you.' Which is final. Command. For a moment the brother and sister stare tremblingly at each other.

'It's time we talked about it openly.' 'What?' 'You know perfectly well. The fact that you want me. Sexually.' Noise of blood draining from my face. Thump of fear in the gut. Nerve tingle, scalp crawl, sickness, stir in the loins: fear. And on to say, composedly and clinically, that she had hoped this conversation would never have to happen. And on, beautiful icy empress of absinthe, to say that she hoped I would have been cured of a boy's infatuation (which is quite natural) in France; and the fear that I haven't. If only, lustre-eyed bride and sister, the fear meant desire. 'Darling, you're not going to psychiatrise me . . .' Oh, no, no. It is emphatically *not* funny. I don't know, my love, when it started: as soon as I was aware of women I was aware of you: your full high breasts, the roundness of your hips, clothes stretched tightly across and around your rhythmic, singing body, the vanishing splendours of your thighs, even the curve of your knee and the fullness of the calf. Never in any other woman the same savage excitement you gave me. I have always worshipped you. I have never really wanted any one else. Or anything else. To lie with you, with your legs about me, to bury my helpless fury between your wide, woman's breasts, to explore and strain and ride and dance, and surge and flow and hate and despair and exult with you and in you and into you and for you, goddess and sister, together, synthesis of all pain and all passion and an unbearable pleasure. Everything else in my life, darling, has been an excuse for not being your possessed slave and for not making you cry out your woman's grief in and need for, and lusting glory of, my defeated, conquering self.

'A very long time ago. As long as I remember . . . I suppose you must have loathed me. . . . ' She will not admit it, but she admits it worries her. All the time careful not to move. No one can sit as still as she can. Careful not to disturb her legs or by shifting her body remind me . . . *Remind* me! Christ, woman, Can't you understand. 'I can't stand you touching me, which is why I shouted the other evening and why I try never to dance with you. It's all very foolish. Almost unprofessional. I hear about incest and incestuous longings all the time in my work. I'm able to listen, to offer treatment, to help. But the moment you touch me, it's absurd, but my skin seems to shrivel.' Dry almost clinical footnote to years of pain and fury, silence and longing. Never herself having suffered such enormous horrors of desire. It has taken her, she says, a long time to even face the necessity of talking to me. Some men have told her that she is frigid . . .

'WHO?'

'It doesn't matter . . .'

'It bloody well matters to me. How many men have you slept with, for God's sake?' Three. In ten years, that's not many. One fairly often will be Grey. So what about Eric Foster? 'Have you been to bed with Eric?' 'No. But I probably shall.'

My sister says that now that we are both living in the same country, sometimes in the same house, we must inevitably see a lot of each other. She has observed, her professional training has made her acute in such observation, that I am still . . . Leaving the sentence finished with a wave of her hand . . . She had also observed that I drink myself into what she calls a state of collapse each night. Succinct medical history in neat handwriting. She is worried not only for me, but for herself. It is getting in the way of her work, because it affects her attitude to patients. And that is no kind of position for an invincible Keller to be in because it materially governs the headlong acceleration rate of success. And it is getting in the way of her ordinary relationships with men. 'How can it?'

'You're not stupid, Paul. I shan't go into details. The point is we've got to come to terms with it. Both of us. I know all about the fantasies, the guilt, the despair. I can't help knowing. And I don't think that you wanting me is evil or sinful or criminal or anything. But it makes me sick. If I'd found out when I was older, perhaps it wouldn't. But that day . . . I was young and I didn't know very much.'

'It doesn't matter that I love you.' 'I'm not sure that I know what that word means.' 'Can we go on seeing each other?'

Of course, it would be foolish not to. She will even go so far as to say that if she thought it would help either of us, if we were different types of people, if she were less revolted, if . . . . . . then we should do it. BUT.

Oh my foolish sister. You now immediately see that you should never have said that. The miserable have no medicine save hope. And I suppose that I, at last, am the calm one because I can see the extent of her despair too, how much I have disturbed her. A shining girl in autumn and sombre decay.

There is nothing to be made of the silence. The Irishman knocks and comes in to fetch a book. He says with charm that we both look awful solemn.

Eric Foster

'Why am I justifying myself to you, for God's sake?'
'. . . understand my sort of jealousy.'
'It's quite absurd . . . '

Absurd?

—I suppose it's all a question of making judgements. And I find that I'm making them in spite of myself. What happened to all those comfortable times when it was possible to be an artist *outside* politics and social responsibility and all these other things.
—Well, things are rather more simple for me. I have never been an artist.
—Now, Jacqueline, you're not going to duck.
—I'm not trying to. I'm a critic. And you despise critics.
—You're a scholar, which is different. Anyway, it doesn't matter what you are and what I am, the point of the argument is 'pure' art like 'pure' science. . . .

The intellectual dummy's dance.

—Jacqueline neat as ever, black and white, slim fitting dress and white collar, slender legs neatly crossed. Unobtrusively feminine, but making no sexual call-sign. Tidily centred in a ridiculously untidy office, mounded with papers, photographs, reports, even pictures propped in odd corners.

—I should have said, Eric, with due respect, that you have always been an artist interested in society. In at least a half of your films.

—I must be wasting your time, Jacqui. You look busy. Unless I can take you out to lunch. . . .

—Thank you. I'd like that very much. D'you mind if I finish this note?

The Managers. National Gallery. 'Q' in the Spanish room. Velasquez, El Greco, Goya, Ribera, Murillo. Moving through the empty room and out through the next empty room, along an empty gallery, long silent, slow.

'. . . trying to educate me.'

'Sharing.'

'. . . and, Eric, thank you.'

—That's done. I'm sure there'll be no problem anyway. Would you like to walk around with me and tell me what you'd need.

—After lunch. It's really very good of you to go to all this trouble. It's an idea I got when I was here a few months ago and it's all to do with the Mantegna *Agony in the Garden.*

—What's the film?

—*The Managers.* It's about Robert Keller.

Your trouble, Eric, is that you make terrific heroes out of people. Then they disappoint you. Inevitably. And you start hating them. You really are most unfair.

Yes, I know that, Ginny. I'm an adolescent still.

'I honestly don't think he cares.'

'. . . surely . . .'

'. . . down in the R.S.G. shelter, if they're still called that, without a thought. That is dispassion.'

Charing Cross on a sunny winter day. Nice curves and levels. Narrow and wide. Hints of green, promising spring. Bustling of taxis. Towers and steeples and domes. 'Q' kneeling on the steps looking up. Impossible angels and turbulence of stormclouds and Jacqueline in a red coat and fur hat, smiling.

—No, I'd have said that, for what they're worth, my films have always been about relationships. *Reciprocals* was and *Scipio* as well, so is this.
—What's your hero called?
—He hasn't got a name. Just 'Q'.
—That doesn't sound like Robert.
—Robert, my dear Jacqui, is not the hero.

> '. . . curious relationship. I suppose I've always liked Daddy.'
> '. . . very likeable man . . .'
> 'Not love . . .'
> '. . . about love.'
> 'Love?'
> '. . . squeak like dolls the wished-for . . .'
> 'No.'

Always this kind of scene that makes me see the buildings crumble. The globe falls from the Coliseum, still spinning and beneath the high buildings crack and split. No noise. The theatres, the domes, the statues, the temples, the palaces. In spring silently crumble.

> 'I'd have gone home to fuck my wife,' grinning through bandages. Gina riding 'Q' as the buildings silently crumble, the pictures sear brown; Gina, still in a light slip plunging onto 'Q', head back, head shaking, eyes shut, mouth open. Roger Lomax tearing the clothes off a Negress in the tube. 'Given warning . . . ' Barbara plunges over me. 'It's your wife who'd need the bloody warning. . . .
>
> Laughter. Robert Keller. The VIP lounge. These passions distract us and obscure our intellectual vision.

> Eric, if you mention bloody Spinoza to me again I'll scream for help.

Go ahead, Ginny. Scream. A mute nearly beautiful thing is your face. . . .

Perhaps an owlish smile. 'Adulthood is not an age but a state of knowledge of self.' Shy, slow adolescence, happy early childless marriage, bitter, civilised divorce, a gently perfunctory love affair—and adulthood still seems far off.

—Just back from California. Stanford or Berkeley, I'm not quite sure which. And he says quite simply that there you have to take sides. I see the point.
—Would you take sides, Jacqui?
—I think so.
—Suppose these wild and stupid children were going to burn your pictures at the Gallery or damaging the books in the Bodleian in the name of some fathead revolution—which side?
—I know that, Eric. But this isn't America. At the moment we are not involved in an absurd and wasteful war. . . .
—Absurd?
—Totally absurd. But it's not just that: it's Wallace and Reagan and Daly and Strom Thurmond. . . .
—That's a pretty mixed bag . . . .
—Exactly. You can see what makes those children, not the wild and stupid ones but the honest and hopeful ones, so desperate.

The problem is one of selfishness. A child on a stony field refusing to share sweets, or using them to buy himself into a game. Once devoured the unhappy kid is beaten and sent home, crying. And other kinds of selfishness, the greatest of all is to fall in love. The words *I love you* are the most extreme expression of selfishness, meaning: *now* you know. I want you for me alone and I do not intend to share you. Now you know I demand your loyalty, kindness, tolerance. Perhaps it is bourgeois. . . .

Laughter.

Do you really mean it, Eric? You love me?
Christ, my darling girl, can't you see?

> '. . . when, how long . . .'
> 'Forever.'
> '. . . no.'

—I didn't expect you to be so passionate. You must talk to Robert Keller. I get nowhere arguing with him.

—So you're making a film to show him?

—No, I'm making a film about a man crossing a bridge, screaming.

—Munch.

—Yes, of course.

—You see it as what?

—I don't know. But every picture I make is about that scream. My commitment is to that screaming thing, neither man nor woman.

> Oh you have a genius, all right, Eric, You have a bloody marvellous genius for isolation.

> A trite tune. Dancing to a cracked record. The intellectual dummy's dance. Rien ne peut lui plaire.

> 'My dear, I promise . . .'
> '. . . I . . . I don't . . .'
> 'Say nothing. No one will be hurt.'

> What win I if I gain the thing I seek? A dream a breath, a froth of fleeting joy. For one sweet grape who will the vine destroy?

—I don't think I have any particular problem, Jacqui. So I hope I'm not over-dramatizing it. Nothing like Andrew's.

—What's Andrew's problem?

—He's an elitist. And because he is also sickened by the world and all the suffering, he is desperately ashamed.

—I suppose I'm an elitist in a way. I believe in minority art.
—High culture. . . .
—All right. The professional left who aren't good enough to write well have tried to make that an obscene phrase, but the really creative mind will find its own way. . . .
—Regardless of the profanum vulgum?
—I've nothing against popular culture. . . .
—I don't believe you.
—Never mind about me. What about Andrew?
—Well, you know how anguished he gets. It seems he's published five novels, all well reviewed and two of which have won prizes as you know, which have sold very few copies. Six or seven thousand.
—But he has his television programme.
—I daresay he's worried about the viewing figures. And it's not his programme. It's why he's decided to write, in fact I think he has written, this ridiculous thriller that Robert . . .
—Oh? Did you know he was going to bed with Sylvie? At least that is what Annabelle Finch told me.
—Good God in Heaven !

(Would you like to?
Of course.
I think I'm a fool. I know Robert does. I'm very fond of you.)

> '. . . you and mummy . . .'
> 'No.'

> 'Q' in his laboratory studying slides. The inevitable breakdown of order. Roaming the city, now no longer empty, the marauders, the berserks of this age.

—I thought you might know. Andrew's a close friend of yours.
—Hardly close. Tell me, Jacqui, is it me or have the entire Keller family as well as most of their friends gone mad?

—They're certainly living it up. Robert's always had affairs, I suppose. But now Sylvie and Paul and Barbara. . . .

That was said tentatively but deliberately. She wants to be quite sure I know that her friend is . . . Why? The neat black and white arms crossed on the gleaming tablecloth, shining glass, bright knives, dark stone (labradorite) on the third finger of her right hand. Calm face with uncertain eyes. I pass it off with a wave of the hand. What should I resent?

—They seem to be collecting all kinds of curious characters as their latest hobby. Perhaps they've decided to opt into the permissive society before it's too late.
—I'm not sure, you know, Eric, that for all Robert Keller's impeccable ethical judgement that he has much moral conscience.
—I don't think it's just Robert. It's a symptom you will find in a certain type of a certain generation. Lawrence Bisset, me, Robert, even David Lawson. We developed an ethical conscience late. . . .

> We knew a falling off of zest; and while the workless topped three million Read Eliot in the pavilion; For us the Reichstag burned to tones Of Bach on hand-made gramophones. . . .

A khaki jacket with medal ribbons. A commando knife. A scarred face. A limp. To speake as the common people do, to thynke as wise men do. Followe thys councel of Aristotle.

> I wonder if her eyes do change as I think they change when she looks at Fingal Grey. Sickens me. Coarse flabby. Flabby mind. 'Q' had this feeling of intimacy with Gina. In a bar, for example, before the holocaust, they would stand very close to each other touching in every way except with hands and bodies. 'Q' sometimes trembled because of the closeness of her physical presence, knowing too that she was aware, although merely comfortably aware, of him.

Now he roams through the city, hearing the shouts of the scavenging, maddened bands, the screams, imagining the ecstasy of Gina violated by a barbarian.

—I think the war meant more to you than to the others. And I for one, Eric, would not say that you had no moral conscience.
—Well, it meant more in the sense that it left me with a stiff leg.
—No, I think more than that.

It's no good being bitter, Ginny.
You're a funny man, Eric, but I admire you. Do you know that? I admire you.

'... hurt you ...'
'I suppose so. I've tried never to indulge myself ...'
'... love ... perhaps ... I ...'
'My darling, hush ...'

And Jasmine Lomax with long black-sheathed legs, delicate gold hair falling soft, curving around pale, tritely pretty features. Black, snagged nylon. Odd the sudden twitch of lust. Desirable to the protective.

Laughter.

Oh, Eric ! You just don't bother. You leave it all to me.
You're so much more competent than I am, Ginny. It makes sense to leave it all to you.
Ridiculous ! You're impossible and I love you.

—I'd have said, Eric, that you want to take responsibility for everything. For every scream on every bridge.
—Twenty screams on twenty bridges are one scream on one bridge?

'So, trust me. No one will be hurt.'

Then *why!* Why? Barbara Keller is a decent girl, a controlled woman, an honest person ... Who fucks with Fingal

Grey. And Christ knows who else. Bisset? Rathbone? The Irishman? He's an attractive man. They've been living in the same house. Gina and the berserk. The torn scream on the face of 'Q'.

—I suppose I've always made a religion of control. I used to read a great deal of philosophy to try and make myself properly rational. My wife used to laugh at me. But that's what I've got against a lot of this new stuff, there's not enough control, not enough discipline. All feeling, no form.
—Well, I'll agree as far as art is concerned.
—Good. It's nice to know there's another dinosaur left to bellow.

I did not want to hurt her. I did not want to trap them into confession. What did I gain except suffering? The agonies of lust and jealousy. Tremor cordis. But not for joy. Not joy.

The most beautiful face can look ugly in laughter and practised smiles.

'Q' searches in the slide of his shaving-glass for the signs of disease, the distortion and disfiguration, abnormality of form. He wears an old battle jacket, with medal ribbons. In his hand a long-bladed knife. He moves through the city.

—It's not that I'm a prude. At least I hope not. But I dislike promiscuity. Of any sort.
—We seem to be back to the Kellers again.
—That's not kind, Eric.
—Aha! But you're laughing.
—Yes. As Barbara's oldest friend, I've lived under her shadow too long not to enjoy a ration of malice.
—I see. For myself I've always envied Robert's amorality, sexual amorality of course. I'd like to have been a good lecher. But I had too much guilt. . . .

Laughter.

Jane West's scrap of skirt high over her arse. Andrea showing, Sylvie touching, Elaine Rathbone straining against tight fabrics, Sally smoothing her dress over her hips, Annabelle Finch rasping one leg along the other contemptuous, Jasmine long black snagged tights, even Jacqui with smooth cool hands caressing. . . .

> And Gina. Slow rhythmic passionate movement. The hairy little Fingal Grey, the slender, golden-haired recklessness of the Irish thug. And the slow movement, glide and ripple, centred upon the splendour of her waist and hips. . . . Slim adolescence that a nymph has stripped, Peleus on Thetis stares. Her limbs are delicate as an eyelid, Love has blinded him with tears; But Thetis' belly listens. Down the mountain walls From where Pan's cavern is Intolerable music falls. Foul goat-head, brutal arm appear, Belly, shoulder, bum, Flash fishlike; nymphs and satyrs Copulate in the foam.

— . . . in fact most often intolerably smug.

—You're very harsh.

—I'm a dishonest man, Jacqui. I have to be harsh. D'you want some more coffee?

—No it's time I was back. Would you like to walk round now and show me what you want.

—Thank you. I don't think it would be very complicated. I'll probably use a hand-held camera for those sequences.

—Will you let me read the script?

—If you can make head or tail of it. You know my esoteric charts and diagrams. . . .

Two o'clock sun on St Martin's Lane, move towards Cavell statue, sweep of hill down past the square, traffic flash. Cut to same same scene empty. 'Q' kneeling on St Martin's steps.

> My hand brushes Jacqueline's hip. She turns. Something precise in her eyes. Serious. Oh.

—Isn't that Jane? Over there. Near the fountain.
—So it is. Pretty child.
—Yes. I have an idea that Paul Keller might be saved from Andrea there.
—Jacqui! I'd never have believed it of you. No. Some mad over-sensitive middle-aged fool will fall for her. She'll marry a computer specialist and become a Helen of social welfare dream in Orpington.

> '. . . not a fool. No. But let's not talk any more. Tell me about the picture.'
> 'It's going to be called *Nocturne*.'

> Eric, don't you make things deliberately complicated? Are you asking me to make nice films that people can understand, Ginny?
> There you are. You see: you're defensive. You cannot take criticism.

—It sounds difficult. What is he doing in the art gallery?
—It has become a sort of symbol of all the things he admired and feared. The inheritance of Western civilisation, if you like. He wanders in. Wanting it to be destroyed and at the same time anxious that it should not be.
—Look, Eric I hope you don't think I'm being cheeky, but is this intelligible to most people?

(Eric, love, it's a *marvellous* idea. Oh, damn, it's closing time.
Let's go to the ML.
We are turning into soaks. Never mind.
Now tell me. What are you calling it?
Gyroscope.
Oh, I think it's a lovely idea, Eric. Tell me all the details.)

> The acts of kindness that destroy . . .

—It's an entirely fair question, Jacqui. I ask it a hundred times a day. What is the point? I think I'm losing my faith in 'Art'. I don't see the point any more.

Yet in his heart of hearts the proud and arrogant soul of Eric Foster thanks an absentee God for what he has been able to do. Hypocrite voyeur.

'Why on earth did you accept the absurd challenge?'
'It's not absurd. I shall prove to him that I can write a damn good thriller.'
'It's a waste of your time, Andrew.'
'No, it's not. I can say some of the things I want to say in a thriller and reach a much bigger public.'
'I think you're going to have egg on your face.'

The gallery is peaceful. Jacqueline black and white elegant; Eric Foster untidy, limping. A few foreigners wandering, a few students, the occasional smiling enthusiast, bored young women being led around by a lecturer.

One afternoon, here with Barbara Keller . . .

'. . . when?'
'I don't think I know exactly. I have to tell you: I love you.'

Down from the waist they are centaurs, Though women all above: But to the girdle do the gods inherit, Beneath is all the fiend's; there's hell, there's darkness . . .

'Yes, I will. I promise. But not now, When its right . . .'

Well you don't say that in bed

Fingal Grey! Emotional instability that gets one into bed is unlikely to change into the emotional stability one needs when one has to get out. Venereal diseases spread. Neuroses spread. Yes, true.

'Q' kneels on the steps of St Martin's, looking up into the coign of the building. Lower down three men lie asleep, or perhaps dead. In the fine square beyond a wild berserk group have just come from Whitehall.

They include David Lawson, Jack Rathbone, Lawrence Bisset.

Robert Keller is in the VIP lounge or has already flown out. Gina Keller is being ecstatically raped across an operating table.

Je suis toujours de mon premier sentiment . . . car enfin je suis philosophe . . .

(Tell me, Eric, we're old friends. Do you fancy my bloody daughter?
Yes. As a matter of fact I do.
I thought so. Be careful that you're not hurt. She's good at hurting people.)

And I have a talent for isolation and hurting people.

«Technique . . . structure . . . form. You can't expect a mere civil servant to be up on those things. I leave that to clever chaps like Andrew and Eric . . .»

—So what do you think, Jacqui?
—I think we just work at what we're good at, doing it as well as we can, believing in it. And if it ends in disaster, it ends in disaster. We try to die quietly. Meanwhile we go on working.

Well you don't say that in bed

A black fog of resentment. . . .

Wlaffrynge, chiterynge, harrynge and garrynge grysbytinge.

Robert Keller

The restaurant was as usual reasonably and agreeably full, pleasantly dim and unhurried. Robert Keller was known there, as indeed he was known in a number of similar restaurants in the West End. He was the first to arrive and was shown to his table, where he ordered a glass of Black Velvet. He sat watching the activity of the room in a mood of relaxed anticipation, ticking off mentally the events of the past day as he noticed this or that attractive woman, the occasional well-known face, one or two amusing human details which he would use in a Carew Sinclair novel.

The day's work had been tiring but satisfactory. Robert Keller had spoken separately and profitably to two Ministers of the Crown, one of whom was an exacting and clever man. He was no longer, he decided, driven by personal ambition, although in no doubt that his services would be publicly recognised, so much as by intellectual satisfaction in solving problems. He had also dealt with two confidential reports on junior colleagues seeking advancement, fairly and impartially. He had completed a full schedule of routine work, but was disturbed from running over this and from the appreciative admiration of a woman of about thirty in a white evening-frock at a table half-way across the room by the arrival of Lawrence Bisset. They had barely greeted each other when they were joined by Jack Rathbone and David Lawson. Punctuality was an important virtue in all Robert Keller's friends.

They agreed that they would all have oysters and ordered more Black Velvet. As usual, Robert Keller said very little in the early stages of an evening with his male friends. He preferred to gauge the mood of each of them, to pick up salient topics and to chart out in his own mind any areas of potential danger.

The conversation was informed, economical, subtly relative. Robert Keller enjoyed his oysters while Lawrence Bisset and David Lawson discussed the trade figures for January, the best for two years. He was amused. Both men were socialists, although Lawson's politics were private and discreet, yet here was a traditional confrontation once more of Whig and Tory. David Lawson's hackles were notoriously sensitive and, for some reason that Robert Keller had never understood but which he was sure had nothing to do with Andrea, Bisset always became prickly in argument with him. Jack Rathbone took a draught of Black Velvet. He was the host for the evening and signalled to the wine waiter.

On the white tablecloth in front of Robert Keller there were two knives, three forks, two dessert spoons and three glasses, as well as a tumbler in which the remains of Black Velvet had made a dark brown lace, reminding Robert Keller of a set of lingerie he had recently bought for his mistress, Sally West, in the Rue Royale. He looked over the gleaming glass and silver with satisfaction, listening to Jack Rathbone ordering wine. The pretensions of his friends to wine expertise pleased him because they reflected his own taste and doctrines. He became aware that the other men were all looking in his direction and that Rathbone had said something.

'Are you intending to maintain a respectful silence?' said Rathbone.

Robert Keller was pleased to pick up the allusion quickly. He relished his reputation as a nonchalant conversationalist who missed nothing, based entirely upon luck and the speed of his mind. He explained that he was in no way concerned with the building of the Q.E.2 and that the counsel of the Minister of Technology (that a 'respectful silence' on the matter was to be recommended) was a matter of indifference to him.

Using the manner of his high-comedy novels, written as Carew Sinclair, Robert Keller became very witty at the expense of several of his colleagues.

Robert Keller chose a *sole normande* and sat placidly back listening to the others giving their orders. He did not in the least mind David Lawson trying to have a little fun at his expense, but he was naturally pleased to have dealt with him urbanely. He smiled, considering Lawson, as he gave his instructions to the waiter a little preciously, noting that, of course, Lawson had always admired Sylvie. They talked endlessly about literature.

Since Rathbone was a serving officer, in Robert Keller's opinion destined to become a Rear-Admiral within the next year or so, and Bisset had also served in the Navy, they were particularly interested in the recent remarks of the Secretary of State for Defence about the Russian ships in the Mediterranean. Robert Keller, who read Russian, quoted to his friends criticism of the Secretary in the Soviet press and Bisset, with his special knowledge of American affairs, began a cool appraisal of NATO strategy. Reminded as they all were of the embargo on road travel to West Berlin at the time of the Federal Republic's presidential elections, they were all disposed to be sombre at the ease with which a tense situation could develop in Europe.

Inevitably they moved to Indo-China and the Vietcong offensive of that very week. Curiously enough, in the eyes of Robert Keller, it was Jack Rathbone who was always most critical of American policy in Vietnam. During the war, it had been quite usual to find officers in any Mess who were left wing. Robert Keller smiled in memory of the contribution the R.A.E.C. and his own Intelligence people were alleged to have made towards the Labour victory of 1945. He was, nevertheless, still mildly astonished when he heard his friend, Rathbone, a senior serving officer in the most conservative arm of H.M. forces, express modestly radical opinions. Bisset, predictably enough, defended the expediency of American involvement and while professing no particular confidence in the new Nixon administration or its promises thought that an end might be in sight. Equally predictably David Lawson, who had served on several missions to the Slav countries in the years 1945-48, brought in the Russian occupation of Prague. In the few days immediately past, another student had burned himself in Wenceslas Square. The conversation turned to the disillusion of the young. Robert Keller expressed the wry wish that his own children might show a little less complacency, aware that Lawrence's Bisset's son had become monumentally disaffected. Jack Rathbone called for another bottle of Genevrières.

'Frankly, I am bored with the cult of youth, said David Lawson. While it was channelled into fashion and pop music, it was entirely tolerable: but when it is turned in a thoroughly irresponsible way to muddle-headed politics and gullible idealism, it is a nuisance. Anyway, all young people are emotionally unstable: it's a simple question of glands.'

David Lawson thoroughly enjoyed parodying his genuinely blimpish attitudes to his close friends. He smiled pleasantly at their regulated laughter.

'The problem is surely that these people are being exploited,' said Jack Rathbone. 'By serious and highly efficient revolutionists. . . .'

'I'm not sure,' said Lawrence Bisset, 'I think there's an enormous amount of quite real frustration and a sense of helplessness, especially among the ones in their early twenties . . .'

'There are a large number of professional agitators,' said David Lawson. 'I was having dinner at my college the other week with Percy Sherwood—you know Percy, don't you, Robert? hardly a reactionary—and he claims that there is a steady minority of activist trouble-makers who manage to stir up the others in sufficient numbers to be seriously worrying.'

'But what happened to all those steady chaps who were working hard or playing rugger and so on,' said Lawrence Bisset. 'Why do they put up with it?'

Robert Keller interrupted to put his view that discontent was a natural condition of youth. He said, further, that there were certainly sinister forces at work upon this discontent, if it was sinister to plan the destruction of Western society at all. It seemed to him that the ultimate collapse of Western civilisation was inevitable, but he asked what should replace it. Equally inevitably, a Dark Age. The choice therefore was between repressive tyranny and anarchy. Their own generation must, of course, Robert Keller claimed, find either alternative repulsive; but the inchoate longings of the young were exploitable. He suggested that while the educational system remained unrevised, the young would inevitably receive muddled ideas from ersatz sages and they would be badly taught by incompletely learned and incompetently prepared young lecturers.

Partly believing his own thesis, it nevertheless gave Robert Keller his customary pleasure to introduce a slightly outrageous note in any argument. Had Eric Foster or Lomax or Jacqueline Benbow been present, he would have built a rather more studied case. The issue was a serious one and Robert Keller was seriously perturbed by it, while confident that in Britain and perhaps France men of his own stamp and calibre would be able to handle difficulties as they presented themselves. They began their third bottle of wine.

Robert Keller, studying the three men around the table, concealed a smile. As they argued amongst themselves, he watched. David Lawson, pin-striped with a white shirt and blue and red tie, small moustached, bright eyed with the wine, made small limitedly vehement gestures while talking in a staccato assertive manner. Rathbone, who had the habit of holding one hand at pipe-distance from his face, its elbow supported by the other hand, whether or not he was actually smoking, never made any kind of movement with his arms; his long grim powerful face occasionally cracked into an ugly smile; he spoke tersely. Fine figure of a man in a more adventurous brown suit than one might expect of a Captain, Royal Navy, thought Robert Keller, married, of course, to a fine figure of a woman. Robert Keller sipped his wine. Lawrence Bisset, with dark watchful eyes and elegantly modulated voice, wore the most fashionably cut suit, although it was by no means obtrusive. Robert Keller watched him with special interest, listening to his defence of the nonpolitical young carefully since he was aware that Bisset was disappointed in the way his own son had turned out. They ate cheese with the rest of the wine and subsequently fresh fruit. Robert Keller enjoyed peeling and segmenting fruit with economy of effort and precision. He gave most of his attention to the excellent Cox's Orange Pippin on his plate.

The progress of the conversation took a much more serious turn as Robert Keller cut the core neatly out of his peeled apple and with six vertical cuts sliced it into eight pieces. Moving from the unrest of students to racial anger, his companions talked about the tense urban situations in the United States. They were sympathetic but fearful.

This topic usually brought grave expressions to the faces of Robert Keller's circle, who knew quite well that they could only stand helplessly by in terms of the American trouble but who all expressed warm determination to prevent such savage antipathies taking hold in Britain.

Robert Keller allowed his precision-controlled mind to fantasise momentarily. Given a 'revolutionary situation' in England, he saw Rathbone and David Lawson resolutely defending the green and pleasant land in which they had achieved modest privileges. Lawrence Bisset and Robert Keller would probably be working out alternative ways of maintaining power. It was not, he believed, cynical to understand that certain men always remained in power; it certainly did not disturb him that he was, and wanted to be, one of them.

As David Lawson liked to stress the importance of good administration, Lawrence Bisset emphasised the significance of democratic parliamentary government, Jack Rathbone praised dedication and discipline in the public service and Robert Keller plugged with deep intellectual and even spiritual sincerity the vital contribution of education.

Over brandy and cigars they discussed the provision made for immigrants at school. Rathbone, one of whose children was at Charterhouse, another at a prep school and the third at a private kindergarten, wanted to know more of Keller's earlier remarks about a revised educational system. Robert Keller dilated.

On these occasions, he was in no doubt about the respect in which his friends held him. They listened attentively and seriously, while Robert Keller surveyed expertly the whole English educational system:

examinations, requirements of employers, comprehensive and private schools in the context of a humane regard for human fulfillment as well as an efficient, integrated, peaceful community. He stressed the importance of the mass communication media, including the necessity of an intelligent exploitation of broadcasting resources and of a responsible serious press.

Unfortunately, though, he happened to make a joke about the demise of *The Dales* and *The Critics*, in the best Carew Sinclair style. Jack Rathbone made some pleasantly jibing remark about the effect of Sylvie's income, since she had been a regular contributor to *The Critics* and the sequence of jokes that followed set up a different rhythm of talk which usually meant that serious conversation, on such an occasion, was over.

'How is Sylvie?' David Lawson asked.

The other two men looked interested as Robert Keller explained that his wife was working hard, but was otherwise well. In fact, he saw remarkably little of her and had seen more even in the days when she had been at the BBC and he had been an ambitious junior civil servant.

'Elaine's talking of getting a job,' Rathbone said. 'Now that Kit's at a school. Don't think I approve.'

'Oh, don't be too hasty, Jack,' said Bisset. 'It's very important for a woman to work. Takes the pressure off. Isn't that so, Robert?'

Robert Keller grinned and waved his cigar tolerantly in the air. He was prepared to admit to himself that he had found Sylvie's desire to work very useful, and no doubt Lawrence Bisset had profited from the spare time that Andrea's antique nonsense had given to him, but Jack Rathbone was a simpler character, basically monogamous. He waited for David Lawson's beaming and irrelevant remark.

'Thank Heavens,' said David Lawson, 'I don't have to worry about these things.'

Robert Keller chuckled obligingly, but Lawson glanced sharply at him.

'It's ages since I saw Sylvie,' he said. 'I think the last time was with Andrew Stone. At the Festival Hall, would it have been?'

'I'm sure it was somewhere acceptably aesthetic,' said Robert Keller.

He had not failed to register and docket the brief glance exchanged by Rathbone and Bisset, but was able to mask any minor prick of irritation without effort. The average woman, Robert Keller contended, was not in the slightest bit selfish, but she was totally self-centred. Men, on the other hand, in his experience, were materially and emotionally selfish but intellectually and spiritually generous. Robert Keller said that all women were competitive in a way that few men were. If they worked in a tough competitive atmosphere, it made them all the more relaxed with their friends. Listening to accounts of their work was a small price to pay for equable domestic weather. He accepted a second glass of brandy.

'I'm not so sure,' said David Lawson. 'Heard that you and Andrew Stone had some kind of challenge. I can't recall who told me.'

'Yes,' said Robert Keller. 'He's going to try to write a thriller. I gather he's already sent it to his publisher. I must say I can't wait. The gothick potential of cyanide and sensibility is devastating to contemplate.'

Robert Keller's friends were suitably amused, but to his annoyance, he found that he still reacted touchily to the mere mention of Andrew Stone. He brought the subject back to Elaine, asking Rathbone if he was going to be emancipated and allow his wife to work.

'It depends on my next appointment,' said Rathbone. 'If I'm given a ship, then fine. If it's Malta or Hong Kong or an overseas shore job in an Embassy, which is what seems to be on the cards, I'll want her to come with me. Naturally.'

Remembering that Elaine had been lonely on the last occasion when her husband had been at sea, some five years previously, as Executive Officer on an aircraft carrier, Robert Keller nodded his appreciation of Rathbone's attitude.

They were now all pleasantly relaxed and although none of them was much disposed to gossip, the substance of what was said became increasingly desultory and trivial. Bisset had been lobbied by one of his constituents about obscene literature. He had, he said, been looking into the matter conscientiously and gave them a witty account of his researches. They discussed pornography in a ribald, consciously red-blooded way with particular reference to the novel *Candy*, which Robert Keller had not read. David Lawson, in his most pedantic voice, expressed his envious approval of swinging London.

'I only wish that things had been as gross for liberal shepherds in my young day,' said David Lawson.

The party broke up in fragmented amusement.

Then in the room downstairs with the high backed stalls which gave onto the street, Robert Keller heard a guffaw that was unmistakable and familiar.

Sebastian Jones was enthroned before an enormous dish of oysters, in roistering good spirits. With him were three young women. Jane West, daughter of Robert Keller's most permanent mistress, a coloured girl whom he remembered seeing before and a third bright-eyed girl whom he did not know. They were all a little drunk and vastly amused by the latest remark of Sebastian Jones. Robert Keller decided it was best to pass unnoticed, but delayed the psychological second or two that enabled Jane West to recognise and greet him.

'Well I'll be a copper-headed one-bollocked phalanger!' said Sebastian Jones. 'It's the four bloody just men in person. Admiral, me old breath of sporting seadust, how are you! Hya, Bisset, how are the bolshies? I don't remember your name, sport, but I know you're a devil for the well-filled panties and you don't need to be the composer Strauss to make a song about that. Robbie, you old Bastard! Hey, mate. Bring some more champagne for these gents, will you. Fancy this as a coincidence, Rob.'

Robert Keller, catching Jane West's eye with world-weary tolerance and ineffable amusement, explained that he and his friends could not stay and enjoy Sebastian Jones' hospitality in view of the next day's commitments. He found, however, that these considerations weighed little with Rathbone, Bisset and Lawson who were contemplating Sebastian Jones and the nubile girls with the brand of vacant grinning benignity that he considered inseparable from middle-aged susceptibility. He sighed.

Surrendering their overcoats once more, they became a noisy, merry party, slightly out of keeping with the easy but conservative atmosphere of the restaurant. It amused him to see Jack Rathbone's face cracked into a semi-permanent grimace of good-humour wedged against the coloured girl, whose name was Ziz, while David Lawson, sandwiched between her and the bright-eyed girl in full sensual bloom, registered the full flush of pleasure at opportune and unexpected contacts. Bisset and Robert Keller, both more sophisticated, acted with more restraint, without in any way dampening the general conviviality.

'Well, Robbie, me old mate,' said Sebastian Jones. 'This is an unexpected pleasure. Would you believe it, though? They have an idea in Australia that you pommies are an arsy-tarsy lot of starched y-fronts. I wish they could be here now and see a bloody Member of fucking Parliament, bolshie or not, two big nobs in the Civil Service and an Admiral having a great laugh with a few sheilas and an old grizzled skink. They'd have another look, Bob, sport, I'll tell you that. Let's have another bottle!'

David Lawson, in Robert Keller's mind by far the most prim and circumscribed of his acquaintance, quite suddenly jumped up and suggested the whole party should pile into taxis and go to his flat for brandy. The idea was acclaimed. Sebastian Jones groped for his wallet.

But as Robert Keller was moving towards the door of the restaurant behind the others, the old man called him back.

'Terrible thing, Robbie, boy. I've left me wallet at your place. Be a mate, sport, and settle it for me and I'll see you won't be the loser and pay you back straight in the morning.'

He went off to join the others while Robert Keller counted out seventeen pounds, flicking each note crisply. He was a little drunk and rather tired, very much disposed not to continue with what had become an unduly rowdy evening. He noticed, however, that the others were in excellent form and caught Jane West's eye. She smiled at him. At the door, he was approached again by Sebastian Jones.

'Many thanks, Bob,' he said. 'I just suggested to the Admiral, we should ring his lady wife and get her along, but he didn't seem to take to the idea. Now, that's a shame, ain't it sport? Ain't it?'

The horny dig of Sebastian Jones's finger into Robert Keller's side underlined the portent of what he was saying. With presence of mind, Robert Keller smiled in a vague and uncomprehending way, wondering, as he got into a taxi with Bisset and Jane West and the bulky tub of guts, how the old man had found out.

Sylvie Keller

'DU COTE DE CHEZ FOSTER'

"**P**erhaps the intransigence of the things that surround us is forced upon them by our concept that they are not themselves and not anything else, and by the incomprehensibility of our conceptions of things in their context. For many years I used to wake up in strange places or on railway journeys with the inescapable sensation that I was moving through a universe which was completely still, whirling my brain into a spiralling dizziness that, as a child, I experienced gazing at my own face in the glass trying to work out who 'I' was, knowing that I existed, that my name was Eric but having no idea how or why I came to be the unique self I knew myself to be without any accompanying vanity; and while I am now able to diagnose accurately this speculative blur of metaphysical imprecision, in those days its seemed to me that I was treading on a gossamer thread of truth, caught by eternal sunlight, which would, if I followed it, lead me inevitably to some sacred and desired understanding of everything, but I always lacked the courage in the moment where I temporarily seemed to lose balance and felt myself plunging into an abyss of mists, losing whatever I did know of myself, even my identity and my self. As I became older these strange sensations, which are the nearest I have ever experienced to any kind of mystical perception of the world, have become less frequent though I am still able to recapture something of the excitement and fear by a process of self-suggestion. Now, when I wake up suddenly in the darkness of an unfamiliar room to find light sliding between the edge of a curtain and the wall in an unexpected place or strange shadows on a patch of ceiling which in my own house would be unlit, I experience, after the first seconds of shock and disorientation, while still etherised by sleep, a weary relief in which I am conscious for a very brief period of intense peace in not knowing what I am or where I am feeling and understanding nothing. Recollected the following day in the cool sunlight of a fashionable street or in a spacious room with friends, these moments seem unreal, but it is only while they last that I have any faint glimpse of eternity.

The relief is passive, a sort of surrender enabling me to make what I will of the unfamiliar shadows on the illuminated panel of ceiling, projecting there the images: things, people, places, which flow with a freedom that seems never to be possible when I am at work, for the labour of recapturing the past is haphazard, fragmentary and unrewarding unless in doing so we are able to make sense of the future. It cannot be ordered or understood, because the frames of memory will not submit to technical logic and the secret flush which began as one of pleasure at an excitement recalled becomes immediately though irrationally one of shame in the nervous torments of the small hours. The rush of night thoughts and images which surge into the empty screen of the mind neither awake or asleep, a febrile state in which the dreamer becomes an idea, a conflict or even an abstract condition, cannot be ordered and I have often awoken convinced that some key image has just presented itself to my semi-consciousness, which is now forever lost and which no amount of daylight discipline and effort can recapture, juxtaposing two events or perhaps dissolving them the one into the other so that, however disparate, they make a new sense, suggest a new meaning, independent of either and yet totally derived from both.

For many years I had not thought of my relationship with Sylvie Keller, save that I had frequently been a guest at her house and had enjoyed a charmingly spontaneous and untroubled friendship with her, in which neither of us made excessive demands upon each other but derived a certain amount of confidence from the unspoken assurance of sympathy whatever the circumstances, when one day I visisted the home of another old friend Andrew Stone, a writer of originality and sensitive delicacy with a small but serious following and a wide critical acclaim, in the early afternoon shortly after his daily servant had been polishing the furniture, using a particular brand of lavender-scented wax. I slumped idly into a deep armchair, weary after a morning in Wardour Street and depressed by the prospect of further meetings of a similar nature, when I became aware of the scent, feeling my whole body respond joyfully as though in anticipation of some exquisite pleasure that I had once experienced which I was about to relive. It took me some time to identify what it was in the room that suddenly induced in me the illogical state of happy and real delight, the details of which were still entirely vague and even when I had isolated the source of my elation in the scent of the furniture wax, it was still not certain that I should be able to focus my memory on the events and sensations that had given me such evident rapture in spite of the mounting conviction that I desired nothing more than to remember intricately whatever it was that held for me the secret meaning of so many undirected years. I sat entranced in the deep chair, inhaling the lavender scent, fearful that in a matter of second the entire experience, the fitful hint of an elusive memory that I wished to cherish, might itself fade and dissolve.

And suddenly the recollection was clear, even as Andrew Stone opened the windows to admit the mingled sounds and perfumes of a March afternoon in Highgate. I was transported to a small pension off the Avenue Louise in Brussels. It was a spring day when the Avenue itself, running between the Bois de la Cambre and the vast platform of the Place du Palais de Justice, suspended like an impossible sound stage above the old city, seemed less like an aortal conduit mechanically circulating the business of a capital city, than a thoroughfare leading to some central festival of metropolitan springtime deliberately decked out by the department of parks and gardens to display the vividly fresh charms of city blossoms and to remind the urban and suburban toilers, tumbling in and out of the city like grains of sand in an endlessly revolving hour-glass, of pleasures and sensualities tasted so seldom as to be forgotten. I gazed about me with an obscure feeling of springtime longing, partly recaptured from memories of youthful delight in such clean, refreshing mornings, partly a new sense of middle-aged wistfulness, mixed with emptiness, the unsatisfied self-pity of someone consigned to a lonely future. Virginia and I had separated finally in February so that I had wandered restlessly from London to Rome to Vienna to Berlin to Brussels, pretending to search for a suitable location for *Puppet of a Dream*, profoundly bored with myself while distrusting the slightest flicker of interest or compassion that I thought I felt for other people; spending hours in corner tables first of all reading then watching and making endless, incoherent notes—lists of titles, images, aphorisms, pensees; blaming myself for the pain and desolation I imagined Virginia to be feeling, yet as totally unable as before to attempt the relatively simple reparations of considerate affection that I had known she needed. Still unaccustomed to looking after myself, perhaps deliberately achieving a form of pathetic dishevellment as an outward token of my spiritual condition, I had brought a tin of lavender-scented furniture polish in mistake for shoe cleaner; and, in keeping with my bored, apathetic mood, I had neglected to change it or to obtain the appropriate stuff, so that each morning, as I applied the wax to my shoes, I was vaguely aware of a strong perfume of lavender, tinctured with the clean, aseptic odour of a recently furbished room.

Now, in Andrew Stone's house, as a result of the obscure chance that his charwoman had used some similar product, I was transported back into a mood of refreshed unexpected happiness, in which there was also a hint of incomplete misery. I became aware of that morning in Brussels when I met Sylvie for the first time in a cafe half-way along the Avenue called La Coupole in circumstances which were to say the least farcical, since the waiter had swept the contents of my glass of beer into her open handbag and I, in my anxiety to repair the embarrassment, had arisen too quickly from my chair, becoming entangled in its wrought-iron legs and falling over with an ungainly crash that fortunately amused even the gloomy *garçon de café* enough to bring about a general emotional amnesty.

As soon as we both discovered that we were English, we became even more delighted by the absurdity of the situation and spent the rest of the morning on the same terrace in the most natural and effortless conversation that I had ever had with any stranger.

And so, for the next few nights, I would take her out to dine, in due course escorting her back to her hotel as far as the entrance, but never farther: because, although I was sometimes persuaded that she would have welcomed me readily enough as a lover, I was anxious not to let the immediate, the unsentimentally innocent freshness of this new relationship, occurring as it did at a time of seasonal rebirth, be tainted by any breath of opportunist lust wafted from some previous disillusion.

Returning to London, I found myself arranging work and appointments that would take me to or near Broadcasting House as often as I was deviously able to manage it, usually at some time of the day when I thought I might catch sight of Sylvie; and, though I was frequently disappointed, taking vain and feverish routes around the old Langham hotel or along Mortimer Street to Great Portland Street and back past the little Nash church, I did sometimes meet her, making a pretence of hurrying or of having some deep preoccupation on my mind that served to make my pleasure and surprise at the chance of meeting her the more emphatic. Later on I took to calling up casual acquaintances who had some connection with the literary world, spending fuddled afternoons in dark drinking clubs in the same area of London while they confided in me their lusts, jealousies, frustrations and failures, and I waited for Sylvie to appear with the softening of her deep brown eyes with which she never failed to greet me. And there can be no doubt that for a time, while I was recovering from the devastation that lay all around me after the angry distintegration of my marriage, at a time when Sylvie herself had discovered that Robert Keller's chronic infidelities had multiplied and degenerated so that friends whom she valued were seduced into betraying her and meaninglessly bracketed with ordinary prostitutes, I thought I was in love with her, recognising in her own response to me, in its candour and the intimacy of her trust, the passionate affection which can easily be mistaken for love until, as often as not, some reckless attempt at a physical expression of it which fails to match the dynamism of the pure emotion ends in an unembittered but inescapable sense of desecration.

It was amazing that the smell of the furniture wax, once identified, brought with it to my memory a rush of forgotten associations, snatches of conversation, a laugh half-heard, the particular flutter of an eyelid caught in the glow of a pink-shaded wall light and the involuntary shift of focus in eyes that would not let a lie pass unmarked. Even after it became clear to me, and also to Sylvie, that we should never risk experimenting with the friendship and admiration which we felt for each other, we continued to meet regularly during the time she still worked for the BBC; and I recalled the particular fragrance that I always associated with her, the especial freshness which I suppose was inseparable in my hidden memory, the subconscious subterranean lake of stored experience, from that first meeting in Brussels so many years before, but a fragrance which had also a great deal to do with the kind of perfume she used which always seemed to have the natural bouquet of real flowers rather than the cloying and synthetic elaboration of odour that is to be found in the liquids marketed by the most famous and fashionable houses, only once causing me anything other than a pleasurable sensation: then the perfume was lavender, exciting me absurdly and, as far as Sylvie herself was concerned, irrationally to make physical approaches to her as well as to ask her to become my mistress. On that afternoon, the small club in which we were sitting became for me like an interior by Murillo in which the characters, all the characters with the exception of Sylvie, were by Goya in the later period when his irony and agility had given way to nightmarish and delirious visions of human rapacity and spiritual distortion, a room of ochres, chromes, saffron, and a multiplicity of sombre browns, relieved only by a huge blind window in which the large square panes had been painted in dubiously bright colours, poster paints mixed by a Matisse or Dufy, in order to brighten the place but which succeeded only in emphasising the drabness of the basic decor and tended to make by its forcible clash of gaiety the mediocre harmony of the little bar appear to be run down and seedy. In this ombrageous gloom, Sylvie, who wore a red and blue cotton print dress, glowed like some coolly exotic flower in the deepest shadows of a forest clearing where the sunlight penetrates seldom enough for the air to seem overladen with a resilient fungoid staleness; and in this atmosphere, Sylvie, bare armed and slender, perfumed insidiously, seemed to me maddeningly desirable so that, no doubt a little drunk, I found myself caressing her thigh and asking her in the most urgent and passionate language to let me make love to her. I saw immediately the quick dart of her eyes, the gleam of excitement, I thought even that I could feel the same excitement vibrate through her body as she moved her leg slightly under my hand and there was no doubt at that moment that she was going to submit to me, with a passionate sensual longing that matched my own feverish eagerness to possess her. She was about to speak, but then from the other side of the dim little room someone called out her name: immediately she became calm, poised, with all the compact charm and assurance that I now understood hid the essentially vivid and emotionally yearning woman and I responded to the change in her, trembling slightly, unable, as Sylvie was, to recover almost instantaneously from the charged, ecstatically painful moment. The moment of intimacy and confidence that Sylvie and I had shared was lost; at the time it seemed temporararily so my disappointment and irritability turned to ironic amusement. I even enjoyed the high-spirited, bibulous evening that followed. But that moment was somehow never recaptured: I never achieved that pitch of urgency about Sylvie again and, for her part, she must have decided, for she was a controlled and imaginative woman well aware of the havoc that suddenly violent affections can wreak when carelessly unleashed, to keep our friendship on a passive basis of respect, understood love which held a suggestion of wistful regret at once sentimental and profound.

And now suddenly all this came flooding out of the past because of the abrupt association of ideas. So lost was I in the indulgences of this reverie, the luxurious but tranquil contemplation of moments in time that can no longer give pain, that I was hardly aware of Sylvie, herself, entering the room. When I realised—it could only have taken a second but it seemed to happen slowly and deliberately—that she was there, it was with a slight shock: the unreal woman of my distant memory was tangibly before me and I must have sat, gaping ridiculously, for a time in silent amazement before I realised as well the implications of her presence in Andrew Stone's house.

For a moment I was unable to speak at all, perhaps the emotional jar that I felt was more than usually powerful because of the sudden appearance of Sylvie in the middle of a clear picture of the past obviously the mistress of my old friend. I recognised, at first, only the sense of envy which is more akin to the deprivation we feel as children at the sight of some desirable toy in the possession of another child, that we might have obtained but which now would lose all its particular charm even though the lingering wish to own it persists, than to the kind of sexual jealousy, insensate, agonising, a torturing desire, that we feel when the object of what we believe to be our love is discovered walking in the street with some obvious rival for her affections, or when we expect to meet her and enjoy the charming delights of her company and she does not come to the usual bar or restaurant, while, at the same time, we notice the absence of a habitué, whom she has in the past flirted with or with whom she has exchanged, real or imaginary, looks of unmistakable significance. Then, as I saw them smiling at my evident, inarticulate surprise, I was able to see that, far from being ever in love with Sylvie, I had desired to be in love with her, as she, perhaps, had also desired to be in love with me. And it was this that we had been able to communicate to one another at a time when our need for affection, our emotional confidence was aching for a gentle response. Sadly it was now the moment to see that the sweet, elusive charm of the play-acting had little to do with the realities of sexual love. I had to admit as much to myself and to confess that the desire I had suppressed for Barbara Keller, which Sylvie had smilingly, delicately, pointed out to me, was no amorous comedy but a tormenting reality. We yearn for reality. But at the moment when it presents itself, unequivocal and unadorned, we fear the transmogrifying intensity of its direct aspect, wishing instead for the subtle miasmal imprecision lent to it by the reflecting surfaces in which our mythomaniac intellects interpret what our whole selves perceive and experience. Perhaps we unconsciously understand that gazing on absolute reality will turn our hearts to stone.

For we are resilient in all things emotional where we ourselves are assailable, once we have acknowledged reality; where once we would have, in solitude and despair, wept impotently over our disappointment and the cruelities inflicted by the less sensitive objects of our devotion, time alone, who has tricked us on one occasion after another, into facing, however briefly, reality immediately, has trained us not to flinch: we become hardened, sometimes callous. And then we are faithful only to ourselves, living in a state of unselfish, even compassionate, fidelity to our own self-respect, able to find rest and comfort, but only in those glimpses of a more fragrant time in our lives when we were young, vulnerable, tender that return to us unexpectedly on spring afternoons, leaving us disorientated, mystified but vibrantly aware of our own fleeting certainty in a world of intransigent objects, things, that may decay but remain themselves when we have departed from the scene."

PART FIVE

Eric Foster

Datelines from Prague, Lagos, Londonderry, Saigon, Cairo. Violence in the streets. Violence in the mind. I do not chip away where I can smash. The bitter wells of intolerance. . . .

> 'Q' alone. Breaks eggs into a basin. Omelette mixture, wooden spoon, stirring images of disaster in a labour-saving kitchen. A single knock perhaps. Gina and the quietness the gentleness: the acts of kindness that destroy. The last evening of sanity. Tomorrow the cracked world in the shaving glass; the scream while crossing the bridge.

But I wish I had kept quiet. . . .

Well you don't say that in bed.

Laughter.

The struggle now is to rediscover something of the old resignation. Shame is positive.

> Eric, I sometimes think that you don't really *like* anybody; anybody at all.
> That's nonsense, Ginny. I love you.
> Not the same thing, darling.

And she was right. All the labour, the laughter, the years of patient reading and learning have been dedicated to the concealment of boredom, the control of resentment, the disguising of envy. Robert Keller, Laurence Bisset, Rathbone, Lomax, even David Lawson, even Andrew; other artists too. But the Keller circle—the *Keller* circle—most of all: the resentment of them is resentment of myself. Hours in the company of men and women whom Ginny could have told me I despised. Violence in the mind . . . Fingal Grey!

I do not chip away where I can smash.

These passions distract us.

At the door in a plain blue suit, white silk blouse. At the moment I was staring gloomily at an advert with a woman in a sexy brassiere. Absurd. Now she is here . . .

Gina sits across the room from 'Q', tall, superbly confident, light-haired, sexed normally and smiling in funny, gentle, relaxed chat. Cut to Temple gardens, autumn, a light breeze. Gina and 'Q' laughing. And then, very gradually, the pose of the girl suggests somehow the whore.
The suave man sits opposite Gina, lewdly spread, seated hands on hips, a little scrap of flowered lace across her tits and a tiny flowered apron, gartered too with flowers and blue stockings with a white flowered pattern. And a wolvish smile, baring sharp teeth, wriggling her buttocks on the chair.

She sits with her legs demurely crossed and tastes her drink. The excitement is out of proportion, ridiculous, but why. . . . ? Why is she here?

—Since you won't come for me, I have to come for you. Where have you been, Eric? We haven't seen you for weeks.
—I've been working hard. On the film. *The Managers.* Anyway, I thought that I'd rather disgraced myself with you.

—About Fingal? I'm not that sensitive, my dear. I'm sorry about that. It's quite true—I have been to bed with him several times, but . . .
—Please . . . Don't think that I feel I have any right to . . . I'm sorry for my tantrum.

Smiling, she moves her head and neck languorously. Suddenly reminding me of Sylvie, the eternally feminine, feline, creature, one morning years ago in Brussels. A Spring morning I think it was, quite obviously interested but not entirely available. Now . . .

(Would you like to?
Of course.
I think I'm a fool. I know Robert does. I'm very fond of you. And there's absolutely no reason why we shouldn't have a happy afternoon in bed, but. . .)

The intellectual dummy's dance.

—Have you been busy?
—Yes. Sorting out other people's problems. Sometimes I go through days of quite shattering doubt.
—I suppose you must.
—Physician heal thyself.
—I don't . . .
—I had no idea you hated me as much.
—Oh, my dear love, I should not put it like that.
—How would you put it?
—Wanted . . .
—Yes, I'm sorry. I'm making a lot of fuss about nothing. After all you didn't say very much. The strange thing was that it hurt.
—I'm very good at hurting people.

Again that languorous movement, coiled laziness, but Sylvie would have contrived something more theatrical, more obviously sexual at the same time tinted with slightly weary resignation. And there is this growing tumescent elation.

> Gina smiling, caressing, stroking her own nipples with the tips of her fingers. Scream. A man, face distorted, rushes towards the camera across a bridge. The sky is scorched and livid.
>
> The professor turns and reads miserably the titles of books, listening to her meaningless laughter. She is drunk and has spilled red wine down her dress. When he turns, however, he is smiling again. . . .
>
> The Latin master strolls to the back of the class. One boy, snickering, hands the book to the other. We look down and see the picture of a semi-dressed woman against the ruled, tabulated page (amo, amas, amat) of a primer. Now from the blackboard, we see it is the Latin master who is gloating over the picture. . . .
>
> 'Q' hits Gina savagely across the face with the edge of a ruler, she laughs. Laughs.
>
> Laughter.

Well you don't . . .

—Do you ever see Ginny, at all?

Startled. Odd to hear her name from Barbara. Almost a frisson of some kind of unnatural excitement . . .

—There's no reason for us to meet. It would only be painful.
—Has she married again?
—I don't know.
—I understand very little about love, Eric. I don't think I've ever loved anyone much. And the trouble is all kinds of men have fallen in love with me. . . . I've gone to bed with some of them, but I'm only really concerned with myself. I suppose I'm totally selfish.

—No. The extreme of selfishness is when you tell someone you love them. It's a simple matter of staking a claim.

—You loved your wife.

—Very much. It's still difficult to think of some of the things we said without pain. For no clear reason we started getting on each other's nerves. She was a gay, rather frivolous girl. Oh, I don't know . . . Vague irritations became whole evenings of silent, fretting anger. Almost suppressed fury. There were no children. There were still occasional days of feverish happiness, and inevitable relapses into glum silence. Neither of us could see that we mattered to the other. Even if we did any more.

> Oh you have a genius all right, Eric, you have a bloody marvellous genius for hurting people. I thought it was for isolation. . . .

—Perhaps loving someone isn't a question of showing them that you do or how much you do; it's trusting them to the extent—just as far as—you think they care about you.

—Eric, my love, I don't think I understand.

—No . . . no . . . Perhaps you don't . . .

—And you never meet?

> Not knowing what I feel or if I understand. Or whether wise or foolish, tardy or too soon. . . . Would she not have the advantage after all?

—No.

> The things that commonly happen in life and are esteemed among men as the highest good (as is witnessed by their works) can be reduced to these three: Riches, Fame and Lust; and by these the mind is so distracted that it can scarcely think of any other good.

—My body is an embarrassment. It's as simple as that. I'm cold, Eric. I'm frightened and I'm cold.

For one sweet grape, who would . . . ?

—It must be disappointing. For the men. I know I look so bloody promising. And I don't dislike it. It's just that I have never felt anything that other people seem to have felt.
—My dear girl . . .
—And the way I walk . . . For Christ's sake, Eric, it's the way I walk! Honestly, I live around this meaningless lump of woman.

Laughter but silent laughter.

Well you don't say. . . .

The excitement is now intense and physical. Barbara Keller is a decent girl, a controlled woman, an honest person . . .

'I'd have gone home to fuck my wife . . .'
Gina! . . . squeak like dolls . . . just as in this room here, thinking of your blue shadowed . . . desiring . . .

She made no single provocative gesture. Only a small movement of her hands; something as well in her eyes. And this I had not seen before. She got up abruptly but gracefully. Of course I was clumsy and stumbled, almost tripping. But then I was kissing her. She responded too fiercely and I had to make her gentle and then she relaxed. Her eyes softened, her body lost something of its tension; she let herself be kissed softly. . . .

Gina turned at the door of 'Q's room. 'Q' saw his face in the hall mirror as he passed—worn, kind. He knew his face was worn and kind. The American teacher started unbuttoning her blouse but did not smile or even raise her eyes. Slowly a light beige-coloured brassiere, the superb breasts swelling out of it. Unselfconscious movement when she was young, now the professor's wife invested the most simple functional action with the calculated despair of a whore pleasing an easy client. Gina's skirt eased down over her hips: dark tights and matching beige panties. 'Q' wanted only to scream . . .

She undressed quietly. I'm not sure but I think she even folded her clothes and put them neatly onto a chair. At no single moment did she stop and show off her body. And I adored her. When she was completely naked, she stood quite still, her eyes on my face: then she moved to the bed. Each step taut and firm. She lay there, not watching . . .

> The Latin master struggles with his tie and hauls it, still knotted over his ear, while the black woman on the bed laughs quietly so that her hard belly quivers and her thighs tremble and Gina laughs riding high over 'Q' and his straining fury and the professor's wife tears his passion into tatters . . .

And then her dark eyes or darkened eyes were on my flaccid, slackened, limping body.

Her lips opened but no longer savagely. Her breasts were full and to touch them was to try to remember their exact shape forever, the stiffened nipples and the perfection of her, silent and soft-eyed. And down the flat velvet belly, around her hips to the strong thighs, the hollow between them, and . . .

> He sobbed onto her breast. . . .

> Laughter.

Absurd. . . .

> As Gina flings her stockinged thighs apart, the berserk man thrusts his head between her legs. She writhes, clasping him tightly, adding to his frenzy. She screams softly, insistently, now writing. And now turbulently heaving and surging her hips and writhing again with wild splendour.

> If it were not for the thin-lipped grimace of her mouth, the wolvish and devouring face . . .

I have been able, after my fashion, to worship you: now I shall possess you, move easily and superbly for my part into you because you have made me magnificent. No. Look at me. Do not close your eyes. Goddess and worshipper. Enclose me and absorb any fury that I can make, but look at me, look at me, intolerably eager to bring you to a fury of possession in the moment of my own cruel delight; as the rhythm becomes faster and faster, my darling, and faster . . . She is murmuring, a moaning sound without words, rippling and plunging beneath, opening her legs wide, stretching . . .

> 'Q''s smiling face vanishes from the shaving mirror. Now there is only the reflection of Gina laughing, tickling the beard of the berserker.

Straining

Absurd . . . Not now to . . .

> The professor's head and shoulders stop moving. He lays down his head wearily. We see that he is sweating a lot. He looks defeated.

We lie trembling, frightened, saying nothing.

> I am the natural fool of fortune. Use me well;
> You shall have ransom. Let me have surgeons; I am cut to the brains.

She moves away. Not looking back, picks up her clothes.

> The Latin master listens to the shower, imagining the whore soaping her black shiny body, gleaming wet . . .

I should weep, but I know that I am dry, arid: dead.

—I'm sorry. I . . .

—Hush, my darling. It was too important. This isn't the time to talk.

—But Barbara . . .

—No, darling. We've talked too much. I'll go now. Don't worry, darling. It will be all right.

> Dear Eric; dear, dear Eric, I could never live without you now.
> Ginny, my own love . . .

> Was it the Goddess herself? Some dense embrace closed like a bath of love about his head; Perfectly silent and without a face. Blindfolded on her bed, He could see nothing but the aftermath: Those powerful, clear hoofprints on the path.

At the door she takes my hand, smiling sadly, and holds it to her cheek. I must look into here eyes. I have to.

In them I read something amazing.

Gavin McNamara

The sap, that Spring and early Summer, wasn't just rising: it was shooting about.

I don't know why it was exactly, but quite suddenly all these bonusbibbers and statusgulps wanted to become part of the swinging scene. There were signs that the Keller dynasty itself was getting tired of the old lumbarpincher, Sebastian, coarse auld git that he was, but their friends had taken to him in a famous way whether he was swilling down their liquor or investigating the posterior plushness of their womenfolk with his primitive hands. Myself I put it down to the end of an era of national confidence, the deliquescence of a jar of boiled sweets, dry rot in the cocktail cabinets of a country that had only just learned about cocktails; but I have these glum moments of philosophical angst from time to time, though I'm no Schopenhauer either.

Anyway, I decided that I wouldn't outstay me own welcome whatever the old greasevat was doing, not having the claims of kinship that he was keeping lubricated by far-fetched references to his antipodean wealth, so I moved into a little place off the Old Brompton Road. I'd made a bit of money by now out of the telvision introductions and from the sale of a few minor canvases of my own hand made to one or two recent acquaintances who were lovers of a good bit of art when they saw it. So, financially, I was independent and I did not re-engage for the summer at the Cricklewood Conservatoire, determined to devote myself to sociological enterprise, the development of my own fragile gift and the fine weather, as and when.

Then, Jaysus, I suddenly got a fierce toothache from nowhere at all. Sally West's compassionate nature was touched and in no time at all I was as prostrate as a spaceman in the electric chair with her conjuring above me with mirrors and brushing me intimately from time to time as she strove with professional ardour to get a better view of a molar. She favoured the kind of loose white overall popular in clinical circles which buttoned up the front and I nearly did myself permanent damage squinting downward over a face that was already dangerously contorted. At last she stepped back and stood smiling, jutting out her right hip like a challenge to a fairy mountaineer and said there was nothing at all wrong with me except perhaps a slight touch of the neuralgia. I naturally stated that I was sorry for taking up her time, but she replied that it was no trouble and did I suffer from hay fever since the pollen count was up and could play hell with the sensitive membranes of the gob. In fact, she said, unloosening the top button of her overall, it was bloody hot. Then, approaching me again she began a sincere scrutiny of one of my front teeth. Bedamned, there was nothing under the overall but a black gossamer of bra: and nature being what it is, while she was scrutinising, I unbuttoned the rest and there was only a matching film of silk and some self-helping stockings. Perhaps it was the heat but in no time at all she was astride me in the dentist's chair and we were engaged in ferocious oral judo, which proved, I suppose, that I was gingivinally sound if nothing else. Now who's to deny that the matter might not have gone a good deal further, but for the fact that I kept my head in a difficult situation and whispered something tactful about the next patient and there being a time and a place. She slid off me and leaned breathing heavily against a tray of instruments, for a minute, looking at me; with her legs apart and a light of unbridled sensual invention in her eye that almost had my principles anaesthetised. Fortunately, however, the moment had passed and she was buttoned into place again by the time her receptionist, a sprightly enough sliver of crème de camembert, popped her head in to announce the next customer.

Naturally, though, I followed the matter up by taking her out to dinner soon and plying her with the best carafe wine to make her talkative, learning in the process that Robert Keller, the paterfamilias himself, under whose roof I had enjoyed copious hospitality, was a favourite sporting personality. She also had the notion that he was always dropping in like a golden shower whenever he had a sign that there was a hint of drought. As an amateur student of social moeurs I was of course interested, and we had several evenings together on the proceeds. I daresay you'd be wondering how the actual ritual fire dance went when the time was right since I've been pretty free with my confidences so far; well, the truth is that, for one reason and another, it didn't happen—her daughter turned up with the faltergrope, Paul; she had metabolic disturbances normal in the female class; the paterfamilias himself called for a game of chess; et cetera. But we're still grand friends.

Meanwhile, I happened to be strolling in the area of the Royal Naval College, Greenwich, one afternoon, when I ran into Elaine. It's a part of London that's come up quite a bit in terms of real estate value and no disgrace at all for a senior Naval officer to have a residence near the painted hall in these enlightened days. Now I've already described Elaine in such terms of admiration that you will have no doubt at the pleasure I experienced in this coincidence. She had always seemed to me to be a little shy and nervous among the top-weight performers, probably because her own origins were upper-middle class and any efforts she'd made consequently, and understandably at that, less estimable, always fighting a losing battle with her short skirt I'd noticed too that she was particularly flustered by the adjacence of the paterfamilias and was unwise enough to mention same to the old rumbleload one evening after a few malts, noticing with regret as I did so the disreputable look of craftiness seeping across his jib.

Now, away from them, it was like meeting a bloody wood-nymph who had escaped from a literary drawing room in her natural surroundings. She was dressed in a blue shirt and a tight skirt of some light floral material, there was a sweet disorder in her long hair like raw silk. And she looked relaxed. It was almost a shame to spoil it by stepping up and saying hello, but if you're bred to courtesy by such folk as the Brothers, needs must, as the saying is. There was that guarded look about her eyes for a second and she blushed like Beaujolais on a pale tablecloth right down to the open neck of the blue shirt, but she smiled as well and asked what I was doing in the arrondissement. I expatiated a bit on the unceasing search of the painter for fresh perspectives which, as far as I could see, aroused the rudiments of interest in her, so we went for a walk in the park.

There are some classes of park that do well for cover and although Greenwich isn't one of them, there is the odd bit of comforting shrubbery lending the shady thought a bit of welcoming shelter. The shyness left Elaine as easily as the morning dew evaporates off a full blown rose, though it would take a fully paid-up lyric poet to describe the sensation of her trembling against me, then melting, then grinding her hips towards me own central fury, using the oak tree she was leaning against for leverage.

The point was that I thought it best to modify the engine revs a bit, so in the appropriately affectionate garnish, I whispered the odd word of warning and caution, referring en passant to that grand example of the bulldog intelligence, her husband, and his work for NATO.

We were lying on the grass by this time, but it did the trick all right because she called me a dear sensitive boy, and there may be something in that, and we lay there, herself unfurled, for a while before she pulled me down onto her most seriously, her body surging under me, like an anacondas' carnival. Then she had to go home to prepare tea, which in the circumstances was just as well. Not that we didn't, in a slightly breathless fashion, tell each other that we'd pluck the first flower of opportunity that cropped up. It never did though, because these things have to be strictly extempore, and we had to make do with secret throbbing in social gatherings of one sort and another. Not that we weren't the best of friends. Damn me, if in the course of various confidential exchanges, I didn't find out that when her husband, Sir

Francis bloody Eiderduck, had been a thousand miles away, the paterfamilias himself had been in his hammock. Weight for age, the paterfamilias had all the resilient versatility of a Brazilian winger, and covered about twice as much ground.

I suppose the nicest disposition was owned by Jasmine. And, given that he was a doctor, her old man was passable pleasant company as well, though with a Midlands chip on his shoulder the size of an executioner's block. He took a fancy to one of my works of art, inviting me round to suggest a place to hang it. They had a nice little house in Chelsea, which is just around the corner from Xanadu and South Kensington, so it was no effort at all. Whereas most of the Kellering were great ones for drinking at home, the healer Lomax kept his finger on the pulse by frequenting pubs and I took to going along fairly regularly for a pint of plain and toasted platitude.

I don't know how we came to be talking about animals which as far as I am concerned are a selection of articles that make me wish to scratch, being covered as they are with bugs of one sort or another. We had a peaceable wrangle which ended in me agreeing to go to the zoo of all places. And it's only fair here to praise all the hard work and shit-sweeping that goes into providing such a facility for outings and education.

Anyway, there she was in a white-belted mack and black tights with her pale gold hair shining in the watery sunshine under a sort of beret gadget. She took my arm and we wandered about amid the bawling blackbirds and herbaceous curlicues like a couple of gossins in a peat-bog only twice as innocent. Elephants, pythons, baboons, crocodiles, spiders, gazelles, coypus, mandrills, panthers. I can tell you there wasn't much that we missed up there on that wild Spring afternoon in Regent's Park. All was well until we came upon a dromedary in a state of high sexual enthusiasm, which is a hell of a sight. I put me arm around Jasmine in an instinctive gesture of protection and felt a tremor go through her as she turned to face me that caused me, unguarded and unprepared as I was, to express certain desires to her in the coarsest way. To my considerable surprise she answered in kind, and we had a conversation that would have had the hair of a chihuahua standing on end and curling. What an imagination! Only the school of English Language and Literature at Oxford University can give a girl that. All this took place on the walk back to her car, where she turned out to be the soft, fondant type: no aggression; warm, tender with no wayward interests. But she had to collect the kids from school and it was getting on for four o'clock, so any further exploration of her and her virtuoso conversational style had to be postponed. And recollected in tranquillity, of course, I couldn't really bite the wife of the hand that bought my pictures very well, could I now? I daresay she must have girded up her linguistics too, because we haven't exchanged more than the odd deep stare in succeeding weeks.

My knowledge of antiques is about on a par with my understanding of the thoughts of Wittgenstein, to name but a few, but as a nation we Irish are always ready to learn and so I responded cordially to an invite from Andrea to turn up at her shop, spelt boutique, and have all the relevant jardiniere explained in words of more than one syllable. In no time at all I was picking out Regency samovars and Second Empire commodes with bare-back nonchalance, until I was suddenly manoeuvred into a limited space between a Julius Caesar wardrobe and a Frederick the Great hatstand to find my hands full of Andrea's titties, looking from North to South, with her hauling at me like the handle of gas main that's rusted up. She was a hell of a noisy woman but very quick, so that it needed an abrupt influx of American tourists, crackling with dollars, in the front part of the shop to restore us to Wednesday afternoon serenity. This wasn't so long ago and I've been lying fairly low since.

Except for a thunderstriking afternoon in the company of Annabelle Finch near the London School of Economics, which is as famous for turning out troublesome bastards of one class or another as any abattoir in the Western hemisphere. I happened to be passing and ran into her, nodding shyly because I wasn't a bit sure of my welcome in this quarter. So it was a pleasant gesture on her part to ask me up for a cup of lap sang suchong. For all the fact that she was such a fine figure of a woman, standing at least five foot eleven inches, with all the relevant heyatoho evenly and generously distributed, I had an idea that conversation would be the main delight of that afternoon with perhaps the odd hot tip on the subject of economics. And sure, so it proved with us exchanging intelligence on the subject of British politics, fiscal matters, the home life of the Kellers and other dangerous topics. Naturally, enough, with herself having an academic bent as you might put it, the entire place was crawling with books. Mrs F. sat in the middle of it, crossing her mighty legs with great, powerful swings.

I can't remember now how we broached the discussion, but it must have been because of my travels. At any rate, we were having an argument about the island of Crete and the scenery along the coast road near the Bay of Armiros. It's amazing how bitter these blue-stocking women get in any kind of verbal slap-and-tickle: soon, nothing would do but that she finds books to confound me. She went into the other room and I could hear her thumping about like a young antelope. Then she called me in.

It was an impressive touch of scenery in its own right, I can tell you. The travel books were on the top shelf and even for a woman blessed with the gift of height like she was, this was bloody near the ceiling. So she had to stand on a chair and had the other leg on one of the lower shelves. To facilitate freedom of movement, she had worked her skirt up a bit; quite a bit, in fact. And now, in this position, she was apparently stuck.

In a commanding voice she told me to lift her down, which, since she was a weighty person, was difficult enough, even though I have meself what's known as a lean and rangey physique. The upshot of this was that my face got pressed into her soft, overpowering presence, as I staggered a bit, making me over-excited. When she was grounded from the aerial circus and we were thigh to thigh and belly to belly on terra firma again rubbing our bodies softly against each other with our hands unemployed and I had begun to think that appearances were hellish deceptive and the next hour or so would be strenuous, the door-bell sounded. It was some students that she'd told to call sometime about an academic dilemma of some kind, and students being the hopeless articles they are, these had chosen this moment. I haven't seen her since, but I daresay it was a moment of folly and the students was what the Brothers would think of as a blessing in disguise.

Which about wraps the Spring up. Being an artist, of course, I took the opportunity of visiting all the great collections in London. The National Gallery may not have the best items in the world, but there's a lot of interest there, so I was delighted to be entertained by such a knowledgeable and charming lady as Jacqueline, a lady all over. Mind you, there was no rude fumbling with this one, just custom-built discussion about the old masters. Not that I didn't detect in odd movements a hypertension that might easily be triggered by the right finger.

I've no doubt that you may be thinking that I'm a lot of shout and no balls to speak of, since I haven't followed any of these acacia-flower fritters up to the golden-brown conclusion. I'm making no excuses, but in a circle of people who know each other and who have very liberal ideas of talk, however self-contained the action, stories get around fast. And my primary duty in return for the warm welcome I'd received from Madame Keller and her lovely daughter was to them. Whatever the temptations, I didn't want the word to be getting around that I was an indiscriminate lecher because that would be almost certain to turn such a sensitive, refined lady as Sylvie against me, as well as frosting the consonants of Barbara. Among any group of people, so far as I can see from my travels, there are always your natural leaders who know where they stand. Such people don't take kindly at all to the second lick at the cornet and it's wise to bear in mind their feelings for a variety of good reasons including self-interest. In my experience of psychology, where women are quite prepared to confess with full dramatic flourishes a consummated relationship, none of them want to publicise a spot of arriviste touching-up.

Sylvie Keller

'TO HAVE IN THE AFTERNOON'

"There was no false spring that year. One day the trees were bare and the grass in the Park was grey and limp. The next day the air was fresh, the sunlight wasn't pale any more, there was that bright, light green everywhere that made the whole city clean. There were no problems except how to work and to be sure the work was good. I had ideas but I wouldn't know how good they were until I had painted them and then forgotten what I'd painted.

And there was so much I wanted to do, I couldn't start, and I would get out a canvas and look at it and open all the windows until the freshness of the morning with the smell of the rain off the trees and the grass in the little square dragged me to the window.

I remember other springs in Paris with the fountains in the Luxembourg gardens and the smell of bread baking in little shops in the rue Notre Dame de Lorette and the water rushing in the cobbled gutters and the men *en bleu de chauffre* with besoms. Or up in the mountains with the hard clear light and the great distances, drinking rum after an ice-cold swim, and watching pine forests on the hills across the valley change from black to green as the sun again rose. That, I said to myself looking out of the window, is called translation of energy. Because I felt good then and my body had never been stale and my eyes had seen into things with a clear gaze. I wanted to paint it all in one picture but I knew it couldn't be done. It was like wanting to make love to all the women I had ever known in one woman. And I knew that couldn't happen either and it made me sad. Yet in a way I was glad about it, because it would mean that all experiences would be over in that one experience and there would be nothing left. Nothing left for these fresh mornings.

So I used to smoke at the window. And the canvas stayed empty until I went out with a sketch pad later in the morning and sat in a bar letting the sketches draw themselves which is not as it should be because you should draw the sketches but I felt very well and it was a good place to be then.

Sometimes I scribbled word portraits. I bought some good white wine and a hunk of cheese and I felt happy because I was doing what I wanted to do and the wine was cold and crisp. Only I wasn't doing what I wanted to fast enough. A lot of beautiful girls came to that bar, usually waiting for someone. I sat next to the door and the girls sat opposite the door, waiting. I used to look up from my work and sometimes my eyes would meet theirs and there was that kind of understanding between a man and a woman that is true and elemental and good. And I would start working again feeling that I was drawing the truest lines ever drawn.

It was warm and fresh most days. Some evenings I went down river and met people in a pub to drink white wine, or I walked across the Park to 83 Hyde Park Square to talk to Eric Foster about images and clarity. He had more interesting things than I had to say, so he talked and I listened and he insisted I had more malt whisky, which he always served in good plain glasses.

One night Sylvie Keller was there. There were other people in the room, mostly talking about writing or painting. I was playing the piano, when I saw her. There was a little joint in Montparnasse where I used to play and I could see the blue smoky air and the small tables with red wine and bocks. I had been playing *Blues Vaugirard* that time when I looked up and saw a dark girl in a red dress that glowed. So I told the guy on the alto sax to take it and went across to her. She was cool and sad and the dance we had was sweet. As I looked up that night, I saw Sylvie in a red dress. She came over and I stopped playing.

'Don't stop,' she said.

'You look fine, Sylvie,' I said.

'Thank you. Don't stop.'

'All right.'

'What's the tune?'

'It's called *Poulet Raspail*.'

'It's a good tune.'

'How've you been?' I said.

'Wonderfully sober,' Sylvie said. 'Who are these people?'

'I thought you'd know,' I said.

'I don't know.'

'You're very cool.'

'No, bored.'

I stopped playing. There was just the sound of talk for a few minutes and Sylvie and I looking at each other and not saying anything. Then someone switched on a phonograph and they were dancing. A girl I didn't know came by with supple movements like a cat. Someone from the film Eric Foster was making.

'Dance with me,' Sylvie said.

'Sure.'

'Dance close, Gavin. Very close.'

'Yes.'

We danced to the quiet music. It was cool and dim in the room and I felt happy. Sylvie pressed close to me, hardly moving. Somebody, a writer who had just been hired for a film, laughed harshly. Robert Keller stood near the small bar talking to a red-head.

'Sylvie,' I said.

'Yes.'

'Let's get out of here.'

'You sure?'

'I wouldn't ask if I wasn't sure.'

'Let's get out of here.'

We stopped dancing and smiled at each other. I went over to the bar and asked for a beer. Keller nodded, moving a step away from the girl. I waited until Sylvie had gone out of the room, then I moved towards the door. Outside in the square we looked for a taxi. She gripped my arm very tight and we were both happy and the night was ours.

We turned out of the square with the orange lights seeming to move across the dark trees into Hyde Park Street and right into Bayswater Road. There were queues of cars and huge square patterns of light from the big hotels. We stood against a wall and said nothing and Sylvie gripped my arm. Then we got a taxi. I told the driver to go to Clareville Street through the Park and got in and slammed the door.

In the park I kissed her. Gently and without any fury. She let me kiss her and leaned back in a corner of the taxi and said nothing. Her head was turned away from me, as we crossed the bridge, looking out across the lake. When she looked at me again, there were tears in her eyes, and I smiled at her and took her hand.

'I've been pretty damn unhappy,' she said.

'Yes.'

'I don't do this kind of thing usually.'

'I didn't think you did. You're unhappy.'

'A lot of the time it's been hell.'

'Don't worry.'

'I won't worry.'

The taxi crossed the busy intersection at Alexandra Gate into Exhibition Road. A lot of people were leaving a concert at the Albert Hall. Girls in long dresses with white, happy faces in the glare of the streetlights and young men trying to be relaxed. It had been a popular, expensive concert, sophisticated jazz or a French singer. Sylvie was looking at the roof of the taxi, quite calm now. I let her hand go and she turned and I felt sure.

The taxi turned into Thurloe Place then round past the station and right into Bute Street where a couple of restaurants and shops were open. She moved nearer and leaned against me but I knew she did not want me to kiss her. I paid the driver and we went into the apartment. Her voice was shaky and she was trembling.

'Well, this is it,' she said.

'Darling.'

'Oh Gavin, love.'

'Come here.'

'Darling, darling.'

'It's all right, Sylvie, Everything is fine.'

'Yes. Everything is fine.'

'Listen. I don't want to hurry about it. It's too important to hurry.'

'Yes. Fix me a drink.'

'Sure.'

I went out to fix her a drink. I made us Bacardi cocktails like I'd learned to make in Miami when I was with Louise and it was summer and I was painting well. I hadn't felt like this since then. A long time ago.

When I got back with the drinks, Sylvie was lying on the bed. She was naked and her face was turned towards the door. She looked me straight in the eyes and neither of us was embarrassed or ashamed or anything and Sylvie's eyes were dark and sad. I put the drinks down and undressed.

'Yes. Now,' she said.

'Yes. Now.'

'Darling.'

'Slowly. We'll do it slowly.'

'Yes. Do you want to talk.'

'If you want to.'

'Yes. I want to. I want to tell you. Ah. There. Do that again. There. Oh you darling.'

'Listen. Shall I do it again?'

'Yes. Yes. That's it now. Oh Gavin, love, Put your hand there. Yes. That's where I want you.'

'Not too fast. Let's wait. Wait.'

'No. Hell! No. I don't want to. Now. Come, darling. Yes. That's right.'

We lay there and then we drank the Bacardis. The ice had melted but they tasted cold and strong and I felt wonderful. So we made love again until I felt empty and happy.

When she had to go, I called a taxi and put her into it and watched it until it was out of sight although I couldn't see her any more. Then I went in and took some more Bacardi and had a shower and lay on the bed feeling tired and clean and a bit drunk.

Next morning the sunlight was bright. There was a fresh breeze blowing when I opened the windows and even in this part of town you could smell blossoms and the new green smell of the trees. I set up a canvas and started to paint."

Paul Keller

Lunchtime lecture. Bisset suave and easy bringing democracy into the heart of Cricklewood, smiling sideways down his nose, watchful-eyed. Prominent in the front row in colour: the Head of Biology, turning every now and then to stare commandingly at sallies of laughter led by Stan, Les, Norman and Graham, nucleus of activism. Bisset explores with smiling patience the Special Relationship.

Parsnips. They were not talking about parsnips. And it was ridiculous to pretend. But what? Surely she can see through McNamara calling to see a mummy about a picture. Three by four evidence wrapped in sacking.

Uncoil the bandages of assurance and there is the custom-staled insobriety of the ageless whore. And my two school fellows whom I will trust as adders fanged. Blandford, Aylmer. Perhaps cultivating the vegetable love of Barbara Keller, B.M., B.Ch., D.P.M., M.R.C.P. Mad.

Meanwhile back at the palace my mother waits, Agrippina the Second of Denmark, studying the latest masterpiece from the studio of McNamara. For what? Lying on a sofa with a nervous headache. And Bisset peeps, voyeur and brothel janitor, at Britannia expertly unloosening Uncle Sam's flies and whispers the excited progress to an eager audience. At least I have shaken off Andrea, which wasn't difficult. I couldn't have been much fun. Perhaps it was just for the benefit of Ragnar, King of the Trolls, charcoal-grey possessor of night and fog, master of the red plague, lord of the deadly shining dust.

Sometimes I know I am already mad. . . .

Now in the Cricklewood Physics Lecture Theatre the youth of England are afire. Pontius Probert puffs cumuli of smiling fragrant smoke. Obergruppenbildungsoffizer Thomas Hoopoe looks pensive as he hears of campus riots, burning banks, intolerable indignities. The orator listens for the mood of his audience to help him find the right, the exact, word. To be fair, Bisset is witty, coherent, intelligent. I wonder does it humiliate him to arrive home as he did and see that pussycat smile on her face. A profession of control as the Ironmaster Troll has made a religion of caution. For what is intelligence without cunning. And malice.

Question time. Les is quick and immediate. Faulted on a detail of fact. So Stan inveighs. The Head of Biology glares and glares, much offended. Bisset easily smiles it away. Calm and able by the single word to trip Stan's rhetoric. The common herd of Stan's contemporaries whom he would lead across the Marcusian Alps like a state-aided Hannibal into the labyrinth of anarchy laugh. Bisset is quite happy to butcher Stan to make an august for the people. Now the sensible questions from the good boys. Stan continues to twitch on his meat-hook. Bisset applies the electric cattle-goad.

What is the point? Such laboured nothings . . . The nightmare vision of Aunt Eric Doom, Jacqueline Benbow brooding about Uccelo as she seals another rivet into her pantigirdle, Rathbone showing the flag, Lomax smarting at the slights of medical politics while fixing a clockwork heart into the NHS, Jasmine and the pediatric horror, Jane West and her looking glass and headful of pop. Mummy and French cigarettes, Welsh cadences carefully spaced, international politics and cosmic culture, reading the days avidly with her flair for prose criticism. And then Pwyll Pen Annwn with his subtle mind and telescopic cock.

In some ways all harmless, no, worthy people. What's wrong with a little private vanity, a featherbrush of ambition, a few drops of affectation. Doing the right thing for whatever bloody reason. Even Daddy. Oh no: charity can go too far. Still Sebastian has shaken them up. 'That idiot,' she said. Cold eyed. They're all getting fed up with him except me, I suppose. But not McNamara! Wormtongue slithers again. And: 'Your trouble, Paul, is boredom.' But then that *frank conversation*. Doing it with Gray and with Foster and with McNamara worst of all: why not with me?

Christ! This must STOP. I shall go mad. Already my thoughts are twisted out of all recognition. Back to Paris and Frankie. Silence, professional fucking. But, Barbara, please do not stand there in that way. Poor, naked cannibals. Scrupulous care. Painful severity.

Our young colleague, Keller. Valuable work. Lunchtime lectures. Producing plays. When it's summertime in Cricklewood. Private Lives. Bravo, Keller. I almost (confides the Head of Biology meaningfully) ran into your father the other day. Thank you, Mr Bisset. Stimulating. Authoritative. Food for thought for the students. 'Are you staying, Paul, or can I give you a lift?'

The Rover. Calm, ironic driving to the commonplace House. 'Doesn't seem a bad place.' No it is not: everyone is trying more or less their best except me and that is not to be sneered at. Yet that is what I do. I lavish upon them my derision. 'I was talking to your sister some time ago, who seems to think you should be working in a University. I told her I didn't agree. You do a lot more good with this sort of chap.' It is quite frightening.

Do you I wonder faultless Bisset resent your wife at all? No, you have stopped caring. Then do you look elsewhere? Mummy? has always found Laurence *très sympathique.* (No, *cariad,* I'm not being affected, I mean it precisely in the French sense. He's not sympathetic, is he, now?) Sally? Obvious choice, perhaps a bit too coarse. Jacqueline . . . Barbara. No. Not that again. A man who has dedicated himself to his work, his career, the good fame that makes the clear spirit clearer of purpose. Like Andrew Stone. So why does the silly bastard go in for competitions with steel-blue Thunderfarter. Who'd read it? Jacqueline. (Rather good. One wouldn't expect Andrew to make much of a thriller.) And Rhiannon herself lilted in with a kind word. Waste of his time. Good writer and Bisset's a good politician and Rathbone is a good Naval officer and they're not all poxed through with sex-obsessions and fixations and I am sure I shall go mad.

Outside the House. 'No, thanks. I have to go to the Tate. I'll enjoy the walk along the Embankment. . . .' Christ, who is this? 'I don't know whether you recognise Oliver, Paul. He is lobbying me in a rather crude way with a view to legalising pot.' His son. Hairy and bright brown eyed and long nosed and grinning. 'Oliver is a very thoughtful son. He looks in every so often to shake his head in sorrow and to offer me his blessing.'

Oliver is friendly, remembering I write poems, and wants to walk with me. Perhaps there is something vulnerable in the hardened core of Bisset, a start of pain in the ironic eyes, watching, watching. The boy is an amiable fool. Odd jobbing his way around the world, strong, unafraid; trying his hand at poems and guitars and paint. 'What I really do not grab is their way of life. So obviously I quit. I have a hell of a time. It's great. I'm not knocking you. If it's O.K. for you, their scene, then that's great. But it's so phoney. I mean Andrea and her objects of art and Larry with his parliament. Not for me. I just want to be me. I don't want to do anything except really see things. That's for me.'

No Oliver you are right and futile. As right and futile as willow-herb, but at least you are having a hell of a time. It's great. And at least your sad father is committing himself to some kind of right and futile future. But let us take four characters in search of a persona: on my right in the blue corner, Fingal Gray, forty-one, Television Cyclops; on my left in the red corner Eric Foster, forty-eight, the camera who does not often lie, wily peregrine vulcan. The one has built a career out of the destruction of reputation, credibility, character; the other has made art out of the debris of himself. Both care vitally for the job. (And for my sister.) They are not evenly matched in this contest. Or take, with the trident and net, Oliver Bisset; with the short sword and armour, Gavin McNamara. Both bums. But what a difference. Here the referee stops the bout before it even starts. No Oliver you are right and futile and harmless. Now take Paul Keller. Aimless posturing foundling dauphin. Yes take him. A quivering moment of painful discontent. The existential whine, incarnate.

'Do you actually dislike them?' 'Who? Andrea and Larry? Jesus, no. They wouldn't harm a fly, it's the crap they believe in. Their woolly liberal ideas. All that art and argument instead of living. Crap. I believe in Rimbaud, friend. Great poet by the time he was twenty and then nothing. When they asked him ten years later about it, he said: "Don't talk to me about poetry. I've finished with all that crap." '

Smiling Oliver is a British Standard Approved bore, recommended by the Consumer's Association, licensed by the Board of Trade (signature of David Lawson) and praised by the Design Centre. Except that he has no way back into the deserving bigtime. At the age of seventeen he went and he will never be quite the same, even when at the age of thirty he starts to write his untidy, prematurely grizzled, pot-bellied memoirs. The untidy clown whom the more intelligent allow to entertain or bore them, according to the mood, in grubby pubs and very seldom invite home. Tolerated outlaw, never alone wolf. Thank God padding on towards Chelsea, cordial of invitation, refusing the robbers' cave of the Tate Gallery. His own man.

And, strangely enough, I feel sticky and dirty.

I am not amused. For once, even Klee doesn't raise a real smile. The kind of real smile that has nothing to do with eyes and lips and teeth.

Today the new regime beings. Jane West. That is a very good idea. She would, I'm sure, and I'd like to. Must have a beautiful body. Tight marble breasts, firm thighs. Young. Perhaps . . . just perhaps a virgin.

Long, shoulder-length brown hair, free flowing; brown clear eyes, sensual mouth and the slightly buck teeth, the wide smile and tiny lines of experience too young, effortless slender movement, undeliberate. Experience of Sally, watching Sally sexing up to all the men, with I know what disgust. So possibly . . . And I might after all learn to love her. And even to suffer over it. Clean, clear girl. And it will help. Help to . . . Now. Temporary secretary at where—Independent Television place in Kingsway. Five-thirty. Bus. In time.

But even now I can see the flowing hair cut and fashioned; the close fitting black dress; handing out martinis, the free smile running along set lines; successful and unfaithful husband she cannot understand having it off with dolly, vulgar typist; inevitable elegance of the room, the scene of so many inevitable silences; children at school somewhere. In a bridal dress; in labour after the callisthenics; holding the first baby; in black at Sally's funeral; visiting the children at University, an elegant mummy, if there are still universities; the years of deserving boredom stretched out before a pretty, moderately intelligent girl who meets the right young men as a matter of course; the lift of brief affairs when someone seems to care, flattering at different ages her intelligence, her looks, her sensuality.

And as I wait in the foyer, hoping to start well with the surprise, I wonder if I can save her from it or wonder if I am only beginning to see how to use people for my own ends.

The lift door opens. She is talking to another girl. Laughing. And now she sees me. She has the most shining eyes in London, tonight.

Robert Keller

As he turned left and crossed the river in the Rolls, Robert Keller imagined Godfrey Sanderling driving the Rover into Buckinghamshire, rather, being driven, congratulating himself on having outwitted a notoriously subtle adversary. He smiled and got into the right-hand lane for York Road. There could be no doubt that the dramatic potential of the Enquiry to be chaired by Sanderling far enhanced that possessed by Robert Keller's and it would bring him a certain amount of attention in the Press. This did not compare with a less spectacular assignment, however, which would bring Robert Keller into frequent contact with three first-rank ministers and into almost daily touch with their departmental juniors over a considerable time. In view of his known political sympathies, always discreetly suppressed, Robert Keller foresaw public recognition as well as considerable power in his future grasp. Since it seemed likely that the huge Conservative lead in the opinion polls would be maintained up to the time of the next General Election and that there would be a new government, he was concerned to put himself in an unassailable position of influence by Autumn, 1970, the probable date. And he would have to be very clumsy to fail. A Cortina swung abruptly out of a side road into his path. Robert Keller braked and avoided it without ado, without subsequently at the next set of lights bothering to glance in its direction.

On most Friday afternoons, Robert Keller would have been driving in a mood of equanimity. On any Friday as satisfactory as this one, he would have allowed himself to feel modestly elated. Nevertheless the minor irritations of the past twenty-four hours kept catching in the fabric of his placidness like a broken nail against cloth. Perhaps the slow stream of traffic in the Putney Bridge Road slightly accentuated his feeling of discontent. He realised perfectly well that Andrea Bisset was a melodramatic harpy, given to fits of hysteria which were dangerous only because of her loose tongue. Yet she was careful enough in certain respects: she had never, for example, admitted to Robert Keller, until the previous evening, that she had copulated with anyone else. He had assumed that she did, of course, and it had not remotely troubled him. What she had offered him was an obscene relationship. Whatever he had offered her had been enough to make her take seriously his warning that if she ever taunted her husband with him, he would immediately break all contact with her. It was therefore perhaps revenge which had prompted her to tell him that she had been fucked (*sic*) by Paul, that she had told Paul of her relationship with Robert Keller and that Paul was an infinitely more satisfying performer (an obvious choice of word), than he had ever been. This last, Robert Keller did not believe. But he was annoyed. The more so because he could not understand why he was so annoyed. It was a kind of spiralling peevishness. Obviously it did not matter that he and his son shared a woman, or *had* shared at one time or another the same woman. It did not matter that Paul knew it, for Paul had not been under any illusions about Robert Keller's sexual diversification for some years and had not seemed to care much. The original afternoon must have given the boy something of a shock, but their subsequent relations had been easy enough. Barbara, he thought, knew nothing: but there was no reason why anyone should bother to tell her, risking the icy scorn that she was mistress of. Sylvie, after the initial squalls of temper and tears, kept her head turned the other way. Yet she must have resented him for years, to triumphantly boast to him of an affair with the ludicrous Andrew Stone. For a moment he was thoroughly amused by the whole ridiculous business and pleased when a pretty girl in a sports-car alongside returned his grin. Sylvie had chosen for years to assume that

Robert Keller leaped into bed with every woman who came his way. She had a particular whimsically sardonic face for these occasions of suspicion. He recalled the evening when she had told him of her affair with Stone and the way she had looked at Annabelle Finch. Robert Keller chuckled. It was all such a nonsense.

He was prepared, now skirting Putney Heath, to recognise that he detested Andrew Stone and always had. It had been no pleasure therefore to hear from Andrea, Jacqueline Bisset and Eric Foster that the thriller which he had challenged Stone to write was a good one. He was content to bide his time on that, but he supposed it was possible. Robert Keller thought that his intense dislike must spring from Stone's indifference to Robert Keller's own skilful writing and the insufferably condescending air that he adopted to anything not to do with art. A woman cannot live with a man for a very long time without knowing precisely who the other men that he dislikes and resents might be, Robert Keller thought, and he was sure that Sylvie had deliberately chosen Stone after years of martyred fidelity, relieved by drunkenly romantic afternoons with dear old Eric Foster or compassionate evenings at the theatre with David Lawson or cheek-to-cheek dances with Laurence Bisset. Not that she had been particularly quiet in the last few months since her uncle had moved in and Paul had taken up with the engaging but patently scheming Irishman. In fact, even the most sedate people, Jacqueline, David Lawson, the Rathbones, had all shown quite alarming appetites for reasonably wild parties. Robert Keller allowed his mind to dawdle over Elaine Rathbone as the Rolls gathered speed in Roehampton Lane. He had enjoyed her greatly but he did not think that she would ever agree to restarting a liaison. She had been younger then, very unsure of herself in the Kellers' circle, and Jack had been a long way away. There was always Jacqui, though. Recently he had found something very appealing in her and wondered why for so many years—twelve or so—she had been more or less unnoticed. He shook his head. Fantasies had always been for Robert Keller a complete waste of time.

He drew into the grounds of his house and saw Sebastian Jones sprawled in a deckchair with a pint of beer in his hand. The old fellow seemed asleep, but the glass was tilted at an angle at which not a single drop would spill. Robert Keller thought indulgently that the glass would inevitably find its own level of stability however much the old man twitched in his sleep. On approaching Sebastian Jones, the absence of any snoring suggested to him that the ancient ruffian either had his eyes shut against the sunlight, or else for some devious reason was shamming. It would be too much to say that Robert Keller felt any real affection for his wife's uncle, but he was quite well disposed to him. He liked old people, especially villianous old people. Having heard no further reference to Elaine Rathbone from the old man, he judged that the sly and apparently sinister remark that Jones had made in the restaurant several weeks before had been simply lucky in its accuracy and at the same time totally meaningless—the sort of lewd, drunken nudge in the ribs that was the stock-in-trade of such people.

Although he had at no stage been unduly disturbed by what Sebastian Jones had said, Robert Keller was at the same time relieved of any likely embarrassment. He was accordingly quite prepared to fulfill Sylvie's demands and start the process of getting rid of Sebastian Jones as soon as possible. Characteristically she had tired of her relation before any of them, except Barbara, whose cool indifference to almost everyone and everything outside her work was in Robert Keller's opinion now exaggerated out of all proportion.

Robert Keller decided not to rouse the old man and began to walk towards the house, swinging his brief-case in a way that usually suggested to him that he was in a good mood. He thought that he might telephone Jacqueline on some pretext or other—there were several: inside information on government grants, an opinion on a picture such as one of McNamara's, a word about Barbara. Then Sebastian Jones called out.

'Christ, Bobby, sport, I'm not asleep. You don't have to be so tactful, mate, in your own garden,' said Sebastian Jones.

'I'm sorry Sebastian,' said Robert Keller.

'I know I was flopped out here like a flaked-out flower-pecker,' the old man said, 'but I was just soaking up the sunshine. This garden's a real boomer, Robbie, and no mistake; you don't have to be the poet Wordsworth to see that. Take an old fellow like me. I could have been as out of place in this town as a saltwater crocodile in Alice Springs, but not a bit of it. You and your cobbers have taken me in with real warm homeliness, Bob. And I'll say another thing that's really made me feel at home: it may be because of my great age and that but a lot of them, especially the sheilas, come to me with their secrets. I suppose everyone needs a shoulder to cry on and an old bald-headed boobook like me's as good as anyone in a thunderstorm, cos he ain't going to seek no fucking advantage.'

Robert Keller was instantly wary. It was an entirely instinctual process which had always proved useful to him and which he thought was a remarkable sensitivity to the inflections of a particular voice at a particular time. At all events, he shifted out of a state of complacent half-attention into one of alert tactical awareness, without for a moment losing a millimetre of lazy composure.

Robert Keller glanced at his wife's uncle with an obvious flicker of interest, observing that such confidences must be fascinating.

'Too bloody true, mate,' said Sebastian Jones. 'You'd be surprised what some of these young blood honey eaters get up to. But then perhaps you might not be. Eh, Robbie? No, son. No need to look alarmed. It's just my joke, old sport. Let me show you one or two bits and pieces, son.'

They proceeded towards the house, pausing for Sebastian Jones to admire some flourishing hollyhocks.

'That's a fine display of purple leaping frillytits you have there, ain't it, Robbie?' he said, 'You know, Sylvia's always liked flowers ever since she was a little toddling infant.'

Smiling, Robert Keller ushered the old man into the sitting room through the French windows. He was amused and while the Australian went upstairs, poured out two glasses of whisky in the sitting room and waited. Eventually Sebastian Jones reappeared carrying an ancient leather wallet about eighteen by twelve inches, which had seen hard wear, no doubt in the Great Victoria Desert among other places. The leather had flaked away here and there and was scratched but still retained a comfortable lustre. Obviously this was the kind of container for private papers and important documents.

'The fact is, Bob, me old sunshine, that it's time I sorted out these bits and pieces,' said Sebastian Jones. 'And I'll be bloody grateful to you if you'll give me the odd word of good advice. Meanwhile, there's this.'

The old man produced a copy of *Country Life* and turned up a particular page on which was displayed a small but excellent house in an acre and a half of its own grounds not far from Goodwood in Sussex. Robert Keller saw that it had three bedrooms, of no great size, a bathroom, separate lavatory, kitchen, and large reception room, giving onto a verandah. It was centrally heated, had several outbuildings and a garage, with various other amenities which were inessential but agreeable. It was offered at £19,750.

Sebastian Jones explained that he had fallen for the area after a trip to the race-course in the company of that Irish bloody villian, whom Robert Keller identified as McNamara, and various others. He had been to see the house and was impressed more by its surroundings, especially the trees, than anything else. He became lyrical on the subject of trees.

Robert Keller's eye, meanwhile, fell on various beribboned documents in the wallet, registering the names of at least three mineral companies at present working in South Western and Central Australia and prospering. He also noted three different bank-account books. There was no question of Sebastian Jones being able to afford the property, it seemed, though Robert Keller would dearly have liked to inspect the documents for himself. He wondered if Sylvie's abrupt desire to be rid of the old man had not been rather too precipitately met by his own response. He waited for Sebastian to show him whatever it might be among the papers and documents that required his advice, but apparently Sebastian was concerned only with the photograph and description in the magazine.

'Now, mate, I haven't a bloody earthly how to begin this kind of transaction,' said Sebastian Jones, 'but I thought perhaps I could rely on you to guide me through it. It's time I was out of your fur, here, anyway.'

The notion was lightly deprecated by Robert Keller with the amused ease that had given many of his professional colleagues a sense of warm reassurance without ever encouraging them to seek a more familiar relationship. Nevertheless he said that he would be only too pleased to help the old man and talked to him of solicitors, conveyances, surveys, searches and mortgages. Mention of the last tickled Sebastian Jones, who picked up a bank book and waved it without opening it.

'I reckon me old pals at the Australia and New Zealand Bank will see me all right, there, Bob,' he said.

Then he put the book back in the wallet, while Robert Keller asked discreetly if there were any other matters where his expertise might be useful. Sebastian Jones was profoundly grateful, but thought that most things were going pretty smoothly, though he was relieved to know that if anything got too complicated he was able to turn to someone with as powerful a grasp as Robert Keller. He then gathered together his papers into the wallet and took it away.

In due course he returned in a mood to tell Robert Keller lewd stories of his early life. Robert Keller pretended to listen, filled the old man's glass regularly and wondered how to manipulate best the situation so that his wife and family might benefit from the old man's wealth. Eventually, Sebastian Jones decided it was time he took a stroll to a nearby pub, where he expected to meet some friends. Robert Keller had no qualms about going to his guest's room and checking on the odd papers and was about to do so, but at that moment Paul came in.

While they were talking, they were joined by Sylvie, who asked for a martini and showed them an advance copy of the thriller that Robert Keller had challenged Andrew Stone to write, with an ironical smile on her usually elegantly composed face.

PART SIX

Sylvie Keller

'NIGHT THOUGHTS'

"**N**o because hes never likely to do anything without some crafty clever motive and all this fussing over Sebastian with the Savoy Grill and no hurry because hes harmless after all must mean he knows the old buggers filthy rich or hes found out something as well as might be I dont give a damn its not as though we needed money after all unless hes getting through it but hes always liked old people Im not really being fair it might only be that not that this one is a very nice old man pawing and pinching and drinking like a sink a bad influence on Paul too I dont see why we should put up with him to please Master Robert feeling every woman who gets in reach and bawling comments brings Paul back drunk all the time there must be something I dont know or he wouldnt have stood for it always very civil service my wife I dont believe youve met Robert Keller my name is though Ive known him to be kind enough to all sorts of people who arent close to him which is what selfishness is all about never considers me and takes no interest at all in Paul perhaps he thinks Pauls a bastard or something shes the same takes after him cold sow and he must be really too never getting any satisfaction and always wanting some new sensation God they did look silly with Andrea bending over and him his hand on her fillies grinning in the kitchen those short legs of hers but I suppose shed let him do anything nothing fastidious and Master Robert likes new quirks not that any of them are much better there was Larry looking at the blonde heifer with the bootblack eyes in the pub with me cool and toujours the gentleman or even little Andy turning round all the time to look at that kid in the seethrough must have been the publishers typist with upper class airs and damp drawers Gavin too little touches and whispers thats all an act with that big thing one day hell go like a stallion and not care a damn how I feel and at least Id know he wasnt putting on a performance you always knew with Robert there was some passion that husky noise in the throat deep somewhere we had a very violent phase not that he likes being hurt only hurting didnt want my nails in him never anyone as gentle as Arthur honestly Christ thats a long time ago have to laugh remembering the delicious shame wishing I was a Catholic to go to confession and say Arthur Evans Father on the mountain shameful in the dark box I wonder if it affects the old priests soft voices murmuring about sin I egged him on Father not much detail how I suppose brushing him and rubbing my tits oh God Sylvia stop it or Ill what Arthur I loathed being a baptist lust in the dusty vestries a bit exaggerated but then all that solemn singing and youd see someones eyes undressing you and meet them give it you right back that one theres a brazen bitch for you in chapel too I loved making the tidy men blush no style at all youve got to say that for the papists theyve got flair and I wanted some panache lasted a long time too even with him laughing at me about the Welsh always needing religious guilt elegant atheism but always so bloody different and exciting poor Arthur not knowing where Id got to at that May ball and next day bruises on my thighes hes always been violent I suppose it suits ones like Andrea degradation thats why Larrys so polite hates her under all the blandness narrowed eyes on the raucous cow someone David Lawson told me in the army after a dinner one married man with three kids said lets go up to Soho and pick up an old cow I suppose its so genteel with a lot of them but for a long time I couldnt understand that story anyway Andrea is a cow and pretentious as well as being the communal bicycle fancy little Andy poking her perhaps that made him jealous and that daft challenge not that its a bad thriller skipped through thats it yes jealous of the little fellow not that size means a thing its application but all this time wasted let alone on literary games I wonder what hes up to there as though anythings easy weve lost a lot more than innocence and respect or whatever its supposed to be not separating us no quarrels ever now who can tell with dandruff and teeth going row over that thing Sally so he changed his dentist just like that vain bugger only wanted an excuse shes a rotten dentist thats why Eric said one afternoon probably a bit pissed only thing as our bodies get uglier is the ultimate pleasure of the act itself when beauty no longer interrupts whos to say its not the last lovely secret so how does such a wise attractive man lose a wife he went on loving and fancy bloody Barbara of all people God help him in the dark in the dark is she a les perhaps might be because Im doubtful about Jacqui and that butch tigress from the LSE yach makes me sick to thinks Im likely I can see so Gavin confident lays me stripped and shuddering third programme sighs obliging little cries in return who cares Ive pretended often enough before I dont understand why suddenly I want it so much serene I should be last fling but then Ive got my work I like and just because hes tripping about like a goat I dont have to prove Ive got the trim sexy body still welldressed graceful and properly made-up so competitive we all are women thats why Im lying here thinking this when my mind should be on Joyce for next Thursday week Giacomo like to meet a real genius perhaps my one saving is Ive never been really jealous or wouldnt have a woman friend left the way he goes at them not that theres no pain see Erics face when you talk of Barbara and that smirking greaser Fingal stupid name but a great tool on him no doubt I hope he bashes hell out of her toffee nosed monster that she is treating Eric like that hes to blame as well not admitting its just lust having to make something of it Robert wouldnt care as long as he had his fuck unless it was a good one then hed be back for seconds no pain with him say goodbye and leave it alone with moocow Andrea like little Andy and Christknows whoelse then the dentist thing and Elaine but that didnt work and Jack hasnt an inkling she coming to tell me tearful too nervous for him I suppose thinking I gave a bugger and oh well I did my bit telling her not to let on to Jack type to get dramatic and screw the arse of anyone from Chatham to Hongkong all rotten they are except Eric and Jacqui perhaps bent I dont know but none of its much good for Paul why cant someone like Jacqui or Jasmine show him one afternoon nice clean fucking no thats not right has Master Robert done them too I wonder because somethings wrong he drinks so much and hes not like her cold he was a lovely affectionate child now with that old fool spotting me and Gavin the other day leering dirty old git funny I liked him at first a lot as a child though never a kind word except at Christmas card time not that Madame Myfanwy would have spared him an acid drop if shed had anything to go on Dad so different thats where Barbara gets it from my mother not that shes in Madame Myfanwys class for malice told me often enough you wait till you have a child of your own Sylvia youll have endless trouble dont say I havent warned you putting on these airs talking with that affected accent theyll say youve lost your head because Arthur Evans is in Cambridge youre still only in Cardiff then pregnant and not ashamed you dirty little slut I wonder would he have married me smiling otherwise poor Dad struggling to the wedding in his cap and Robert was very kind hes always been kind to Dad not the boys weak bastards under Mams thumb Barbaras much more beautiful but the same coldness and the same showing off Madame Myfanwy with her voice and Barbara with her body but frigid Id guess certainly no socalled morals would you like some t said the duchess Robert always let her get away with anything like I could always twist Dad when the boys couldnt get anything out of him they understand each other intelligent and definitely his but Paul perhaps not in the old wartime days of golden radio features when no one actually laid a finger on it but Pauls lucky not to be like him or me handsome boy razorcut quiet used to worry me shed walk about in front of him showing herself no secret of anything then suddenly all coy and badtempered when the boys eyes were like chapel hatpegs old army phrase of Roberts and Robert too smiling at her in her slip perhaps she matured late a mother should give the benefit of the doubt to her daughter after all and I hope it hasnt had any lasting effect because hes never had a steady girlfriend which is why I wish some older woman would I wish I could myself no thats ridiculous but its what I mean you know build him up give him confidence so that his poems would grow too that he never shows us any more and Ive asked him he says not ready getting dark and silent perhaps Sallys daughters innocent enough though shes nothing like her mother if thats the case I doubt it no she might hurt him someone older not Andrea please God let his father do what he likes there from Allsouls to breakfast but it would revolt Paul the thing is Jane Wests thick wanting to be a model of all things when youre young intelligence counts for a lot more and Pauls a snob intellectually like me that would solve a lot I suppose brazen bitch some would think it unnatural to think of a son in that way but I care about his happiness if hed stayed in Paris better though theres a chance he might be inverted no just shy its no good Im never going to sleep lying here thinking of Jesus I wish Gavin could finish me off now Id better get my mind off wheres the switch and read Bronze by gold heard the hoofirons, steely-rining Imperthnthn thnthn sirens in wartime when Robert was on leave must have been when we started Paul six or seven times then Horrid! and the gold flushed more marvellous feeling it was then to love and say all right it would be right tonight to start a baby in such love Blew. Blue bloom is on the started going wrong almost then early as that soon after and now never with me a call pure, long and throbbing. Longindying call though he doesnt seem to bring them home thats something and Ive lived without but not any more Im not the kind of woman who dries up passionate always as a girl oh come Arthur come come isnt it nice oooh when did he last kiss me not a peck kiss A moonlit nightcall; far: far. used to want to do it with my knickers still on suppose I went and give him all the old display he likes until he got a hardon allworked up and I told him good now Im going to be fucked by Gavin as I am because Id like him to know Im getting it and its good still Last rose Castille of summer left bloom I feel so miserable alone oh concentrate Sylvie Id better start again Bronze by gold but hes Pauls friend suppose he told no Paul musnt think Im a whore it would upset him and Electrabara would poison him against me no because hes sensitive enough to care and maybe I shouldnt see Gavin or anyone no because its really wrong and no even that time in Cambridge was an accident when he took me away from Arthur into that other mans rooms with champagne and I said no not any more drinking out of the same glass not any more Robert no and then he was kissing me touching my breasts and slipping the bodice down in front of a mirror and whispering no I was gasping all excited with a big fire inside me wanting it quenched no I said Robert no it would be wrong but he was smiling on and undressed me standing and all I remember is saying NO."

Eric Foster

—Perhaps the first thing I have to do is explain why I am here at all. I was naturally flattered to be asked to come and talk to you about my pictures, but susceptibility to flattery isn't a good enough reason to pontificate in public about anything. And I've always disliked the idea of academic cinema, because I am not a good critic and because it's always seemed to me, up to now, that pictures are not made out of theories, whether these are general concepts about aesthetics or precise technical ideas. So I have always avoided theories while trying to master the craft of making pictures and composing structures of related images which observe life from a certain perspective, seldom my own but nevertheless not easily separable from my own. Yet there must come a time in the life of anyone who has been involved in fiction, whether literary or visual, perhaps as a result of some private crisis, when he finds himself taking stock of what he has done in terms of ideas, themes, techniques. He might well ask himself what it amounts to and whether what he has presented to others is an accurate version of experience, rather more vaguely and uncomfortably whether his perception has been 'true'. He might also wonder how he is to proceed, if he is going to make anything else. Is he going to develop earlier themes and ideas? Has he after all anything to say? Or will he merely create beautiful objects which have their own integrity, but nothing more? I have recently, I must confess, asked myself this kind of question. And since the discipline of explaining oneself to an audience whose knowledge is assured and whose goodwill may be assumed obliges one to speak honestly and think clearly, I was more than grateful to accept this invitation. These prefatory remarks may also excuse the fact of my having chosen to illustrate my talk exclusively from my own work. This is not vanity. I ask your patience in making with me a retrospective journey of exploration into a labyrinth of ideas that may very well lead nowhere.

—I'll begin by showing you a clip of film . . .

> *Black and white. Leicester Square. Falling leaves. Dusk and lights begining to flare out of deepening natural shadow. No heightened effects. Hurdy gurdy twanging as leaves fall. Shakespeare in the middle of the garden, quizzical. The man and the girl appear quite suddenly on the left. He is out of breath and she is laughing kindly at him as she runs into the garden and turns to wait, holding out her hand. He exaggerates his exhaustion and clasps for her hand. They look at each other, the music comes up. Cut to Hippodrome Corner, now brightly lit, brash noisy music. He puts his right hand to his ear and grins as they approach . . .*

> A question of gentleness . . .
> I'm not that sensitive, my dear . . .
> Squeak like dolls . . .
> We've talked too much . . .
> I've never wanted to risk anything . . .
> . . . talent for isolation . . .
> Laughter but silent laughter.

. . . accompanied by a short film (57 minutes) by a new director, Eric Foster, who served his apprenticeship at Ealing. The theme is simple, an essay in lyrical disenchantment. A middle-aged man leaves prison and is taken up by a kind but romantic upper-class girl of twenty. Inevitably the idyll (which contains some of the most honestly frank love-making we have seen) comes to an end. To say more would be to spoil a quietly beautiful climax. Shot around London, without artifice, using music as it happens in the street with buskers or in bars on juke boxes, *Song in Late November* is an extremely promising movie, which . . .

More people. Veering smiling faces. Hot-dog stand. They buy two, thickly splattered with onions and walk past the smart people going to the theatres self-consciously unselfconscious, laughing. The girl bumps into a man in a dinner jacket, very splendid and severe; she spills onions onto his shoes. But makes him laugh . . .

End of clip.

—When that picture was first put on, the critics who noticed it at all tended to think that I was making some kind of social point, either about the man leaving prison or about class differences in Britain. In so far as I have opinions about both, perhaps I let these colour my picture in ways of which I was not especially aware, but my main purpose was lyrical. I'll try to explain myself more precisely later, but for the moment, I'd like to show you some more film . . .

> *The actors are coming down the hill from the old barn theatre to the fields where the tents are pitched, laughing, singing, carrying lamps and torches. The two lovers, who have been lying quietly together, start up in some confusion and whisper. They go off into the trees in different directions. We cut to the actors, all dressed fantastically either in the costumes of the play or in odd scraps of theatrical finery . . .*

>> . . . do not see the point in making this sort of pretentious nonsense. The plot, for what it's worth, seems to be loosely based on Shakespeare's *Dream*: a troupe of young actors take over a barn in a seaside village and persuade unsuspecting holidaymakers to come and watch them. Meanwhile, as is the way of young actors, they laugh, quarrel, fall in love, undergo fits of jealousy and fury. And when it is all over, they go away. Foster is certainly capable of making pretty compositions, but they are all so

deliberate, so contrived, that they remind one of the studied insincerity of Watteau or Fragonard, all very well for them, but completely out of place today . . .

Laughter and confusion . . .
. . . a job, not particularly, interesting . . .
The figures of the dance . . .
I wish I did not love her . . . still . . .

When the actors come into the field of the tents, John, the man of the two lovers, is kindling a fire. They all surround him. Conversation is distant, heard in snatches. Some of them sing, very quietly. In harmony. John begins to look around for Jessica. She doesn't appear. The jollity of the others grows. John starts getting agitated . . .

—It's only fair to tell you that nothing dreadful happens to the girl and it's all intended to be funny. At least no one accused me of having any social purpose in that picture. It was called *Midsummer Comedy* and that's all I wanted it to be. We did hire a barn in a seaside place and we did put on *As You Like It* and a sort of hotch-potch of scenes from Shakespearean comedy. The whole picture was shot on location and a great deal of the dialogue was improvised. Where you see audiences, they are real, and so forth. I wanted the picture to be beautiful to look at, a little fantastical, funny and lyrical.

—The second time I've used that word. So I'd better start explaining. It seems to me that all artists are basically concerned with reality—either in the interpretation of reality or the understanding of reality. I think that the novelist John Fowles says in his book of aphorisms something about metaphysics having passed from the philosopher to the artist—that is to say the kind of problem, as I understand it, that involves the pondering of essence and the essential. For me, there are three kinds of reality. The first of which is lyrical. This is the moment of pure, highly personal, identification with the rest of the world in terms of a particular mood, a glimpse of harmony which is mysterious and in no sense reasonable. The idea of order. And yet, not ideas about the thing but the thing itself. It is something that most of us here tonight will have experienced. Yet, it is the most difficult experience to express and to transmit, because it is almost always adulterated by other kinds of reality which I shall discuss in a moment.

—I once went to a small fishing village in Scotland at the end of summer. The kind of little place that has quite a lot of people on holiday in the season and then huddles up for the rest of the year. You have several of them, say in Fife, on the eastern coast. Very pretty, decorated with little lights and what have you. I got there at the end of the season, in a pretty melancholy frame of mind. One day I saw an old man in a seaman's jersey and a peaked cap smoking on a bench; a little boy all on his own trying to catch a crab; a youngish, big man leaning on a sailing boat fitted with an engine which took people on trips, yawning; two women, middle-aged and a bit faded, standing above the little beach in the autumn sunshine. And there was me, sitting on some rocks eating a tomato. We were all quite separate and some of us were not aware of the others, but we were all a part of a particular moment. I made a short film called Once More Around the Bay about this little scene and perhaps because I have an aptitude for melancholy I've spent as much time as possible wandering around places like Le Touquet and Newquay and Aberystwyth ever since, hoping to make something longer.

—I remember telling a friend of mine that I had no point of view, that I was merely an observer. For a long time I believed this, but I can now see that in my fourth picture I was already, unconsciously, formulating the artistic premises which, for what they are worth, have been the basis of my later pictures. I thought at the time that I was still exploring a simply lyrical reality. Let me show you a bit of it . . .

> *The clarinettist leans back, watching the smoke rising from his cigarette, smiling slightly, faraway. The accordionist has been listening to the story but his eyes are now moving between the two groups at the other tables in his line of vision. As he looks at the businessmen roaring with laughter, they become the thugs who beat the clarinettist up. His eye dwells on detail: around the bar. The glass brooch of the girl with the truck-driver,*

who becomes suddenly the clarinettist; spilled beer in front of him; the drumming of the guitarist's fingers. The clarinettist's voice, quiet and cool, dawdles on; commenting on the end of the story, simply. A girl from the Salvation Army comes up with a paper: the clarinettist and the accordionist ignore her, the guitarist gives her money but will not take a paper, shaking his head . . .

Car enfin je suis philosophe . . .
A child on a stony field . . .

—That film, *Three Musicians*, was the first one of mine to receive what might be loosely called critical acclaim. This mattered at the time because it put, in one way or another, more money at my disposal. Anyway, I still didn't have a social purpose, but I wanted to make a less personally lyrical picture. So I made the clarinettist a free-flowing romantic, to whom things happened and ideas came easily. The accordionist was much more involved with other people, but only as an observer. A highly sympathetic observer, but because he was himself a totally dedicated musician, very much apart. The guitarist, by far the quietest of the three, worried and cared. The idea was to intertwine the three lives, as they are revealed in the bar one evening, until ultimately even the clarinettist is incorporating the other two into his memories and inventions. I don't think it was a very good picture: it was technically clumsy and pretty obvious. But it is important to me because it indicated to me now, not much enjoying the benefit of hindsight, that my ideas were taking shape vaguely; and also because I started getting interested in detail, large numbers of people glimpsed fleetingly, packed sequences of events within a basically simple but dramatically charged plot. What I am now proposing to describe as epical reality.

—It was a pity that my next picture, made at a time of great stress, was much too personal and self indulgent to make any use of these new ideas. It was called *Puppet of a Dream* and those of you who know Meredith's *Modern Love* from which that phrase is taken will realise how much better he handled the same theme. Nevertheless the picture did make me determined to abandon the private and personal. —Here's another clip—from the film that followed it . . .

Boulevard St Germain on a summer evening. Dark. A lot of people, mixture of fashionable, beautiful, derelict, with tourists, bourgeois. Packed pavements. A mime, painted up, working hard as a chicken laying an egg, surrounded by a crowd which, seen from his point of view, look like so many masked heads, grinning menacingly. There is enormous bustle. In this we pick out Ivan, walking on his own, apparently unaware of the gaiety, but never bumping into anyone although his progress is somnambulistic . . .

Lame man with no hymn to sing for any reason . . .
Talent for isolation . . .
It's true, I have been to bed with him several times, but . . .
. . . long bladed knife . . .

> . . . new film by Eric Foster is a mess of images. No one has ever denied that Foster has ideas, and this film is full of visual distractions, some of which are delightful—a blind man staring fixedly in front of him until a young girl with a prodigious hip-movement passes, some ducks pursuing a small boy along a path; and there are some equally diverting phrases—'Would you require a matching chasuble?' asks a treacle-voiced assistant at a religious outfitter's. But these are lost in the headlong jumble, the helter-skelter of sounds and scenes, that Foster keeps hurling at us in a psychedelic orgasm. The central story of the murderer who knows he has killed someone, but cannot remember whether it is his wife or his mother, is merely a silly vehicle for the director's grotesque self-indulgence . . .

> I'm good at hurting people . . .

Well, you don't say that in bed . . .

Eric, my love, I don't think I understand . . .

—Let my try to explain what I mean by epical. I use the word instead of epic, because I want to be quite clear that the central characters in my pictures are not in any way heroic, but they are in many ways archetypal. Their behaviour is probably dictated by one or two simple accidents of circumstance, temperament or of fate: but it takes place against a backcloth packed with incident and some of the characters who inhabit that backcloth world often step out of it and become directly involved with the central person in the story. And whereas these people are not important, for example, to my murderer in *Gyroscope*, from which that bit was taken, he is involved humanly with them. He has killed this woman and the shock has totally thrown him, but he would not be able to treat anyone else brutally, and the details of anybody's day in a large, savage city—and all cities are savage places—help to establish the extent of his humanity and the enormity of his guilt. What I was trying to do in *Gyroscope* was establish a tight, densely packed central world moving at great speed on its own axis. Around this was the orbit of Ivan, my murderer. As isolated as an astronaut, but a part of the central coloured blurred sphere, an inescapable part of it. And then holding the whole thing together: Ivan's received ideas of goodness and evil, right and wrong—not only his, of course, but the moral notions and premises on which orthodox Western civilisation are based. The critics didn't like it.

—Since some of the criticisms seemed to me to be accurate, I tried to profit by them in my next two pictures. I tried to limit the backcloth and was aided in this by the limits imposed on my budget by other hands than mine. I also tried to make the central character less dramatic than Ivan. In *Reciprocals* he was an academic whose marriage broke up and in *Scipio's Friend* a lonely Latin teacher, pathetically shy but highly sexed, who leaves a fantasy world for reality in the course of what I hope is a comic holiday with a group of boys in Italy.

—The title, by the way, is from one of his non-erotic fantasies, brought about by one of those sentences which children used to have to grapple with: The friend of Scipio is frightened by the stories of the pale husbandman. I was accused of becoming sour in both these films, mainly by the very few people who had enjoyed the early pure lyrical stuff. I thought I was still being lyrical but I had added something more.
—Now let me show you this . . .

> *Theatre bar: interval. First night, crowd very elegantly dressed and made up. We look down from central circle at stalls foyer, which is even more brilliant. We fix on Piers, grey-haired and confident, with Lisa bubbling at his side. Remaining with him we hear, but do not see, spoken in the midst of the hubbub: 'Poor man . . .' 'Absurd he should be so unhappy . . .' 'A man of that intelligence . . .' 'Why does he allow it . . .' 'She is so totally stupid . . .' All the time we are on Lisa flirting with two men who are playing up for the benefit of Piers. One of them turns noticing his fixed gaze and we cut to the blonde withthick tangled hair who is getting Piers' message very clearly . . .*

> We're all ripe for a spot of moral anarchy . . .
> . . . adolescent still . . .
> These passions distract us . . .

—I tried for the first time in this picture to tackle the third kind of reality which is moral, using the same sense of the word as in moral philosophy, which, as I take it, means the regulation of personal behaviour by general custom for the general good. This is why I called it *You and Spinoza*, though I must admit my original title was, *You and bloody Spinoza*. The highly successful Piers in that picture was by training a philosopher who deeply admired Spinoza, drawn to the tiresome but vivacious girl, Lisa, who becomes desperately ambitious for him and puts up with his multifarious infidelities. Some people welcomed the fact that it was less complicated than some of my other pictures and even found it funny, which is what I had hoped. But nevertheless it was based on something serious said by Spinoza himself: The things that commonly happen in life and are esteemed among men as the highest good (as is witnessed by their works) can be reduced to three: Riches, Fame and Lust; and by these the mind is so distracted that it can scarcely think of any other good.

—Perhaps some of you will remember that in *You and Spinoza*, Piers writes a play which Lisa sells for him. He, it seems, would have been perfectly happy as an obscure teacher, but his success develops. Other women become attainable. Lisa has the success that she has coveted, but is always afraid that Piers will go for good. Piers wallows in self-contempt. But it was intended to be funny.

—My last two films have been less simple. Here is a clip from *The Wanderer*, which is the picture of mine most universally loathed . . .

> Unless bloody art means something to reasonably educated people . . .

The sweep of conifers up a steep hillside brushed heavily with mist; a beautiful girl alone in rumpled lingerie; four people at a bistro in London smiling; close up of a face with heavy lines, bearded, a patch over one eye; turbulence of stormclouds; a khaki jacket with medal ribbons worn by someone whose face we do not see, holding a long-bladed knife...

You haven't a logical mind . . .

The sweep of conifers and the lined, bearded wanderer. Out of the mist and dark trees come four hooded murderers. Close up of the mutilated face of the victim. Next time we meet him (on the Marseilles waterfront) he wears a patch over one eye and the scars show beneath it.

Absurd . . .

> . . . outside politics and social responsibility . . .
> An absentee god . . .
> I am the natural fool of fortune . . .

—My most recent picture, *Nocturne*, while equally unpopular among the critics—obscurantist, pretentious, esoteric, arcane—take your pick, was rather different and, I thought, the most lyrical that I'd made since my first. In it, a man who is particularly happy sees a girl hit by a car. He is some distance away and he is not sure whether she killed herself or whether it was an accident. It is a beautiful night in early summer. Rather like tonight. It's only the third film I've made in colour so I was pleased with it. The man cannot approach the body, although other people have now arrived, because he is afraid that it is his own girl, the reason for his happiness. Why is he afraid? The picture explores this.

—I have finished one other picture called *The Managers* which is about a research doctor, mentally unbalanced, and a fantasy he has concerning biological and chemical warfare, but I won't say any more about that.

O the sciagura d'essere senza . . .

—It seems to me at this stage of my life that whatever moral posture we are twitched into by invisible strings of desire or self-interest and however we are jointed ethically to respond to tugs of remorse and guilt, the supreme difficulty for all men is to die quietly in a world that has no God; and to reconcile himself to personal defeat is a prefiguring personal difficulty for each individual. Each one of us is writer, director and actor in his own life. How often do we begin by observing, a part of some circumstance but apart from it; we become involved and it might sometimes seem that we are able to arrange and control events to some desirable end; then, almost always too late—we realise that we are involved, that we are, however unwillingly, actors in the scene waiting for the murder, the custard pie, the oracular revelation.

—Thank you for listening. You have helped me a great deal.

Robert Keller

While he was amused at the whole idea of a series of articles on 'The Anatomy of Power,' Robert Keller was pleased to have been invited to contribute to it. At the briefing lunch, that afternoon, he had learned that the other contributors would be representative of the political parties, industrial management and the unions, all much more in the public eye than he was: so that his own design of becoming selectively better-known was furthered.

Robert Keller considered the bare page on his desk and unscrewed the cap of his fountain-pen, reflecting that power was one of the things that really meant something to him, but there were, for him, two quite separate kinds of power and indeed two quite different but equally seductive theories of power. The first was highly personal both in execution and and in conception: it involved expedite, confident decisions whether planned or improvised; since no such system would be fallible, it involved a degree of self-critical absolutism, a truly pragmatic system in no sense restricted by ideological doctrine or whim.

Robert Keller wrote:

'William James asks: "What, in short, is the truth's cash-value in experiential terms?"'.

As a young man, Robert Keller had occasionally cherished fantasies of absolute political power, which had in due course been modified by increasing knowledge of the modern despots. But he had no basic faith in democratic processes although passionately in favour of the democratic illusion in which he actively participated.

After all, as his whole life and career testified, Robert Keller believed passionately in the right of the masses to express opinions, and equally passionately that they deserved to live in a decent, beneficent society which took care of their needs and offered overyone the opportunity to excel. His distrust, his scorn indeed, for the political fecklessness of the masses did not affect these beliefs. Robert Keller accordingly described himself as a socialist and a democrat. But he believed that the democratic processes should be controlled by those people in any free society who proved, in different ways, their ability to shape and administer the ethic and legislative code of that society. He smiled: these were the senior politicians who served a parliamentary system, the top industrial managers, the union leaders, a few people in communications and most important of all the higher civil servants.

Robert Keller genuinely admired the Civil Services of the United States, France and most of all his own, while fully cognisant of the flaws and shortcomings in each of them. It was they who protected the masses from the manias and paranoias of dictators or potential dictators, as well as from the anarchic and self-destructive forces in the masses themselves. It was they who undertook to govern the engines of government, so that nothing was in excess. Everything in Robert Keller's own background made him despise the old-fashioned Establishment, but he was happy about a quasi-Platonic quorum of influence in the hands of men of proven talent. He grinned. He would tolerate more artists with a great deal of freedom.

These reflections did not disturb him by any hint they might contain of cynicism. Society must know itself. He wrote:

Inevitably when one discusses administrative power using terms like 'cash-value', one is open to charges of cynicism. But knowing the cash-value of policies, that is to say the price of them, is the business of the professional public servant. He must be watchful and sceptical, without becoming inhibitingly suspicious . . .

Nevertheless, Robert Keller allowed his wife, Barbara and Paul to do more or less as they pleased, and had always done so; but he knew quite well that it had suited his purpose, and that their particular desires had seldom conflicted with his own. Among his friends, he was acknowledged leader in that they adjusted to him, rather than he to them: David Lawson, Jack Rathbone, Laurence Bisset, even Eric Foster, had at one time or another sought out his advice. Certainly, in his relations with women, he had always done more or less as he pleased. Here, he was prepared to acknowledge some psychological lack, or need at least, in himself. A new, attractive woman was always a challenge to him and he enjoyed the sense of emotional and, eventually, physical power that conquests of this sort gave him.

He began to write rapidly and fluently, developing with restrained wit the idea of the civil servant as a dutiful cynic in terms of politicians and the electorate, gradually tapering off the slightly bantering tone as he approached questions of social welfare and order, postulating a common agreement among all sane men in positions of authority that society should be humane, uncorrupt and progressive.

Recalling a snatch of conversation with Eric Foster, Robert Keller remembered describing himself as a Hegelian. He had been trying to bait Foster mildly; and certainly viewed Hegel with as much interested scepticism as he held for every other professional philosopher, and no more. But at that moment of writing, he recalled snatches of Hegel's thought and realised that many of his own concepts relating to his work might well have been adapted from the philosopher. He was intrigued and leaned back in his comfortable chair, smiling to himself, gazing at the shadows which were now lengthening.

Beginning with the premise that any world view, political, ethical, functionary, must be compatible with human reason, as opposed to mystical revelation, Robert Keller thought that good government, aiming towards perfect government, should come from a process of refinement, a progressive revelation of itself in its assimilation of its own historical experience.

He took up his pen and began to write again, delighting in the flowing movement of the nib on the creamy texture of the paper. The importance of the immediate task was to formulate that idea in concrete, assimilable terms, readily comprehensible to the reader of serious Sunday newspapers, but he was distracted from his search for an apt example by a fresh thought, again relating to Hegel; the idea that the task of philosophy was to consider 'that which is.'

Robert Keller, deciding that what he wrote would in any case only serve as a draft, continued:

The task of philosophy, according to Hegel, is to consider 'that which is' ; so the task of administrative government is to concern itself primarily with that which is. It can only guess at that which will be. So its provisions for the future must be flexible to say the least. In this way, in government as much as in other things time past and time future are both perhaps present in time present. We progress experientially; we forecast imaginatively: and meanwhile the show goes rationally on. Hegel, feeling himself to be alive at a time when civilisation was drawing to a twilight, saw the owl of Minerva taking wing at dusk. There is no reason for us to be as pessimistic and we must not assume that the refining process in government is at an end: what we must arrive at is a form of administration which is humane as well as efficient, considerate as well as decisive, kindly as well as rational.

He lay down his fountain pen and read through the text so far. With his usual intelligent use of detail, he thought he would illustrate his argument in so far as possible from minor parables on the difficulties of running a complex modern state.

At this point, Robert Keller observed Sebastian Jones through the window. The old man was pursuing with amazing agility a somewhat raffish matron, herself possessed of a fine turn of speed, around Robert Keller's garden. Robert Keller shouted.

'Hi, there, Robbie, sport,' said Sebastian Jones. 'Meet Cherylene. She's from Wangaratta.'

'I wish to speak you you, Sebastian.'

'No sooner said than done, and no mistake about it, Bob, old mate. It's opening time, so Cherylene can take her evening glass of fruit-juice in the pub, while you and I transact a little business, eh, son?'

Robert Keller waited, having decided on a firm and decisive line. He thought that Sebastian Jones was a little frightened of him and intended to take full advantage of it.

The farce of the situation struck him as his eye ran over the last sentence he had written:

. . . in the best of worlds where careful conceptual thinking along disciplined and scientific lines is matched by genuine enthusiasm, flair and virile action . . .

Paul Keller

The bat-wing of madness. I cannot name the precise hour or even the particular day, but it was unmistakable as it brushed over me. And knowing my body to be whole, to be sound, the knowledge was accompanied by a sense of filth and weariness, of fever and unclean humours. The generic family of the disease may be labelled guilt, but there is something more. Self-pity, boredom in a world that throbs with pain and has become weary. In need of Prometheus.

I have endured the voice of thunder . . .

Worse I have endured the smooth inflections of the huge Thunderfarter himself and their reverberations. Caligari of the North Atlantic. And the silent shadow-stepping raptor in the sombre corridors of the decaying schloss hammering the entranced diaphanous starlets, who scream and succumb and squirm with corrupted ecstasy. Yet outwardly the respected margrave, descending into the village where gay peasant folk greet him with deferential smiles. And feel his protection. But there are rumours, legends, about the schloss and what goes on. None of the villagers have ventured in, except the servants who now live there and who are surly, silent, long divorced from their families.

But I can no longer stay in the darkness . . .

Cloistered virtues of David Lawson, Bisset: the coldly well-behaved, the controlled, nothing in excess, middleweight brigade, whom the gods will drive mad in subtle ways; heirs of the disinherited gentlemen who took the weight of government on their elbows always: these I cannot respect for their assumed chastity, their wistful, yearning restraint. Blue-filmed eyes and scrabbling fingers flicking behind the ramrod backs, the ascetic smiling. And yet I know there the answer lies somehow: in chastity, or at least in purification. D. H. Lawrence in Plato's cave, for Christ's sake!

It is time to seek a lost, lost track . . .

What was the idea that women are more naturally inclined to piety? Oh, yes! The pussycat-smiling; cariadcarrying, fully-paid-up literary lunchers; the fiscal Sapphos; and those who are too gay, tending the fires and suckling the young while the lithe hunters roam on the plains from Cro-Magnon to the high Medoc. It all depends, my dear Pythagoras, what you mean by piety.

Leaving the warm scents of upland caves . . .

For the yellowed brilliance of fine summer days? Ay, there's the rub, as they say, the brush of the round, compatible hip and it's just bad luck that she happens to be your sister and it would be viewed in most circles with painful severity. Oh but that is triumphantly over. The pain and weariness of that has been conquered. And there *can only be* violent emotions, from which we escape by purification. But perhaps not yet? Jane . . .

> *Et le printemps et la verdure*
> *Ont tant humilié mon coeur*
> *Que j'ai puni sur une fleur*
> *L'insolence de la Nature.*

Here, intellect and passion pull in opposite ways. As they say, action and reaction are equal and opposite, but some are more equal than others.

And there will be muttering Shrouds
On the road and raving men will cry out . . .

More, surely than the mere infusion of spleen. The worse corrupting, the unforgivable. Yet it was there, the irony of the sun tearing my flesh, the craving, quite suddenly, to deflower. Ha! Too late, old cock, too late! But there was something. . . . *Chéri, je vais très bien avec toi.* . . . Where are the Frankies of yesteryear? No, my love. The emotions and the passions must be more violent than that. And there must be pain and there must be weariness. Eric Foster perhaps is the consubstantive. And McNamara. . . . No admirable serenity in him, just the menacing calm of a psychopath about to move. Yet, and yet, the vibrant certainty, the pulsing of the blood, the violence of feeling. It is odd that of all of them Eric, tortured and limping, is the only Promethean, mingling intellect and passion, breeding flowers out of the sterile ground. And that both of us suffer, have suffered, addiction to the same false heroine.

Worse: tentacle voices out of white mist . . .

I'd like to put my hand up Keller's sister, Blandford, wouldn't you? Ooooh yes, Aylmer: I bet she's very hairy, don't you. You'd have a job finding it. Is that true, Keller? Now, Keller, temper, temper, Diddums feelums sexy sister, then.

Flies slow on putrid, mutilated flesh . . .

That will not do. A nice man with nasty ideas. Hatred unquenched over years and years. The squat fat boy with huge strong wrists and the easy athletic bully: a small-town solicitor and a prep-school sportsmaster whom I still wish to murder.

And over all the stench of futile spleen . . .

Violence even of wicked passions, that will not be denied but from which there must be a liberation. Against such fantasies of torment, against the urge to corrupt, what is the desire for a woman who happens to be my sister. The fat Fingal, the easy McNamara. All right, let them be forgiven, and forgotten.

The woman made of carnivorous blossoms . . .

No. Jane West is not premier cru anything. Light, flavoursome, sweetly scented, fairly alcoholic. An easy passion, an instinctive response. And a passion and a purity altogether out of keeping with the experienced eyes, the already ruptured hymen. However I should have felt, I did not. And there is the fragrance. It could not be, but it seems to have happened.

The tempters and the innocent victims . . .

And so, with the first flecks of snow in the winter air, we leave autumn and shining decay on the transport back to summer, knowing that these patient men and women are preparing to sit out the cold, dark months, in the hope of next year's spring. Next on BBC 1 you can see *The Good Old Days*, while just about to start on BBC 2 we have Part III of *The Rise of Silas Lapham*. If you only knew, Jane, what hope I have imagined in those clear, brown eyes, and what leprous patches are hidden by my clever, clever words, I think you would admit defeat and trip away, now, from unhappiness.

> But they will not be avoided, their laughter
> Erodes the will, their luck is stillborn
> And I have endured the thunder too long . . .

It is not really a question of personal neuroses. Spread-eagled on the supple trunks of intellect and passion, there is some kind of journey to be made, if one survives; if one is cut loose before the ropes that twine the bent trees are split. And there must be no expectation of reward: hard work and a good life in which the most one can hope to do is to hurt as few people as possible shall no longer have their truffles and champagne, gift-hampers and pneumatic blissmates. It is all pain and weariness: the reward is in having tried: having suffered. *Les vrais voyageurs sont ceux la seuls qui patient pour partir.*

> I do not know what I shall find in ruins
> Whether I shall survive alone, unwanted . . .

Standing apart in churches, huddling my felt shroud of guilt around me, watching the worshippers go grey-faced away, having lit candles in the side-chapels to the saints most in demand, I have learned nothing yet. From what I have seen of tolerance and endurance and understanding and uncertainty, I am inclined to guess that admirable serenity and quietness are very different in kind. I am opting for quietness.

I can no longer stay in the darkness.

Gavin McNamara

I recall reading somewhere that the man and woman who lives more civilised in behaviour than feeling is sure to find rationality in irksome virtue.

But to get back to the gist, which is that there's a savage beast not far below the surface in all of us, my own experience in the cultivated borders of the Kellergarden proved that this particular sage was a striker in the £200,000 class with guaranteed opportunities on television as an expert to follow. In fact, if all the bastards on the world's surface were to be gathered together in a single island and that island was to be recognised by the United Nations Organisation, it would be represented there by the paterfamilias, in person, Robert Keller. That, at least, was the opinion of Andrea Bisset, freely expressed, and a number of other members of the gentler sex, after the elfin storyteller, Stone, had walked slap into the paterfamilias' tiger-trap where he was discovered by sundry savage lion-hunters who had him for breakfast on Sunday and flayed his skin for the spare bedroom parquet.

This, no less, was the upshot of the famous literary competition and it's no secret at all that the poor little sod was as furious about it as a pixie who'd walked into a bumble-bee backing up. And there was quite a lot of partisan feeling generated by the whole celebrated cause, with many of the opinion that the paterfamilias' little joke was nothing but a mean and low malice, though I was strictly impartial myself.

I suppose it was all a question of professional pride, which, without the adjective, as a deadly sin must rank as an absolute nap selection. Anyway, the paterfamilias, having issued the challenge, as the course of the action ran, also furnished the poor bloody purple fritillary with a plot, craftily not telling him that it was one of his very own, already published, turned arse over tit, so to speak.

Since Stone aself was far too highbrow an article to read rubbish like the paterfamilias' books, and since he had only shown his thriller to people who was either themselves as highbrow, such as Jacqueline and Sylvie—this one making rather a point of ignoring her husband's oeuvre, or else to thick bitches like Andrea, he hadn't discovered the old ringmaster's little ruse. Bejasus, though, the critics did! And just in case they didn't, as I heard it whispered by a friend of mine himself a member of the journalist class, the paterfamilias slipped a joking word to one or two top gossip-writers in the course of an interview about something or other to do with the hobbies of a top scientific civil servant. As I've already mentioned, I was taking a strictly nonaligned position in the whole tomcobblery like a Burmese undertaker.

Anyway it made quite an interesting change for a few days before it quietened down into nothing again, of particular fascination to an historian of the human foible like meself. This is what put me in mind of the words of the sage, whoever it was, that I mentioned. My own life and times has taken me here and there about the world, but among this high-grade range of comestibles there was a fibre-tearing savagery that would have frightened the hell out of many people used to actual violence.

Most of the confidences of the women I heard in intimate circumstances, to tell the truth, because after I had established as the main subject an allegro risoluto with Sylvie, the whole Summer symphony began to unfold with very lush orchestration and nearly all the women of the Kellering started to perform a sort of Sally Grand National. And for a couple of weeks towards the end of July, my modest room was like one of those sheds they keep the bull in back in the auld green country across the wather, a scene of hot-eyed energy and basic exuberance. I won't go into tedious detail now, though even I am tempted by the memory of Mrs Anabelle Finch and the Graeco-Roman enterprises favoured by her, purely as a sociological document. I think that on the whole she preferred women, but there couldn't have been many strong enough to match her. And I learned a hell of a lot about abuse and economics. Anyway, after a while, of the immediate circle there was only three remaining: Jacqueline, Jane and the beautiful Barbara. The most glittering prizes, as it would seem to many, no doubt, in the noisettes de veau Orloff stakes, whoever the hell Orloff might have been But lust as a modus vivendi is awful tiring, so let him who's not getting his share cast the first custard pie.

It would be fair to say that I was never as close to the men of the group under study, and I'd go so far as to say that Ponce de Lawson and the Grand Admiral himself didn't take to me at all, but from the hanging gardens of Hampstead to the hortillonages of Hampton Wick I was made free of the thought and inner drives of most of them, directly or indirectly. And I must confess to bafflement.

First of all you have the paterfamilias there, advising the mighty of the land on themes such as death, disease, famine and destruction, but taking time off to play japes on the gnomic aorist of modern letters, your friend and my friend, Stone. Not only that, you have that intelligent item falling for the whole shower of garbage about friendly rivalray which is as fragrant as forgotten carrots in a polythene bag. Now Sylvie herself had told me that Stone had bejewelled her own fair bosom with kisses, and it turned out he had tumbled Andrea as well, so it could have been that the paterfamilias, for all his arietine capers in the pens of his neighbours, was jealous. From my own reading of the situation, however, I thought it had more to do with envy, since Stone having one of the most fluent nibs in the trade was frequently being invited into the seraglios of contemporary ethics by bishops, life-peers and clubmen philosophers as a signatory to letters to *The Times* about people being pissed about by the governments of less fortunate lands. The paterfamilias fancied his conscience to be of a size matching his bollocks, but the invitations seldom forthcame his way. And that I think was part of it too.

But in any case there was all the others. Now an interesting feature of the whole social physiography was the way in which they seemed to have changed since the old balderbluss and subsequently meself had appeared. From the most reliable sources I had it, that whereas the paterfamilias had been round them all, there had been very little cuisine paysanne otherwise. The elfin Stone had had the life frightened out of him by Andrea, who herself suspected the graven public image Bisset himself of the occasional trip into the upper air regardless of votes. Now, the word on him, from Sylvie, was that he was great on passionate, narrow-eyed looks and the occasional lingering hand in the slow fox-trot, when and as; from Elaine, that he responded normally to close contact with rounded surfaces; from everyone else that he was a fish-eyed, politick bastard with no more life in him than a white paper projected by the previous party in office. I'll say this, meself, that I always found Bisset watchful but courteous, with a keen eye for pictures.

They all suspected Eric Foster of having had the best of Sylvie in the great days of the third programme, but there was an almighty confusion about dates in this respect, and Sylvie herself told me that apart from the elfin one and my own discretion, no one else at all had penetrated her silences. Mind you, said she, many's the time Eric might have, had he looked like making an offer, but he was always destroyed by memory (of his ex) or expectation (no secret: the marzipan infanta, Barbara) and that put her off. There was in her opinion a debilitating intellectual aspect to him that turned his current awry. Notwithstanding the consensus was not convinced; but my own editorial opinion was that he hadn't even noticed.

There they all were. Rathbone—a Rear-Admiral in the last Birthday Parade; Lawson, rich enough to buy shares in a specialist pub in Earl's Court; Lomax—curing the sick before new generations of silky-haired nurses; Fingal Grey, weekly renewed in his own image. The slopperjaw, Paul, seemed always to be busy writing wee poems and in a terrible dichotomy between decadence (as it was) and liberation (as it seems to be), which as those of us who have travelled a bit know is the perennial problem.

Now, a lot of yez will be asking why a fellow of such sterling savoir-faire in the region of moral notions should not have rescued one of the

Ariadnes available from this island of Noxos and headed back, like the clappers, to the Cote d'Azur: here you have in a nutshell the dilemma of the social historian who wants to know how it's cuttin' on several planes at once. The truth is that the urban commotion is a source of endless inspiration to me. And although I had more in common with that timeless gabledecock, essentially speaking, it was absorbing to see what made the computer hum.

I began to ask the odd question. But only of myself. I don't go in much for the statement of intent or even belief, seriously discouraged by such people as the Christian Brothers, let alone princes, courts, covenants and the United Nations Organisation, but I suppose the time has come for me to declare that I'm in favour of all that expands, unites and says Yes, as another sage (James, W.) puts it. And there are many like me about who always seem to set the top spinning. I don't condemn easy and, if fact, I don't give much of a damn what people are up to because I'm never going to stop them: the damned, the perverse, the stupid thrill-flickers, the sick, the euphoric, the anaesthetised, the enchanted, the kind, the visionaries, the transported.

When you think of the results of rational thought, ideological control, civilised habits, you should think of the history of the twentieth century. And if you're going to spit on Descartes, you know what to do on Marcuse. They're all the same. And it isn't often I lose patience. I don't have to. My kind survive.

PART SEVEN

Robert Keller

On entering the room, Robert Keller was slightly surprised and moderately amused to see his friend, Jack Rathbone, now a Rear-Admiral, glaring and pipe-sucking against a wall. Robert Keller smiled confidently and heard himself warmly hailed by Sebastian Jones.

'If it ain't you, Robbie, you old yellow-footed rock wallaby,' said the old man, 'come and fill your tankard at the billabong of all delights, mate.'

Robert Keller wondered, once more, whether his wife's uncle was not too ridiculous a caricature to be authentic, and the thought made him glance, serenely, around for his host, whose Irishness sometimes reeked of provincial repertory.

The flat itself was small, but not as small as Robert Keller had expected. McNamara liked to pretend that he lived in a shoebox, but the basement premises were in fact comfortable and probably, when not packed with an extraordinary array of people, reasonably spacious. Robert Keller took a glass of wine, sipped it prudently: it was, however, palatable.

He joined Jack Rathbone and greeted him with a tolerant but sardonic comment about the other guests.

'What possessed this chap to invite us?' asked Rathbone.

Robert Keller said that he understood from Sylvie that McNamara was anxious to return some of the hospitality that he had received.

'Can't say I've ever cared for the chap,' said Jack Rathbone, 'but Elaine's very taken with him. You know how women are.'

Smiling understandingly, Robert Keller said that he was surprised that the wine was drinkable.

'I shall never understand these drifters,' said Jack Rathbone. 'Well, Robert. How have you been keeping? What's this about you making an ass of Stone in the papers?'

Robert Keller chuckled amiably and explained the situation with understated skill, so that Rathbone's grimly handsome face cracked into the fanged, ugly smile which was much esteemed by many women of Robert Keller's acquaintance.

'How's he taken it?' asked Rathbone. 'Always struck me as a bit neurotic.'

As Robert Keller shrugged his shoulders lightly to suggest that little harm had been done, that he did not much care, and also that Stone had been somewhat petulantly upset, there was a whoop from the other side of the room, distinguishable as coming from Sebastian Jones, although the old man could not be seen.

'I see,' said Jack Rathbone, 'that you still have your wife's uncle alongside. My God, look at this fellow.'

Rathbone's glaring eye was fixed upon a youth with long silky hair dressed in clinging trousers of pink jersey with a ruffled white see-through shirt posturing before an overweight, lumbering man in tweeds with a public school accent, whose lower lip trembled in anticipation. Robert Keller was about to say something suitably tolerant, when he saw his daughter come into the room alone. It was crowded enough for her not to be noticed, but Robert Keller was able to catch her eye and she squeezed her way through the press of bright-eyed, jawing party guests, as Jack Rathbone uttered short grunts of pleasure, removed his pipe from his mouth and cracked his face into welcome.

'Hullo Daddy, Hullo Jack,' Barbara said.

'Good to see you, Barbara,' said Jack Rathbone. 'You look splendid, as usual. Very pretty frock.'

Beaming, Robert Keller listened to his daughter receiving bluff Wardroom flattery that disguised perfectly usual lust, watching her own intelligent, deep eyes sparkling with humour from time to time. He did not really overestimate his daughter's actual sense of fun: in fact, he thought she took herself too seriously, but, unlike Paul, she had always shared Robert Keller's sense of irony and it had given him a sense of gentle pleasure often to catch her eye during a conversation and with no more than a flicker of expression exchange a witty footnote to some absurdity. While he looked at her, however, he became aware that she looked tired, even strained. He asked if she had been working hard.

'Pretty steadily,' she said. 'How are you, Daddy? Outmanoeuvring the rest of the Civil Service as tirelessly as usual?'

They all laughed.

'I hope,' said Jack Rathbone, 'that my daughters don't grow up as sharp as this young woman, Robert. Reads you like an open book . . .'

'Talking of which . . .' Barbara began.

She was cut short by another prolonged whoop from Sebastian Jones and distracted into a sequence of acid comments on the subject of her great-uncle.

'Since that old ape has come along, everyone seems to have gone completely mad. Paul appears to be turning into an alcoholic, Mummy is . . . Oh God, here's Fingal. I'm going to disappear through here. Is that where Gavin is?' Barbara said.

Neither Robert Keller nor Jack Rathbone knew, but they exchanged a significant look at the intelligence of Barbara's implied rift with Fingal Grey. For his part, Robert Keller thought it a pity, since Grey's undisputed influence as a television celebrity was a considerably more useful commodity per se than the modest talents at the command of McNamara. Nevertheless, he was able to appreciate the fascination and charm of McNamara's personality, as well as the undoubted force of his character.

'I must say,' said Jack Rathbone, 'that fellow must have quite a way with him, if he can get through to a girl like Barbara.'

Robert Keller agreed and asked Rathbone where his wife was.

'That's a point,' Rathbone said. 'Better go and look for her in case she needs rescuing from one of these shits.'

He nodded towards a nearby group, not discriminating as far as Robert Keller was able to tell, between an Irish novelist of middle age, a hippie from the Board of Trade who worked for David Lawson, a gaudy and loud young man who clearly worked in publishing and a Scottish barman, who were laying siege to two self-advertising girls from the BBC. His departure enabled Robert Keller to make his way to Sally West, in conversation with a flamboyantly bearded man of about thirty with wide shoulders and confidence. Robert Keller had seldom seen a black man with so much poised indifference. As he joined them, the man turned huge lustrous eyes on Robert Keller, who realised that their extraordinary glowing glassiness was caused by contact lenses rather than drugs.

'Hullo, Robert,' Sally said. 'This is Jerome. This is Robert Keller, who is very important, Jerome, and who controls some part of everyone's life.'

'Hi, Robert, baby,' said Jerome. 'You having a good time, are you?'

Robert Keller said that he was having a good time and asked what Jerome did. Jerome was a dancer, but recognizing Robert Keller as a member of the white establishment became aggressively determined to talk about Black Power. Robert Keller, aware that any statement of his real opinions—that the movement was inevitable, essential; and, in the longest term, useful to sensible world government—would anger Jerome and bring about a hot and tedious tirade, took the offensive. Incisively and authoritatively he put the point of view of White power, refusing to yield to the bazooka-fire of Jerome's interruptions. The upshot was that he and Jerome got on very well.

Robert Keller was intrigued by Sally West's response to the argument. He knew quite well that she cared as much about Black Power as she did about Vichy water, but she was attentive, almost eager. In her eyes there was the liquid softness of a woman consciously displaying the relevant signals of sexual excitement. The superb black man was indifferent, but Robert Keller was attacked by a pang of jealousy that resembled a sudden sharp pain in the chest—an intimation of mortality. A minute, bird-like lady led the splendid Jerome away in mid-sentence. A girl in a string bag filled their glasses, touching Robert Keller's arm with her almost bare breasts as she leaned across to serve Sally.

'How are you getting on, Robert?' Sally said. 'You've been conspicuous by your absence, lately.'

'I've been unusually busy,' said Robert Keller.

'New secretary?' asked Sally. 'Or taking the piss out of harmless little novelists? Eric Foster told me that poor Andrew Stone is on the verge of a nervous breakdown.'

Then he asked what she had been doing.

'I've not been pining away,' Sally said. 'It's amazing what one finds to do.'

Deliberately but with a show of absent-mindedness she rubbed the inside of one thigh with the other knee, gazing off to the left. It was her very coarseness that most appealed to Robert Keller: she actually enjoyed all the erotic byplay more than the tender denouements.

'I understand that Jane and Paul have something going for them,' Sally said.

Briefly he had a picture of Jane West, firm and nubile, in a short black nightdress that he had noticed in a shop window and wondered how he would behave to her as a daughter-in-law. Until now he had behaved scrupulously to all the younger women in his immediate circle, with the exception of Elaine, who had married into it, and Jasmine, who wasn't all that young, but at this particular party he was, for the first time, aware that time would soon be running out.

Sally was drawn into a benign and receptive-looking group consisting of an ageing South-African expatriate communist, who was incidentally and accidentally rich, a New York Jewish film producer called Woody Holly, a poetess, a long-haired, long-dressed Brigadier's daughter, a philosopher and a woman in a sari who programmed a computer. Robert Keller stood listening, behaving with a reflex courtesy, smiling cleverly, interpolating the odd wise chuckle; drained of all energy. For a moment, he wondered if there was a real pain across the top of his chest. All the while, he mechanically, as a result of long habit, registered details: the pattern of the sari, the contour of the Jew's five-o-clock shadow, a mole on the chin of the wealthy communist, the philospher's lips, a faint and inexplicably enticing scent of perfume and sweat from the Brigadier's daughter.

It was one of the most amazingly mixed gatherings to which Robert Keller had ever accepted an invitation. McNamara, while a guest at Robert Keller's own house, had shown evidence of picking up strangers of alarming diversity. This talent had filled all the rooms, as far as Robert Keller could see, of the basement flat with unlikely but presumable bedfellows. The picture of Jacqueline Benbow pressed into a corner by a hairy-chested labourer, and ostensibly relaxed, served as a symptom of the remarkable symbiosis. Robert Keller reflected wryly that his wife, never slow to remind people of her origins in the working class, would be glorying in the situation. Yet, as he looked around, his eye falling on a ripely dissipated woman with a vast *crinière* of chestnut hair, Robert Keller felt his enthusiasm rising again. The pain in his chest had been imaginary. He flexed his left shoulder and arm and drained his glass.

'And how are you, Mr Keller,' said McNamara, at his elbow, filling the glass again. 'Enjoying yourself, I hope. There are some undignified bastards up and down the room, including a sizeable troupe from my own homeland among whom the word seems to have got round, but I trust you'll forgive all that. Hey, Kevin, that's enough of the fucking holy polemics. I don't care what sort of witness he is, go into the bathroom and you'll find Eileen and Rose fighting off two Wicklow men . . . That's the trouble with these boys, Mr Keller, they get the sectarian bit between their teeth and they're off!'

Robert Keller commented with ironic admiration on the range and variety of the guests, asking if they reflected some spirit of sociological curiosity in McNamara.

'Not a bit of it,' McNamara said. 'I'm just a bastard for getting to know people, and once I do, give or take the odd one that falls by the wayside, I seem to know them for life. Mind you they're interesting enough as you say. D'you see that girl making up to Mr Bisset, M.P., now? She's a very interesting person, what with her being a strip-tease artist and her sister being a nun. I'm sure you don't bother with that sort of thing yourself; but she has a magical way with a brassiere, as technically assured as Yehudi Menhuin on the fiddle in its way. And that fellow in drag used to be in the Special Branch, believe it or not, until they found out his proclivities. But, sure, he's amiable enough. And you would have been delighted to see Fingal Grey almost making a dreadful mistake.'

Laughing, Robert Keller allowed his glass to be filled again and said that he had not yet had a chance to speak to Grey.

'It may not seem very tactful inviting him at all,' said McNamara, 'what with the strain between himself and your lovely daughter. But there, I said to myself, they're both adult and sophisticated people; and being grateful to him for some television work he put in my direction, while, at the same time, thinking no party would be complete without herself's adorning it, I took a risk.

'Mrs Finch,' said McNamara, suddenly, 'is out in the hallway. I must say it's a fine figure of a woman, that; if it's not an indelicate observation.'

At this point he was called enthusiastically by some lurid girls in short, shiny, revealing dresses. He filled Robert Keller's glass again before departing. Robert Keller noticed a girl who had opened her blouse to the waist and who was wearing nothing under it, and gradually as his eyes tracked around the room began to wonder if he might be hallucinating, as more and more people seemed to be compromisingly displaying their bodies or to be unrestrainedly taking part in some form of erotic contact. The scene had all the dim unreality of an orgy designed by an old master with a pretty comprehensive knowledge of sexual license, with additional touches by Fellini. At this point, Robert Keller's eye stopped on the lonely, miserable but obsessed eyes of Eric Foster, gazing about with the deep intelligence, the weary fascination of a minor artist unable to forget his work; editing, assembling, cutting, mixing, framing sequence after sequence into yet another masterpiece that would never come off. Foster saw Robert Keller and limped awkwardly, pushing diffidently through the shrieks, laughter, warm, soft, sweating, rubbing, palpating bodies, towards him. Since Foster was a long-standing friend of Andrew Stone and since Robert Keller knew that he would not refer directly to the joke, he anticipated an uneasy but interesting exchange. He had never liked or understood Eric Foster, but he respected his dogged industry, his patient cultivation of a very fragile gift. It puzzled him and sometimes even troubled him. Robert Keller was a much cleverer man, who sometimes doubted that he had achieved as much. But not often. He waited for another of their protracted, inconsequential, edged conversations. Then abruptly Foster touched Robert Keller's daughter. The two of them swung to face each other, clearly not expecting or intending any such contact. Robert Keller watched, fascinated. Barbara and Eric Foster could not have held the look for more than a few seconds, but it made an indelible impression of terrible pity on Robert Keller, who did not often experience such feelings and who could not imagine what has passed between the two. Foster had forgotten about Robert Keller. He pushed on out of the room, his face contorted with a blind anxiety to be gone. Robert Keller's daughter made a small gesture with her hand and stood staring after him, but a moment later was fighting off the encircling arm of a North country actor, newly established, whom Robert Keller recognised. He decided not to go and talk to Barbara, adhering to his policy of never prying into his children's lives. But he had always been fond of her, perhaps compensating for her mother's indifference, and he was not able to forget quickly the look of misery on her face.

'Well strewth, here you are, Robbie, you old wedge-tailed eagle. What's come over you, sport?' said Sebastian Jones.

Robert Keller realised that he was drunk. He stopped listening to Sebastian Jones, although the old man continued to babble raucously and obscenely on. He left him, without a word, still talking, when he caught sight of Jacqueline Benbow, slightly ruffled, making for the street door. Passing through the lobby or hallway, as jammed with people as the other rooms, he noticed fleetingly David Lawson giggling against the bosom of Annabelle Finch, both attended by half a dozen indeterminately pretty young people; Jack Rathbone, himself, with his gothick grin, surrounded by women and holding up, unmistakably, a pair of flimsy panties; and talking very seriously in the middle of all the riot and confusion, the thick smells of tobacco, drink, pot (no doubt) and human bodies liberally cosmeticised, Barbara and the Irishman, McNamara.

He went out into the area. Jacqueline had disappeared. He climbed the steps, but there was no sign of her. Deciding not to return, but to try his luck at her flat, Robert Keller began to move away. Then he heard sobbing beneath him from the area.

It was a young man and in due course Robert Keller made out that it was his son, Paul. The boy began to retch. Although he remembered well that he would have hated to be discovered in such humiliating circumstances, Robert Keller judged that Paul was very different and made his way down the steps again.

Paul Keller

Seven foot tall, steel-blue. At the gateway of the garden of delights, the angel of death, without his sword, stands, recruiting those who pass out. Firm hand, clammy heart.

Lychanthropic litter. There about him. Beast masks grinning in lust and triumph or snarling, yellow-fanged envy, red eye, whimper and deep-throated growl, slaver drip and stiffened hyaena hair, scenting the corruption and the lewd blood. All about him. Dancing, slipping, threading his way through them, with the mad red wine in his hand, he goes. His eyes stare bright blue and there is the fixed triangular smile on his mouth. Laughter without mirth. Lust without passion. Tall, fair, slender, he moves among them and their animal yelps, the skitters, jeers, chirps, mewls, barks, brays, whinnies, howls, blares, yaps, snorts, grunts, bleats and hisses of his people.

And outside the angel of death, the night stepper. With the seductive erlking-father comfort. More powerful, yet unable to exercise power at the height of the other's rites, for fear of the fury of the celebrants. Waiting only to sweep up the weak who have to run away from the fierce games. Da Bog, demon daddy, out of the dark.

That slum redhead, shivering glass laugh, soft fronted belly massage, gutteral obscenities about a bastard family and giggling suggestions. And vindaloo blood Indians groaning with pleasure at the thought, while she, shrieking, with blunt, scoured fingers, prods the buttocks of an epicene white-faced clown, like one I saw as a child, empty eyed music maker asking where he keeps it. Sly faces of Dublin intelligents, starving thin chins lengthening, eyes narrowing in a malicious joke. Thick-thewed buckoes from the bogs, mouths overbrimming with smoke-salmon and sausagemeat, slurping at a pint, chomp, eyes glazed with huge see-through tits, or tight satin over jelly arses. Cruel-tinted bullfighter veronicas beside an Arabess in satin pyjamas, thick ringlets of dark shining hair and sharp teeth just gleaming through heavy sulky lips and smoked eyes. And Welshmen who loathe and drink and insinuate with nasal voices, cherub faces, swarthy dog leers, groping with lithe hands while talking of 'Home'. Chinese fertility charm, slit to the waist, takes off pure white silkies and hands them to red-faced goblin who sniffs as at a rose, to shrieks of laughter. Streetsweepers of the soul and emotion's garbage-men, touts of sentiment, pimps of the intellect all gather around him. And whores, petty criminals, fifty-seven varieties of addict, gamblers, con-men, cheats, poets, music-men, painters, dancers, players, performers. And the unlucky, those who were caught.

And glimpsed in the middle of them, towering calmly, the stoned philosopher beaming fatherly function. God it was a ridiculous night. Ceremony of desecration. And with that fixed blue triangle of a smile, he had them all preside over the debauchement of their wives and women. And how many others of their kind that I did not know packed into that instant-whip of carnal, boozed, souped, grassed, sent, bent, twisted, turned on and out and over, fixed, iced, snow-blooded madness. Act of hatred. Which they deserve. For he is the shaman of the dispossessed. Faces spilling laughter, the obscenties of noise as the music gets louder and the lights flash and the room starts to spin and the colours whorl creamily into a sick-centred vortex.

Placid features of Elaine wolvish, pushing back her shoulders and thrusting tight breasts at the man sweating over her, rather flabby pale face and streaming together spirals of ochre and puce where Jasmine, delicate gold and timid, glitters, leaning back into the man whose fingertips meet along her loins and he stretches back his scrawny scrub of beard and quivers. Huge bright eyed birds perch knowingly about and cry in raucous voices harsh sounds, meaningless piercing.

French-letter balloons float upward, squeakers sneer, wine splashes and the record player blasts away as Medico, Roger Lomax, is installed as Cock of the Walk by clapped out Queen of the Light and Bitter, Elsie the Bull. Said physician Lomax: 'It sure beats healing as a hobby.' Meanwhile trigger-tempered filmster, Eric Foster, takes one long look at the bilious spectacle and makes for the upper air, telling reporters: 'It may be a harmless giggle for some, but to me it reads like the gibbering of the undead.' Spare a blush for the slumming novelist, notably absent from society host, Gavin McNamara's wine-in and pot-luck, Andrew Stone, author of seven prestigious but low-selling *romans a clef*, licks his wounds over critical mauling after publication of his first thriller, *The Man with One Sandal*. The story goes that the whole thing is an elaborate joke on the part of Robert Keller, polymath adviser, civil servant, writer and now deadly adversary, but either way *Sandal*, according to Sunday yarnbibbers, could use a lot of restitching.

Mr Gavin McNamara, the host at Friday's charity soiree, was in conversation with Dr Barbara Keller.

Grotesque split eyes, flailing or frotting bodies, unzipped smiles and laddered conversations. Torn fibres, parted seams. Tumescence of sound: music, stridences, snicker, giggle, tomtom beat, shatter chatter, screech, bubble, retch, in waves, tangible as hot air blown through a ventilator, causing sickness at the spine. Stink of excited flesh, fluids and lymphs released.

Rear Admiral J. Rathbone, had his hand down the tights of a young psychology student.

He stands there with Barbara, febrile triangle of a smile on his lean-lined face, watching with victorious eyes the easy transmogrification. Reptiles squirm beneath the stamp of feet, rhythmic stamp to the insistent drumbite and noiseless slither of the supple green plagues underfoot. He stands and smiles. She, tranquil, beside him. Unmoved but unappalled.

Whitehall's most stuffed shirt pinged its poppers last night in leading Board of Trader, David Lawson's one-man argosy into the *dolce vita* of

South West Kensington. Accompanied by handsome financial witch, Annabelle Finch, 5 ft II in whose vital statistics (38½-26-40) match the ones at her fingertips, the ebullient bureaucrat smiled: I've never grabbed anything so much since Naples.' Tucking her rhinestone handled whip into her girdle, Annabelle demurred. 'He's got his wopsical hat on, tonight', she snarled appreciatively. London's Royal National Orthopaedic Hospital reported that Mr Lawson would be back at his dictating machine after the operation.

Running of mud-coloured clayclinging sludge. Oily waters slow and sedimented with pink effluent. The grey trees leaved with putrid fronds of flesh. No wind. Only the big eyed friendly birds, huge, gay finches and cheerful canaries to enjoy the blinding serenity of the clear sky, placid blue vapidity without sun but daylit. Canals and scarlet sluices of the bloodways pumping the polluted fluids tirelessly around the decaying fields.

Mrs Sally West was sharing a joke in the area with a West Indian friend.

Ziz, gleaming-eyed, invited me into her. . . . Gripping those strong black arms, I staggered downwards making beautiful music. She said.

Launching her latest one-handed monologue, *The Sensitive Virgin*, Jacqueline Benbow, peripatetic connoisseuse and tireless bargain huntress for U.K. art bunkers, said: 'I'm strictly an amateur. The thought of doing it night after night horrifies me. I just like to amuse a few friends.' So saying, she made a dignified exit, complaining about the heat. Not making it as a stand up comic, on this occasion at least, guffawing teletheomancer, Fingal Gray, lay back quoting Confucius, before being carried out into a waiting hearse, converted into a holiday home by three pneumatic teleramaniacs. Supine, he was still joshing an hour and several secretaries later, pinned to the cushions by an admirer. On top of Old Hokey?

And lug the guts into the outhouse. Purple faced, like some monstrous crowing infant, foreshortened fat limbs rubbery, burping and puking slurred trills of satisfaction, Sebastian, unbuttoned as Noah, inanely droning a pitch of pleasure; one fat cow asleep against his paunch, a totally pissed girl leaning against her and another drooping over his blunted paws. Orange and peagreen vibrations prodding the brain under the soft lobes of gristle at the back of the skull bluntly but insistently, padded jabs of dizzy itching pain, tickling the base of the fibrillating spine. The guts crows again on his dunghill a spittlekeen of recognition.

Mrs Robert Keller, critic and reviewer Sylvie Hart, was playing angels on horseback with a young Polish businessman.

The room is full of Blandfords, Aylmers; the secondary modern gang with horseshit catapults, waiting behind a tipsy vase or a cracked jug; the Maoist students laughing when *I* spoke.

Oh Frankie. . . . Still they are they, he gleaming a blue fury of secret exultation, and she relaxed at his side, unmoved, always at his side, sticky and dirty. Cockroaches in the cellar I was locked in, by Blandford, dry paper-rustle in the blackness. I . . .

They were playing a name game in the green-tiled lavatory where antique merchant, Andrea Bisset, sat comfortably on the knees of U.S. Army Major on diplomatic duties in Europe's major capitals. 'It is' said la Bisset, 'so crowded everywhere, we came in here to talk of mutual friends.'

Are you all right, Paul.

Lizard movement. Mauve cymbal-bursts inside my head between the root of the nose and the bit where the skull screws on to the neck, shimmerpoint of nausea.

Jane and Laurence Bisset. His hands on her, and that smile into his narrow bead-brimming dark eyes, licking over her fresh clean body; that sure smile she gave him, promising to match with wise tricks any whim. The movement of her hips communicating her intricate knowledge of the most exotic carnalhouse, whispering into his hairtufted ears on tiptoe as his stiff fingers pressed rabbling upward the clean young breasts. She shuddered.

Yellow and black retch of night and death. Please. Aagh. Oh, sweet Christ, no. No. Last night. No. Kill me now. And laying his furred hand gently on me, the smiling reassurance of King Demon.

Gavin McNamara

There's no doubt about it that the small party that I threw was a great success with all the fine people to whom I owed a touch of hospitality in return. They all came except for the wee pookie, Stone, who was resting his nerves in the bell of a cowslip somewhere and it was a very eventful evening.

The whole proceedings had borne out my own theory that the most respectable people on the outside have the same basic ability to cut loose the inhibiting elastic as the rest of us, however high-up and even famous they are, as long as they know that the place is free of journalism and that they're all in it together.

Take these people who had befriended me, as an example. Apart from the old slaverduct and the paterfamilias, personally, as I have already testified, nothing went beyond the occasional fantasy when there was a velvet cushion to stroke or a passing cucumber. Sure, the jejeune falterclutch, Paul, confessed to me a sordid arrangement in the city of Paris with some kind of ground-staff professional; but that's neither here nor there in the life of a young thoolermerawn of his class, weight and handicap. Oh, I daresay there had been a bit of *fin de siècle* breathing and the occasional wag of mixed spice over the casserole, but not much action outside the strictly private magic lanterns of each individual mind.

The lank streak of hand-held photoplay, Foster, was honest enough in a misguided and disgusting way to put most of his fantasies, as far as I could see, on general release, causing a lot of disturbance in the upper brackets of British intelligence; and plodded through the temptations of

Saint Anthony with the demented courage of a Don Quixote. But the whole Sancho Panza Division that rumbled on half track behind the poor pasta-whiskered git on his vitamin deficient nag through the atmospheric despairs of every European purgatory from Oslo to Athens relied entirely on pastries specially imported from Denmark to keep their health and efficiency up.

Yet, at that small ceilidh I originated, they was all wearing ribbons down their backs and no mistake, even the ruler of the Queen's Nay-vee and, for a panting, blushful moment, the Duchess of the Deathray Corset, Jacqueline. Do you know that by the end of that tolerant night, apart from celluloid lyrist, Foster, and the miraculously preserved Barbara, weakening though she was to my fingertip precision as I listened to the tumblers clicking, all of them had shown an animal side to themselves, blaming it on the wine I was serving, which was the best the paterfamilias' own stockist could provide. For the first time, ever, the paterfamilias was the only one left out, having had to break off his pursuit of Jacqueline to see to the vomiting simperjunket, Paul.

There was the profound Bisset and young Jane; her old Mother and the hippocratic oather, Lomax; Jasmine and Lord Admiral Effingjoy; Elaine and the pocket commander of the parlour inquisition, Fingal; David Lawson carried off in one cup of Madame Finch's brassiere, like a babby in swaddling clouts, screaming delightedly; and Andrea and Sylvie both helped me tidy the place up, along with a few others of a friendly and sociable disposition. It only goes to prove that behind every sober frontage there's a very well appointed house of pleasure, given the opportunity or the excuse.

The wonder of it all to me was the predicaments and dilemmas that would be cropping up in the consciences of all these gamesome hotspurs in due course. Because it was the whole ethical panorama that had me baffled, with or without a table of orientation. I can't pretend to have frequented the same billiard-halls as Jean-Paul Sartre, Albert Camus, and the like, as a lad. We Celts aren't strong on philosophy of any sort, let alone the moral variety, though we do a nice line in mysticism. No, it isn't that I'm setting meself up as an expert: it's simply a question of human observation and an Irish eye for paradox.

During the next week or so, I was as grata a persona as you could wish to see in almost every one of the postal districts of the great metropolis. I noticed the paterfamilias was a bit more distant and I heard from the ancient bloater-bulge that there were signs of a more hardline attitude as regards himself, though the dear knows that wasn't before time with his lewdness and revolting habits. We heard a lot more about the old hooligan's hidden wealth, though no one that I ever heard of had seen any of it. It turned out that some time before, when he had first inflicted his grossness on the Kellergattung, he had acquired an advance from the paterfamilias and then another pending the settling of his papers. There was also a lot of blether about some house near Goodwood and a confusion among certain banks as to which was to have the privilege of dealing with his affairs. Now the paterfamilias was a great one for casting his bread upon the deluge, but, bejasus, he expected it to rain bloody doughnuts pretty soon after. You wouldn't exactly call it avarice, as mortal a sin as a man can put a name to, so much as business acumen.

I wasn't bothered myself, though interested enough to see how it would all transpire, being of the private opinion that the old gruntandgrumbleload was spinning leg breaks and googlies when it came to the matter of lies, but the wanderlust was on me again and I was thinking of moving in the near future after transacting a last bit of business.

To be quite honest about the whole tarradiddle, I was eager to contract a beautiful friendship with Barbara Keller, herself, before departing, to sustain me in the long desert nights or in the alien darkness of murmuring jungles with gentle thoughts of past passion and bliss to come.

I spent the intervening days, between the party and the projected date of my temporary exile, dashing off a few ephemera for courteous friends at a decent profit, as well as doing the rounds of my less fortunately endowed mates who was all anxious to do me proud for an evening from

Acton to Oakwood and from Tooting to Canons Park. On one of these celebrations, I was honoured by the company of Jane West in thigh-length boots, and I swear it was the few inches of sheer stocking-material between the end of the boot and the hem of the skirt that seduced me from my resolution. She was a strong, supple, advanced girl when you got to know her, Jane. But of course it was in the blood and, given a lucky marriage, she'll have a regiment of kids to keep the public school system supplied with fodder.

It was my passion for neatness made me go for Jacqueline, plus the momentary glimpse of her disarranged at the famous party I gave. Before enduring the frozen blasts of Antarctica or the oppressive steaminess of certain Sumatran swamps, I thought I might manage to reduce her to a platinum bangle and the scent of expensive soap after the opera one night, so I looked in at the National Gallery from time to time and fixed a night for *Götterdämmerung* or some such bit of Germanic howdyoudo calculated to rouse the magic fire in a Nordic woman.

But since I'm being frank, I won't disguise the fact that the principal objective was the goddess herself, the more desirable because I knew that she did, but had only been remote and unattainable in my direction so far. I took her out to a jazz club, where I was a bit known, returning her to her cloistered cell, opposite the hospital, without a fingerprint on her. An evening in E flat, moderate tempo, with only the occasional minor chord. We drank wine and did not dance. At the end of the evening she stood there, in the autumn smokiness, her full and lovely body as lovely as it would ever be, the beautiful slightly arrogant face with its clear honest eyes smiling up at me, the silky hair brushed back catching the light. Jasus, for the first time in my life, I was worried at the empty, tingling sensation around the heart, wondering whether it was love or cholesterol building up. Barbara Keller laid her hand lightly on my arm, very lightly, expecting me to draw her towards me. I didn't bloody move! And let my face go serious. She was too high class a woman to do the same and look charged or dramatic. She let the smile brighten.

'Good night,' she said. 'Thank you. It has quite truly been a wonderfully enjoyable evening.' Still smiling.

'Don't forget the music.'

'I don't think I shall.'

Then she took her hand from my arm and went inside, without turning round. I stood still, for a while, looking at the door where she had gone out of sight, then I lit a cigarette and went on standing there in case she decided to have a peep through the window. Then I went away.

Next day she telephoned.

Sylvie invited me round for the Saturday and I couldn't think of any way of avoiding it, though quite clearly I had to evade any of the old extracts from the red book of Hergest or whatever she might have had in mind without arousing suspicions. As luck had it, the whole family was there. The paterfamilias brooding darkly in his study about bacteriological weapons, or the decline of liberal humanism, or a diabolical gambit in the departmental war-game; Paul, the daisyflop, alone and palely loitering in the rosegarden; the cool and beautiful Barbara reading in the pine room so called; they were all there. Thank Heavens, though, Sylvie had decided it was her day for being sophisticated, so there was no untidiness of thought, word or deed in the way of undignified scuffles in the scullery or loaded conversation. Sylvie lilted her way through us all with the enigmatic mixture of charm and intelligence that had brought her all the way from Merthyr Tydfil to her present exalted and influential position in the world of culture.

She was specially solicitous for the welfare of the bunny-floss, Paul, who I must say looked as transparent as a bit of rare porcelain held to the light. She spent a fair bit of time in maternal cossetting and, in due course, went walking around the spacious lawn with him, arm in arm, with the poor fellow looking as if his nerves was connected personally to the national grid. I took the opportunity of slipping into the pine room.

Barbara was still there giving enough attention to Dostoievski to have made the poor chap feel positive had he but had the chance of meeting her. She put the book down and gave me one of the slow assured smiles that meant I was a popular figure in the latest opinion poll. She put *The Possessed* down.

'I'm not disturbing you?'

'No,' she said. 'It's very nice to see you. I didn't expect you to be here.'

'Your mother was kind enough to ask me round. I think with the idea of cheering up your brother.'

'Yes. I'm worried about him. Is he drinking a lot still, d' you know?'

'A fair bit. He's a nervous lad.'

'I think it was a mistake that he came back here at all and that old ruffian, Sebastian, has only made things worse,' she said. 'We must seem a strange family.'

'Well, you spend a lot of time here, after all. You can't be so bad.'

That had the intended and desired effect of making her laugh and even blush a little.

'I get on well with my father,' she said. 'Oh, I know he has his faults, but he has a sense of humour and a good mind. It's a sort of refuge: not only from work, but from people. There are always enough people around this place to get right away. Friends of Mummy's or Daddy's or even both.'

'Tell me, if it's not too rude a question; you don't have a very high opinion of them, do you?'

'What, my parents?'

'No, no. Your parents' friends. The Bissets and Rathbones and Lomaxes and Lawsons and Stones and so on.'

She shrugged her shoulders. In most people that's a commonplace enough movement of no great beauty. She performed it like Pavlova at her lyical peak. This bloody psychiatrist woman was having a bad effect on me, unlocking certain floodgates of sentimentality which should have rusted fast years ago.

'I don't dislike any of them,' she said. 'Except perhaps Andrea. Jacqueline used to be a close friend, but we're both fairly busy and we don't see much of each other these days. Eric is . . .'

'Yes?'

'I have a lot of respect for him.'

'The thing that's always rather surprised me is the heterogeneousness of them. They're all quite different, aren't they?' 'Except in one respect. They're all successful.'

'What do you mean?'

'Well, all of them, Daddy and Jack and David Lawson and Larry came from relatively humble beginnings and met at roughly the same time, so they've all got on together. And Mummy picked up people like Andrew and Eric when she was about half way up and they were more or less beginning. Film directors are, of necessity, late starters. I suppose they are all a bit smug and self-satisfied. Paul thinks they are. But, after all, they have worked for their success. I don't think one makes any more friends after a certain age: there are only new acquaintances whom one quite likes but whom it's quite easy to take or leave.'

'That sounds uncommonly austere.'

'Does it? I suppose so. I'm not saying that one can't fall in love, or, for that matter, have affairs. I've no evidence, in all my experience, clinical and otherwise, for supposing that any of us gets the slightest bit wiser emotionally.'

And she gave me the slow assured smile again, though I didn't think that made me even joint favourite as yet. Anyway I wasn't crowding the hurdles at all.

'Yes,' I said, with some thoughtful vertical movement of the face. 'I suppose it's a question of sharing certain values. I can understand Paul's point of view, mind. I have no particular yearning for status or possessions myself. I remember listening in amazement to someone in oil telling me about his servants. What would I do with servants? That sort of thing.'

'It's not just material values,' she said. 'It's ethics. Even Jack Rathbone's a socialist, you know. They're all impeccable liberals who haven't yet given up hope that the world isn't going to survive along civilised, liberal lines. I think Daddy probably has private doubts, but I'm not sure that he'd confess them.'

I was thinking to myself that if the rest of the world was going to emulate Daddy's idea of civilisation, I would buy shares in all available systems of birth-control. But I nodded my head in a grave and sage way.

'Look at this room,' she said. 'This is where my mother works. Look at the big windows and the pine panelling and the spare, elegant furniture and the right books. All the right books. And over there: her own little case of Favourites, where you'll find very evidently read and a bit tattered poetry and politics and popular philosophy and psychology and easy history. And very little evidence of any intellectual *taste*.'

She said this quite sharply and I was obliged to look alert. She laughed at herself and shifted her legs so that I couldn't hear for a moment or two, but came back to awareness with herself saying that what she'd said was dangerous priggish talk and typical of her nasty side.

I thought a few nights before, after we had been to the little smooth jazz club, that I'd never see her look more beautiful. That afternoon, she was. Relaxed in the chair, sitting erect, yet with the firm round outlines of her body, the clean, long superbly shaped legs crossed just above the knee, the soft fairish hair framing the serene, confident face. Calm as she was, in a white suit, elegant, playing it as always *her* way, there was something that happened now and then in her eyes that made me almost bloody desperate to have her at that very moment. I wasn't quite sure what it was, it occurred fleetingly and I might even have been imagining it. It was something secret, something which was her own, not without despair.

'I can't get over the fact that such a beautiful woman as yourself should be so cerebral.'

'I don't think I am,' she said, smiling. 'When you're brought up in a certain atmosphere of talk and allusion, you find out about things and at a certain age you either accept or reject them. Do you know the Bisset son? He has rejected. I've accepted. Paul doesn't seem to have made up his mind. It seems to correspond to the difference in age.'

'I'm not concerned with Paul. At least you will not deny that you're beautiful.'

'I'm obviously attractive to men.'

'What does that mean?'

'Oh, don't mistake me. I'm a straightforward heterosexual.'

'Yes?'

'That's all. Perhaps a little deficient in what is called human warmth. I wonder how much that matters.'

'Your experiences haven't been entirely happy? Or is that too delicate a point?'

'I don't know.'

'Shall I tell you what I think?'

She smiled at me, her eyes laughing with a deep glitter of merriment. At least I thought so. She inclined her head a little to the left. It was an untypically carefree movement.

'You musn't cast me in a fairy tale,' she said. 'I'm quite used to being a character in someone else's fictions, but I can be effortlessly disappointing.'

'For me, you'd have to prove that. I think you are the most desirable woman I have ever seen. It would be silly to pretend I haven't seen a great many. And only one of them has worried me as much.'

I had quite a shock when I realised that I was telling her the absolute truth.

'Well,' she said. 'I won't pretend either. I won't pretend you don't attract me, that what you've said doesn't please and excite me. At this moment I feel happier than I have for some time. And I'm not going to pretend that I trust you.'

She got up from the chair in one perfect movement like Salome shedding the first veil and smoothed the skirt over her hips. She held out her hand to me.

'Come,' she said. 'Let's go and get a drink, then you can play some music for me.'

I laughed, looking up at her. For a second then, I almost felt properly innocent. It was something peculiar at any rate that my memory had never recorded before. I went over to her and took her hand.

'I meant what I said.'

'Perhaps,' she said.

I took both her arms in my hands and she rested her fingertips lightly on my arms. She did not resist or move away, so we were standing very close, looking into each other's eyes. She was smiling. I was losing the battle about kissing her, knowing that she was not going to object, and confident that I had the cunning of purpose and strength of will to leave it at that for the time being in favour of the drinks and music, when there was a sort of choking noise behind us.

I turned and there was Paul, looking white and mad with fury. Barbara said something and I stood aside smiling as affable as morning sunlight on a clear brook. And the young bastard picks up a fucking ornamental knife off the bloody table and stabs me with it. . . .

Sylvie Keller

'LAST NIGHT IN THE LABYRINTH'

"The dark red stain spreads on the white surface. At first it moves quickly outward, even in contour, as a blob of ink on some absorbent paper, but soon, as the point where the liquid and the surface are in immediate contact becomes saturated, the stain spreads more slowly and the supersaturated place becomes bright and wet. The red stain continues to grow, however slowly.

The body is lying in a corner of the room, where it has fallen in the angle of the two panelled walls. The wood of the panelling is pine, smooth and unstained, treated but unvarnished, with an even grain and very few knots, those that occur here and there have been deliberately placed to create a certain effect. The plain wood gives the room a clean, light appearance.

To the right of the body, in front of a big window about six feet square, there is a simple table of the same type of wood. It is elegantly designed but austere and unadorned. Two upright chairs are drawn up to the table, one on the side nearest the window and the other on the shorter side, furthest away from the body. A third chair, of the same light wood, but with a curved backrest and arms, lies overturned on the short side of the table nearest to the body, pointing away from it at an angle of about one hundred and twenty degrees. There is an open book on the table, four or five pages of which project upward in the shape of a partly opened fan. Farther away, near the window, there are more hard-covered books in one pile as well as paper-covered books of the kind published on the Continent in another; beside these books there is a thick shorthand pad with a spiral of wire at the top. To the left of the open book, towards the centre of the table there is an ornately decorated sheath, made of leather, about a foot long and curved.

The knife to which the sheath belongs is on the floor in front of the body. It has a bright chased blade about eleven inches long, curved, stained now with blood, brownish in colour because of some trick of light catching the brilliance of the metal. The hilt of the knife seems to be made of ivory, elaborately carved. From the nature of the symbols and the decorations on the handle, the knife appears to be of Arabic or Islamic origin. The curved tip of the blade now points to the sagging body in the corner.

It is the body of a tall, lean young man, dressed in a white roll-necked shirt and tight-fitting trousers of faded blue denim. He is not dead but appears to have fainted. The shoulders are wedged in the corner of the wooden walls, where he must have slumped to the floor. The right arm rests limply on the floor, the left arm is bent across the ribs under the wound from which the blood is still flowing steadily, so that the stain on the shirt is getting bigger. The right leg is bent and the right side of the body bears most of its weight, the left leg extends straight in front of the body, slightly spread, so that the tight cloth emphasises the outline of the young man's well-developed genital organs.

His face, which is tanned and quite deeply lined in the triangle formed by the bridge of his longish but not prominent nose and the wide, thin-lipped mouth, is slightly contorted. What at first seems to be a grimace, perhaps of pain or fear, at a second glance might be interpreted as a twisted or wry smile. The eyes are closed, the eyelids minutely wrinkled; several lines converge on each of the outer corners of the eyes, suggesting that the young man is in the habit of smiling a great deal, or that he has spent much of his life in bright sunlight. Apart from a single deep furrow running across the middle, the forehead is smooth but very high. The gold wavy hair, which may be receding a little, is fairly short and roughly parted on the left side. The head lolls a little to the right.

All the walls of the room, apart from the one which holds the big window, are fitted with bookshelves. On two of them, the one opposite the window and the one to the left, which also contains the only door, these shelves run from floor to very near the ceiling. There are lower shelves, at about waist height for an average-sized man, under the window and at about elbow-leaning height on the remaining wall. The books are all mixed together, paperback and hardback. Many still have brightly coloured dust-jackets. The total effect is haphazardly colourful. Across the room from the wounded young man, at a distance of about twelve feet, there is a single armchair, near which there is another moveable bookshelf, in which most of the books have either torn jackets or none at all. In the farthest corner, diagonally opposite the young man, there is a miniature set of library steps.

Two people stand looking down at the young man, while a third person, a well-built, fairish-haired girl, kneels beside the crumpled body. The girl's hands move confidently but gently, removing the white shirt from the waistband of the denim trousers and drawing it up to reveal an ugly wound, just beneath the rib-cage, from which the blood is welling. The girl begins to apply pressure to one point and then another on the flesh of the wounded man. She turns her head and speaks to one of the other two people. Her face is pale but her voice is level and she shows little emotion other than professional concern. Her white suit is spattered with blood.

The other two figures are both men, or rather a man and a boy. When the girl speaks, the man, very tall with heavy shoulders and a powerful frame, kneels on his left leg and hands her a clean white handkerchief. His face has lost none of its normal ruddy colouring, but shows about the eyes an intense and worried concentration. The boy appears to be dazed. His face is greyish and the mouth is slack and drooling slightly. The eyes are wide open, almost staring, and he is whimpering slightly but if he is trying to say anything, the words are unintelligible. He is standing quite still, his gaze fixed on the body in the corner. The knife on the fawn-coloured carpet, flecked with spots of blood, lies at an equal distance from the wounded figure and the motionless boy.

The eyes of the wounded man flicker and open. For a moment, he has difficulty in focussing, then he sees the girl kneeling beside him and tries to smile. Although she tries to restrain him, he attempts to move. This causes him evident pain. He seems to be having some difficulty in breathing and a dribble of blood shows at the left corner of his mouth. The girl speaks quickly to the man kneeling on her right, who rises quickly and pushes agitatedly past the motionless, impotent boy, out of the room."

Eric Foster

A long-bladed knife.

Between the idea And the reality Between the motion And the act Falls the Shadow . . .

Something has to be salvaged. These are people that I care about, after all.

Oh, Eric, dear! You'd never do anything really violent. You'd make a convenient myth out of it and write it all down.
Sometimes I'm not so sure, Ginny.
Aren't you? Well, I am.

Between the idea And the reality . . .

And now.

Frowning, black-browed face of Roger Lomax. 'Jesus, I don't know how the bloody idiot managed to miss. The lung and God knows what else. Oh, yes, he'll live! The trouble starts bloody here, Eric.' No, no. I know, poor kid.

At least I think I know. There are certain irrational acts of violence that I understand too well. The defence of the helpless which becomes murder and the rational refusal to put your hands about the throat of your wife's lover.

Absurd.

Poor kid. Barbara Keller is a decent girl, a controlled woman, an honest person. Repeat it often enough. Make enough lists. Define and describe it minutely. It will cancel out the event, but it will help to render it painless. Lists are opiates. Poor 'Q'. Enters the room and there Gina and the curling, questing beast. What did he see?

Beside the point. Forget it. Eric, help us. Please, help us. What happened, Roger? Can you do anything? Jacket, limp, medals, long-bladed knife. It might so easily have been me. No. Not possible.

> No, Eric. You are the type who invents concentration camps. But you could never staff them.
> You don't believe that, Ginny?
> Oh, I do! You have such a fertile divergent mind, you could justify anything. Fortunately, you aren't much of a man of action
> . . .

—Oh Eric . . .
—Sylvie. Come here. Have a sip of brandy.
—What will they do to him, Eric?
—Nothing for the moment, Sylvie. Now you musn't worry. Robert's here and he's looking after everything. Roger and Barbara have taken McNamara to a private clinic. There won't . . .
—Gavin. How is Gavin?
—He's hurt, but not badly. Now, Sylvie. You must sit down.
—Where's my boy, my darling boy?
—Jack Rathbone's with him. He's all right.
—I love that boy so much, Eric. They've never understood him. He was always too sensitive. I knew. Robert wanted him to go to a boarding school, but I wouldn't. And she's never been kind to him. He had to grow up with there always being this thing of her . . . Oh ach, Eric. I never . . . She's a whore, that child, Eric. Have nothing to do with her. I knew she was in there. I knew what they were doing. I sent him in there.
—Now, Sylvie, Hush. You mustn't upset yourself.

—It was my fault, Eric. I sent him in there. I wanted him to see what they were like.

—Now, Sylvie. Now. Take a little more brandy. It wasn't your fault. It would have happened sooner or later with someone else. We're all stupid about some things. We're all capable of some sudden fury. It's just a question of seeing it in perspective.

—Gavin was my lover . . .

—Yes. Well . . .

—Why should I grow old, Eric, without anything. Andrew. Him. Christ knows I made it plain enough to you. But no. You wanted my bloody daughter. Oh I saw it in your eyes. And in his eyes. My Paul. Always watching her. And she knew it. She used to . . .

—Stop, Sylvie. Stop! Not for me. Not for her. For you. Don't say any more, now. We'll talk again. We can talk about everything, quietly. Together. We've always been able to talk, haven't we? Listen, my dear. Jacqueline's here and she's going to stay with you. So just rest, will you? And I'll come back in a little while . . .

—I must tell you, Eric. I must talk to you . . .

—Yes, Sylvie. Yes. I'll come back . . .

Contortions of grief. The convulsive mind adjusting to hopelessness with spasms of fear and anger dying away.

> *Les chagrins secrets sont encore plus cruels que les misères publiques . . .*

Can you manage them, Eric? I could almost laugh. Set, concentrated faces. Roger will fix the treatment of the mutilated body, Robert will fix, will fix, will fix . . . And Eric will manage.

—Did I kill him?

—You've come pretty close to it. Roger Lomax has taken him to a hospital. I think that unless something goes badly wrong he'll be all right.

—I'd do the same thing again.

—That does not surprise me. You've made things bloody difficult for yourself.

—For myself? Oh, no. For Mummy and for Daddy and for my sister. That's what you mean, isn't it? What are you doing here, anyway?

—I'm doing what I can to help. And I'd better say at the outset that I couldn't give a damn what happens to you, so I'm not going to listen to any self-pitying drivel. You aren't Meursault, you're not Raskolnikov and least of all are you Orestes. You're a rather boring and stupid young man As it happens I understand what you did and why you did it. Or I think I do. And the other members of your family are people I value one way or another.

—I'd have done the same to you.

—That doesn't interest me.

—What is Daddy doing? Pulling strings? Getting on the blower? Setting it straight for the record?

—I imagine he's doing his best to keep you out of prison. For which you should be grateful. You wouldn't get on well with the others: they'd break you. So let's not have any heroics. If McNamara brings a charge, it's attempted murder. And if you plead provocation, you will have to be explicit. Understand? You don't want that, do you?

—I don't care. Why should I?

—Nor do I. As far as you're concerned. But it would hurt and damage Barbara, it would seriously disturb your mother and your father has better things to worry about. And I want to be certain that you understand where your histrionics are likely to lead.

—Ha! I'd have thought you'd be more sympathetic. After all you've made a trade of compassion.

—You'll get less sympathy from me than anyone. I've been a self-dramatising fool too often. Try and spend the next few hours growing up.

> Think well, deeply, generously . . . An old nonsense. Poor
> forked animal. Weak and defenceless. In the laboratory, studying
> slides. Whom madness consumes and in the V.I.P. lounges Robert

Keller and other wondrous necessary men remain calm, until touched privately. . . . The ultimate value is reality.

But, Eric, what can *we* do to help?
I don't know. Just be there if either of them needs someone .
Oh, God, Eric, it frightens me . . .

Reason is useless and there is nothing beyond reason.

—Jacqueline . . .
—Hullo, my dear. Do you know what's happening? I've left Sylvie sleeping.
—The boy's in there. I think he's in a bad way.
—Upset?
—Acting. But in a dangerous state of mind, for all that. I hope Barbara will know what to do. I suppose that's too much to expect.
—She seemed in perfect control when I saw her.
—Did she telephone you?
—No, Robert did.

Absurd.

That my own heart should leap up to hear something as unimportant at this moment, standing in the debris of my friends' lives. This calm, level-eyed girl with worry in her voice and a concentrated wish to help, gentle, takes my hand.

—We'll do what we can. It would be best if she got one of her colleagues to treat him.
—What on earth's going to happen, Jacqueline?
—I don't know. I haven't registered it properly, you know. It's the kind of thing that happens to other people.
—It is.
—Yes, but . . .
—I know what you mean. Will you go and talk to Paul? I think I was a bit rough.
—You?

—Yes, I lost my temper. It's not easy to explain why. He needs someone who's not going to.

—What did you think of Gavin?

—I didn't think much about him at all. A drifter. Remarkable knack for living every moment up to the hilt, like all his kind. Not much warmth.

—I didn't know there was anything . . . Sorry . . .

—With Barbara?

—Yes . . .

—He's an attractive man. Isn't he?

—Yes. I find him attractive. I shouldn't have thought he would have much effect on Barbara.

—No, well, it's difficult to predict what people will do . . .

> Peleus on Thetis stares. The creature in whose company we are seeking amusement . . . that is the creature whom henceforward we shall love . . . With regard to Lust, the mind is as much absorbed thereby as if it had attained rest in some good: and this hinders it from thinking of anything else.

Poor boy.

The houses that we know so well suddenly become strange. This room is now like a set where people are going to talk about the act of violence that happened somewhere else. What happens? Someone rings your doorbell. Can I come in? I've left my wife. The years, the sense of waste, the tears, the boredom of someone else's self-recrimination, the grief. Or the unbidden guest is pissed and uncertain. Or there is a sudden death in someone's family about which you feel nothing. You catch yourself singing over some domestic chore and stop and start because it was hypocritical to stop when there was nothing for you to feel. Now, in this room, the scene of so much theory of compassion. An impossible event. The unreality, the absurdity, is overpowering. But the urgent need to help, somehow, persists.

Sylvie rocked backwards and forwards murmuring the boy's name over and over and over. Why did she send him into the room? The only things really in our power are our thoughts. . . . 'It's your wife who needs the bloody warning, Batch.'

'You know, my dear, for an intellectual you're not desperately intelligent.'
'You are enchanting . . .'

Long-bladed knife.

Perhaps it was somewhere in my own mind.

. . . Fortunately, you aren't a man of action.
I don't want to lead the pack.

—Ah, Eric. Good of you to come. I think things are sorting themselves out. Where's Sylvie?
—She's asleep. Barbara gave her something.
—Paul?
—In the sitting room, with Jacqueline.
—Hysterical, I imagine. The whole action was hysterical. I suppose I should have foreseen it. Paul has always been unstable and McNamara was a febrile character . . .
—Was . . . ?
—Oh, he's not dead. Roger Lomax got him into some private place run by a friend of his and, as I understand it, he's comfortable. I used the past tense purely because I imagine that our relationship with that young man is over. We'll know pretty soon whether he intends to bring charges. Did you go to that party? Yes, you did. I remember seeing you. You didn't stay long.
—No. There was a reason for that . . .
—You've got more common sense than most of us, Eric. What did you think of what you saw?

—It seemed a fairly usual party of its kind. If you collect a lot of exhibitionist people together, you can expect that sort of thing. I must say, Robert, most of the people we know seemed to be enjoying themselves.

—Yes. Now, Eric. I'm going to be absolutely frank with you. We have never been particularly close friends but I like your intelligence and I am perfectly well aware that you are fond of Barbara. I shall try to buy this chap off. One way or another. Ethically, that is inexcusable, but we have to be pragmatic. As far as Paul's career goes, it doesn't matter very much, though I daresay his health would suffer. Sylvie is highly emotional, as you know, and much too involved with Paul: it would be very damaging for her. Her television reputation would make it certain that the press took an interest, whereupon they would find that I was involved and that Barbara was. While it would not necessarily damage either of us professionally, it would certainly not do us any good. More importantly, it would do positive harm to our work.

—So? What are you asking me to do?

—Nothing, Eric. I am simply putting you into the picture of what I intend to do. I shall allow McNamara the chance of making up his own mind. We've been generous to him and he may not be a malicious fellow. If he wants revenge, I shall attempt to dissuade him by reasonable compensations. Failing that approach, I shall exert force. I hardly think that I am cynical enough to describe it as *moral* force, but it will be something of the sort.

—How?

—David Lawson and I both have a certain amount of influence which can be unobtrusively brought to bear. But I'm sure it won't come to that. I hope I can rely on you.

—To do what I can to help your daughter and your wife, yes. I've seen quite enough emotional wastage. As far as McNamara is concerned, it depends on how far you go.

—It depends on how far I have to go.

Easy smile. The managers know how to order things. Mine are the swollen lips that speak of doom. Laughter.

«Technique . . . structure . . . form. You can't expect a mere civil servant to be up on these things . . . »

'And the way I walk . . . For Christ's sake, Eric, it's the way I walk . . .'

I suppose it would be best to go away. She hasn't come back and I am here for her, but Jacqueline is more use and will hurt no one. Limp away, old man, *Croyez-vous . . . que les éperviers ont toujours mangé des pigeons quand ils en ont trouvé?*

—For the sake of all the blessed saints, will someone tell me what the bloody hell is going on round here?

A fool and jester. The sly old man sniffs fear in the air and blusters. The common, vulgar opinion.

She comes back, weary. Drained of energy. With her someone brisk and bearded and competent. She tries to smile and it is time for me to go. He will be able to get things done. I can telephone later . . .

Eric, Can you please come here? I need your help. Can you hurry, please?

I am the natural fool of fortune. Actors in the scene waiting for the event. Overprepared.

PART EIGHT

Gavin McNamara

In the first place there was the element of surprise. Who would have believed that the young clatterballs would have stopped beating his luminous bloody wings in the void and swooped down like a flying serpent into my bosom? That alone was enough to set me thinking, propped up as I was in snowy-white splendour attended by dusky nurses with a touch like a concert pianist, every one of them. Oh, I must say I lacked nothing in the way of care, attention and champagne during the period of my recovery and convalescence, from which I gathered that it must have been a close thing, but I was well on the way to rejuvenation. And when you think of the headlines and nastiness that the newspapers is capable of, I could see the point of view of my benefactors. In fact, when a member of the press did penetrate past the frontier guards and three-headed dogs they kept about the place to ensure that it retained its exclusive nature, I was as bland as cucumber rhaita, explaining the whole unpleasantness away as an accident. I couldn't help marvelling all the same how the news of my indisposition had reached Fleet Street, unless the old schemerboam himself had been gossiping when pissed or flying speculative kites.

I saw quite a bit of him during the weeks of enforced rest as, bit by bit, everyone began to show less concern as I improved in health and had accepted the paterfamilias' generous offer of financial aid. The old dodgetateur had been given his cards shortly after the incident for general looseness of behaviour. This was a hard decision, since, apart from his foul language, drunken habits, coarse volume and the urge to grab a handful of any shapely female arse that happened to go wiggling by, he was a quiet old bloke. I suppose what did it was the paterfamilias discovered that all his papers was the mere dreams of an ancient failure who had spent his life scrabbling in the hard grit of the desert for a fortune that was never to be his. Sure, the bankbooks he had were real enough, but they were all out of date, since the squandercoot had long since spent whatever he had put by, about seventy-two hours at the most after putting it there. It was a hard decision on the part of the paterfamilias, as I said, particularly as he himself was doing very well financially and in other ways, as I understand it, what with hot tips on the stock exchange and various other tides in the affairs of organisation men. Nevertheless, for old times sake, I took the ancient batterbulge under me own wing. Not unmindful of the precepts of the Brothers, as you will be able to judge. True enough we discovered that we had knocked up against each other from time to time in the past but that was hardly a coincidence with two such wandering spirits as ourselves. Anyway, it was strictly temporary as an operator in his class always finds a bed of roses somewhere with adjoining bath and asses' milk in the h. & c. system.

But to get back to gist, the falling off of the mainstream interest in me was on a grand scale. Even the healer, Lomax, in whose stubby fingers had dangled the cord that suspended me above eternity, as you might put it, became a custom more honoured in the breach. And, while during the early days of my infirmity I was visited by the paterfamilias, the woolly lion of the nation's trade, the chancer of the azure main, the voice of parliamentary democracy, and the tiger-tailing terror of television, all showing a touch of patronising concern, they were soon safely back at the business of life, liberty and the pursuit of happiness on behalf of the folk whose guardians and representatives they were. Barbara came once with the interminable icicle, Foster: a restrained and reconciling handwashing display of nohardfeelings. The little cocksparrow of polite literature, Stone, called several times, though. Always with a smile, a stammer and some little gift in the way of grapes or liquor, that was uncalled for since I had never been much of a mate of his. Jane West came too, but they reported what happened to Lomax, who must have forbidden any further visits in case they might do me an injury.

Apart from a note and some flowers sent by Jacqueline, that was that. Not a single peep or chirrup from all those other gentle creatures to whom I had brought either a little spark of afternoon excitement or the vibrant thrill of a July dawn: not Sylvie, or Andrea, or Jasmine, or Sally, or Elaine, or Annabelle. And, after all, why should they? Things are difficult enough for women in a man's world and while I haven't any sympathy at all for these liberation groups with their stridency and flop-fitted obtuseness, you have to see they have a point of view. The upshot was that I left in splendid isolation, since most of the other people, such as attended the party I gave, were strictly casuals who do not go in for hospital visiting. The secret of the whole phenomenon, of course, was guilt. I've sketched the broad lines of my sundry relationships already, so it would be very coarse-grained of me to go into further detail, but it's a sad fact of human behaviour that we're always bloody minded to those who accommodate us in the departments of lust and license, often to the point of brutality, just as we start loathing the sight of people who hear our confessions, unless the cloth is cut on the cross, and we even freeze over the day after alcoholic affection.

The paterfamilias finally showed up a few days before my discharge to settle the future with a certain modest generosity. The sleek Brazilian jaguar of British franchise was with him as well as the magnificent man on the flying trapeze of administration, who had legal training. So had the paterfamilias. I signed a few depositions or affidavits or whatever. And that was that.

I didn't mind, particularly. They were a lying, cheating, conniving, humiliating, deceiving, grasping, scheming, fornicating, hypocritical and meaningless bunch, secure in their own good esteem. And the ones who weren't, like Foster or Jacqueline were either natural enemies of my kind —sooner or later, or else, like Barbara and Stone and Jane, in the process of being corrupted.

The day they let me out of the nursing home, I met the old gulpbubble and we set off, with excellent prospects, for another fine harvest of pomegranates.

Eric Foster

The autumn light falls through the window with a gentleness that matches the mood of the people in the room. A tall, balding man who limps across towards some bottles, carrying two glasses, and a beautiful girl with fairish hair and a serene poised manner, who is sitting in an armchair. The tall man pours out two drinks and hands one to the girl. They smile but do not speak. Their movements are precise as though they are especially careful not to touch one another. The girl is sewing a button onto a shirt. The man limps across to a rocking-chair and picks up a book.

> 'But Dionysos as a universal power does not belong to any particular age or generation. It is not merely that emotional forms of religion are still known today: for such religions tend to be but a particular direction of forces which are active also in other than religious groups and even in the isolated individual. So when Dionyos is manifested in the play as the purveyor of drugs of many kinds, as the source of ecstasies and disasters, as the enemy of intellect and individuality and the defence of man against his isolation, as a power that can make him feel like a god while acting like a beast, as a spirit that partakes of the beauty and the callousness of man's natural environment, this is a god whom all can recognise . . .'

—I've finished the shirt.
—Thank you. Is the drink all right?

—Yes. What are you reading?
—It's a book about Euripides and Dionysos. Shall I stop?
—I thought it might be nice to go and have lunch in a pub. I've got some shopping to do.

Every movement of hers is slow and beautiful. The sunlight is very bright, but it is cold. A November day when leaves and papers are briefly stirred by the lightness of the breeze. People are wearing scarves and topcoats. Children have pink faces, lagging to look at Christmas windows, already arranged. The mean streets are highlit and shaded, irridescent reflections of glass on dusty pavement, dark glamour even of puddles. Saturday morning in London with barrows of fruit and backchat, pigeons and fanciers. Sunlight.

—Do you want to visit your parents?
—No. Do you think I should?
—I think your father would probably like to see you.
—Will you come?
—Yes. I'll talk to your mother.
—I don't think it matters much. He's probably so busy that he doesn't notice. And I'm sure he'll have found some way of amusing himself. Mummy's probably still living some piece of fiction she's currently soaked in, something suitably depressing.
—I think she was very badly upset, you know.
—Inevitably. I'm sorry I can't be more sympathetic. Surely you were bored by being cast in some totally unreal part that she'd chosen for you?
—I used to think it was amusing. Remember, I'm something of a mythomaniac myself.

> ' "Can anything be plainer," he might say, "than that I light my twopenny candle on earth and that the sun then kindles his great fire in heaven? I should be glad to know whether, when I have put on my green robe in spring, the trees do not afterwards do the same? These are facts patent to everybody and on them I take my stand. I am a plain practical man, not one of your

theorists and splitters of hairs and choppers of logic. Theories and speculation and all that may be very well in their way, and I have not the least objection to your indulging in them, provided, of course, you do not put them into practice. But give me leave to stick to facts: then I know where I am." The fallacy of this reasoning is obvious to us, because it happens to deal with facts about which we have long made up our minds. But let an argument of precisely the same calibre be applied to matters which are still under debate, and it might be questioned whether a British audience would not applaud it as sound, and esteem the speaker who used it a safe man—not brilliant or showy, perhaps, but thoroughly sensible and hard-headed. If such reasonings could pass muster among ourselves, need we wonder that they long escaped detection by the savage?'

Robert sits at his orderly desk, the single sheet of paper before him, half filled with neat, straight handwriting. The autumn sunlight floods into the room. The books glow. Robert talks easily and placidly about the Middle East, Vietnam, peace initiatives. He sticks to facts, analysing them meticulously from the point of view of the government and nation whose servant he has chosen to be.

—Did he say anything about Paul?
—Not to me. You didn't see him?
—No. Well, I did for a moment. But he went away. He had to meet some friends.
—Your mother was relaxed. Pretty much her old self.
—Yes. She is resilient. Daddy says she's reading vast books of psychology and coming up with new theories about various authors and painters.
—No harm in that. They seem to be easy enough with one another.

Every movement she makes is slow and beautiful and yet there is urgency and passion. It is as simple and easy to exult in the supple rhythms of her fierce desire, her pleasure in her own responding body, now a little flushed, as it is to weep tears of affection.

—It's a relationship that I shall never understand.
—I think it's a perfectly commonplace one.
 ⸜ —That is a thoroughly depressing thought.
 ⸜ —A marriage of sensibility and technique. It's curious that they should have both and yet that your mother seems to stand for the one and your father for the other.
—They're giving a party. Do you want to to go?
—If you do.
—No. I'd rather go the pictures.

> 'In everything that can be called art there is a quality of redemption. It may be pure tragedy, if it is high tragedy, and it may be pity and irony, and it may be the raucous laughter of the strong man. But down these mean streets a man must go who is not himself mean, who is neither tarnished nor afraid. The detective in this kind of story must be such a man. He is the hero, he is everything. He must be a complete man and a common man and yet an unusual man. He must be, to use a rather weathered phrase a man of honour, by instinct, by inevitability, without thought of it and certainly without saying it. He must be the best man in his world and a good enough man for any world. I do not care much about his private life; he is neither a eunuch nor a satyr; I think he might seduce a duchess and I am quite sure he would not spoil a virgin; if he is a man of honour in one thing, he is that in all things.'

—I think I'll start a new picture, if I can raise the money.
—Good. It's high time you stopped idling around. Too much reading isn't good for you. What's it going to be?
—Well, do you know, I'd really like to make a sort of thriller. Quite simple. Where the good chap wins.
—You will have to be careful. You're getting soft.

> 'Each tells the other that he is not God. . . .'

London street. Winter promised in the afternoon sky, grey and orange streaked with straggling daubs of cloud. Looking westward from a high window, the blank towers of the skyline rear blind-eyed above the tumble of roofs, domes, spires. It is at street level, where the sensations are blurred, that we discover when and how mythology is possible.

> '*You speak. You say*: Today's character is not
> A skeleton out of its cabinet. Nor am I.'

—Sometimes you look at me in an odd way.
—Do I?
—Perhaps that isn't the right way of putting it.
—Perhaps it's just amazement that you are there at all. And that this moment has passed in this way.
—I'm not sure that I know what you mean.
—I mean that you are Barbara Keller and I am Eric Foster. And that the way you walk is the way you walk. And that that is enough.
—Whatever happens?

> 'End here. Us then. Finn, again! Take. Bussoftlhee, mememormee! Till thousendsthee. Lps. The keys to. Given! . . .'

—Yes. Whatever happens. That is enough.

Sylvie Keller

HER OWN WORK

Dear Dad,

Thanks for your last letter. I'm glad that your rheumatism is better and that everyone else is all right. We are much the same as when I last wrote.

As I told you then, Sebastian Jones has gone at last and we have seen no more of him. I don't know why he didn't come down to see you. And I don't know where he's gone. He left in a huff after Robert had had to tell him firmly what was what. He might decide to come down, but a lot will depend on what he thinks I may have told you. Whatever happens, I must warn you that he's jovial enough but a terrible drunkard and, as Robert found out, an even worse liar. I don't suppose this is any news to you, but I'm letting you know so that you'll be prepared if he does turn up.

Robert is very busy with one of his committees. I'm not sure what this one is, but I think it's quite important behind the scenes. Robert gets on very well with most of the cabinet ministers and they trust him. The snag is, of course, that when there's any difficult job going, they always think of him, so he's always up to his eyes. How he finds time to get on with his books as well, I don't know. But he says they keep him amused, which is the main thing.

I've been quite busy myself and I shall be on television fairly regularly throughout the winter on an arts programme and a new discussion thing. The first is on BBC 2. And the other is BBC 1. You *must* get a colour set.

Tell Mam that I said so, and if she argues you buy the one you want and send me the bill. It's a present from Robert and myself.

It doesn't surprise me that there's still a row going on between Sidney and Watcyn about the Prince of Wales' presentation. It is ridiculous when you think of how bad things would have been if anything had gone wrong, that those two should be so petty. Robert went to the Palace the other day to some official do, but I couldn't go because of television. We both went to a party in Number Ten, though. There were all sorts of people there and it was very enjoyable.

Otherwise things have been pretty quiet. Paul is doing well at his job, but he hasn't been at all well. I think it would do him good to go abroad again. He is very well qualified, after all, and would do very well in America, where he has an offer of doing research, from someone that Robert knows in the University of California. It's an enormous place and he hasn't made up his mind, yet, but we think it would do him a lot of good, as I said. Robert has always thought he's wasting his time at the place in Cricklewood, but he can be a very stubborn boy. A few years in America, together with his experience of France, would stand him in excellent stead when he decided on a job over here. We both hope he'll settle down in academic life, somewhere. That seems to be his natural talent.

We've seen very little of Barbara lately. She is a glutton for work, as you know, and recently she has been going about a lot with a nice man called Eric Foster. (I think you met him once with me, years and years ago, when you were in London. He makes films.) They seem to get on well together, but God knows she's a difficult child when she wants to be.

The weather was fine until a few days ago, but it's raining at the moment and our garden looks a mess. We're having one of the rooms redecorated from floor to ceiling and so we're at sixes and sevens indoors as well.

Robert sends his best wishes and hopes your leg will be strong enough for you to come and see us in the spring. That's all for the moment.

Love, Sylvia.

Robert Keller

At the end of a satisfactory morning's work, Robert Keller took his two principal assistants, Christopher Jarvis and Emrys Anthony, to the Caprice. There were a number of reasons for celebrating: the Enquiry had wound up its proceedings successfully the previous day, Robert Keller had been sounded out in relation to the New Years Honours List, he had been asked to make a fact-finding tour of certain areas of the Middle East, with a view to H.M.G. taking an initiative to ease tensions in the area and it was the Christmas season.

Jarvis and Anthony were industrious young men of modest origins, who used their quite different aptitudes with tact and intelligence. Jarvis, behaved with the effortlessly supercilious courtesy that he had picked up at Eton and Oxford. Anthony had retained his Welsh accent, suitably tempered with an eccentric delivery and occasional gouts of acid wit. Robert Keller was fairly certain that neither of them liked him particularly although they were amenable and amusing companions; at the same time he was sure that they respected his ability and were genuinely eager to learn from him.

Their conversation was as enjoyable as the food. All three men were well-informed and enjoyed the conspiratorial intimacy encouraged among those who share exactly the same secret information, enabling them to gossip with malicious humour as well as to exchange perfectly serious ideas informally. Robert Keller was half-way thought his duck Montmorency, when he noticed a wicked light of merriment in the vage blue eyes of Jarvis.

'Isn't that your picaresque relative?' said Christopher Jarvis, nodding his head towards the opposite side of the room.

Before Robert Keller had turned round, he heard the distinctive whoop of Sebastian Jones and felt his own body stiffen involuntarily. Nevertheless, he was determined not to put up again with the slightest nonsense from his wife's uncle. Explaining that Christopher Jarvis had chosen an appropriate word to describe the old man, he began an incisively comical account of the unscrupulous and meddlesome ways of the ancient layabout. The two younger men were delighted. But Robert Keller's luncheon was made uneasy by the imminent knowledge of Sebastian Jones' unpredictable presence.

As things turned out, his digestion need not have suffered in the slightest. Some twenty minutes later, Sebastian Jones, in the company of two broad lean men, who were calling him a crazy bastard in the long-bow twangs of Australian hard-cases, waddled past the table. He disdained to recognise the husband of his niece, but had clearly noticed him.

'I'll tell you one thing, mates,' said Sebastian Jones to his friends, 'whatever you fuckin' do, avoid the pommy civil service. Toffee-arsed queers, the lot of them, with about as much common sense as pissed flying foxes in a bush fire. It's a mystery to me how the Old Country hasn't sunk into the sea or been over-run by barbarian hordes, what with bolshies and poofs in every nook and cranny. Now I know a grand little place not far from here, where the hostess is a personal friend of mine, and . . .'

'Boisterous old chap,' said Emrys Anthony. 'Is that the one?'

'The very same,' said Robert Keller. 'It's a pity in a way that so much talent has to be wasted. We could find quite a lot of work for a confidence trickster of his skill and experience in the department.'

Over cigars and brandy, Robert Keller allowed his subordinates to talk, aware that they knew perfectly well what he was doing. It was an interesting game watching them preserving a careless insouciance, while slaving away at scoring points. Robert Keller had always enjoyed such games himself, and was pleased to see that both Jarvis and Anthony entered into them with dispassionate enthusiasm. He thought it a pity that his own son was such an earnest and humourless young man, noting the happy sense of relief he had begun to experience since Paul had finally decided to go to the United States.

The train of thought carried Robert Keller with it back into the highly unpleasant period which had followed the stabbing of the Irishman. Robert Keller had never needed to keep his nerve steady and his intellect working more than at that time, when surrounded by panic and hysteria in his private life. Compared to that, professional and public matters of concern were as nothing. He recalled vaguely some saying of Voltaire's which was frequently quoted by Eric Foster, but failed to remember it accurately.

Now things were more or less back to normal. There was perhaps a slight constraint between the Kellers and their friends, but once Paul was out of the way that would probably dissipate. Robert Keller had learned to value David Lawson, Jack Rathbone and Laurence Bisset and had profited from the cool advice, the cool and ruthless advice, of Annabelle Finch. His relationship with his wife was unchanged, but she had been sufficiently distracted to forget her anger about the nonsense with Andrew Stone. As his eyes travelled around the restaurant noting item after item of furniture and decor, his mind ticked off the balance sheet documenting the events of that ugly period. He was disposed to take a cynical view of the relationship between Barbara and Eric Foster, which seemed to him to be doomed.

Having approached Sylvie about entertaining more lavishly but more selectively in view of his forthcoming elevation, he had found her remarkably receptive to the idea. Her own growing reputation on television was an asset, undoubtedly. Without discarding any friends, whom they would see regularly but at wider intervals, Robert Keller thought it was a good moment to plan the extension of their acquaintance. The entirely fortuitous luck that had attended his investments in metal shares, recommended by Sebastian Jones, had made him almost a rich man. He would capitalise on his success and looked forward to the next ten years, knowing his health to be sound and his energy undiminished.

Throughout this private reverie, Robert Keller had by nods or a few neatly interposed syllables kept the exchanges between Christopher Jarvis and Emrys Anthony alive in apparent importance. It was now time to leave. He called for the bill and went back with them, at his most urbane and epigrammatic, by taxi.

Reminding his secretary to arrange for flowers to be sent to Jane West, whose bikini-clad debut in a television giveaway programme had occurred the previous evening, Robert Keller gave all his attention to Nick Waterlow, who had prepared a report on the political implications of a new research site.

'Two small hamlets,' said Waterlow, 'which are really too close for comfort, but I'm sure we can do something about rehousing the yokels. Good thing it's not anything to do with bloody Nationalists.'

'True,' said Robert Keller. 'I'll take it up with the Ministers involved.'

'By the way,' said Waterlow, 'are congratulations premature?'

Robert Keller held the door open, smiling, and said nothing. Waterlow had a lot to learn. '

Paul Keller

I have endured the voice of thunder
But I can no longer stay in the darkness.
It is time to seek a lost, lost track,
Leaving the warm scents of upland caves;
And there will be muttering shrouds
On the road and raving men will cry out.
Worse: tentacle voices out of white mist
Flies slow on putrid, mutilated flesh
And over all the stench of futile spleen;
The woman made of carnivorous blossoms;
The tempters, and the innocent victims.
But they will not be avoided, their laughter
Erodes the will, their luck is stillborn.
And I have endured the thunder too long . . .
I do not know what I shall find in ruins,
Whether I shall survive alone, unwanted:
I can no longer stay in the darkness.